Praise for Donna Leon's
Commissario Brunetti Mysteries

'The appeal of Guido Brunetti, the hero of Donna Leon's long-running Venetian crime series, comes not from his shrewdness, though he is plenty shrewd, nor from his quick wit. It comes, instead, from his role as an everyman.... Not so different from our own days at the office or nights around the dinner table. Crime fiction for those willing to grapple with, rather than escape, the uncertainties of daily life.'

—Bill Ott, *Booklist* (starred review)

'The sophisticated but still moral Brunetti, with his love of food and his loving family, proves a worthy custodian of timeless values and verities.'

—*The Wall Street Journal*

'In her classy, literate, atmospheric Commissario Guido Brunetti series, Donna Leon takes readers... to a Venice that tourists rarely see.' —*BookPage*

'Brunetti... is the most humane sleuth since Georges Simenon's Inspector Maigret.... He is a decent man [who achieves] a quiet heroism.'

—*The Philadelphia Inquirer*

'No one is more graceful and accomplished than Leon.'

—*The Washington Post*

'If you're heading to Venice, take along a few of [Leon's] books to use for both entertainment and travel directions.' —*Pittsburgh Post-Gazette*

A PENGUIN / GROVE PRESS BOOK

SUFFER THE LITTLE CHILDREN

Donna Leon, who was born in New Jersey, has lived in Venice for many years and previously lived in Switzerland, Saudi Arabia, Iran, and China, where she worked as a teacher. Her mysteries featuring Commissario Guido Brunetti include (in order of publication) *Death in a Strange Country*; *Dressed for Death*; *Death and Judgment*; *Acqua Alta*; *Quietly in Their Sleep*; *A Noble Radiance*; *Fatal Remedies*; *Friends in High Places*; *A Sea of Troubles*; *Willful Behavior*; *Uniform Justice*; *Doctored Evidence*; *Blood from a Stone*; *Through a Glass, Darkly*; *Suffer the Little Children*; *The Girl of His Dreams*; and *About Face*, the latest book in the series.

Donna Leon

Suffer the Little Children

A PENGUIN / GROVE PRESS BOOK

PENGUIN BOOKS

Published by the Penguin Group

Penguin Group (USA) Inc., 375 Hudson Street, New York, New York 10014, U.S.A.

Penguin Group (Canada), 90 Eglinton Avenue East, Suite 700, Toronto, Ontario,
Canada M4P 2Y3 (a division of Pearson Penguin Canada Inc.)

Penguin Books Ltd, 80 Strand, London WC2R 0RL, England

Penguin Ireland, 25 St Stephen's Green, Dublin 2, Ireland (a division of Penguin Books Ltd)

Penguin Group (Australia), 250 Camberwell Road, Camberwell, Victoria 3124,
Australia (a division of Pearson Australia Group Pty Ltd)

Penguin Books India Pvt Ltd, 11 Community Centre, Panchsheel Park, New Delhi – 110 017, India

Penguin Group (NZ), 67 Apollo Drive, Rosedale, North Shore 0632,
New Zealand (a division of Pearson New Zealand Ltd)

Penguin Books (South Africa) (Pty) Ltd, 24 Sturdee Avenue,
Rosebank, Johannesburg 2196, South Africa

Penguin Books Ltd, Registered Offices: 80 Strand, London WC2R 0RL, England

First published in Great Britain by William Heinemann, The Random House Group Limited 2007
First published in the United States of America by Atlantic Monthly Press,
an imprint of Grove / Atlantic, Inc. 2007
Reprinted by arrangement with Grove / Atlantic, Inc.
Published in Penguin Books 2008
This edition published 2010

1 3 5 7 9 10 8 6 4 2

PUBLISHER'S NOTE

This is a work of fiction. Names, characters, places, and incidents are either the product of the author's
imagination or are used fictitiously, and any resemblance to actual persons, living or dead, business
establishments, events, or locales is entirely coincidental.

THE LIBRARY OF CONGRESS HAS CATALOGED THE HARDCOVER EDITION AS FOLLOWS:
Leon, Donna.
Suffer the little children / Donna Leon.
p. cm.
ISBN 0-87113-960-X (hc.)
ISBN 978-0-14-311361-4 (mass market pbk.)
ISBN 978-0-14-311711-7 (trade pbk.)
1. Brunetti, Guido (Fictitious character)—Fiction. 2. Police—Italy—Venice—Fiction.
3. Venice (Italy)—Fiction. 4. Physicians—Fiction. 5. Kidnapping—Fiction.
6. Pharmacists—Fiction. I. Title.
PS3562.E534S84 2007
813'.54—dc22 2006052610

Printed in the United States of America

For Ravi Mirchandani

Welche Freude wird das sein,
Wenn die Götter uns bedenken,
Unsrer Liebe Kinder schenken,
So liebe kleine Kinderlein!

How happy we will be
If the gods are gracious
And bless our love with children,
With darling little children!

Die Zauberflöte
The Magic Flute
MOZART

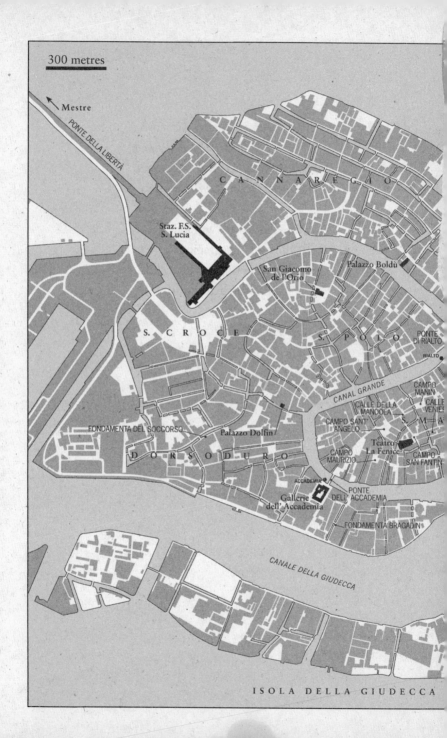

300 metres

Mestre

PONTE DELLA LIBERTÀ

C A N N A R E G I O

Staz. F.S.
S. Lucia

San Giacomo
de l'Orio

Palazzo Boldù

S. C R O C E

S. P O L O

PONTE
DI RIALTO

RIALTO

CANAL GRANDE

CAMPO
MANIN

CALLE DELLA
MANDOLA

CALLE
VENIER

CAMPO SANT'
ANGELO

S · M · A

FONDAMENTA DEL SOCCORSO

Palazzo Dolfin

CAMPO
MAURIZIO

Teatro
La Fenice

CAMPO
SAN FANTIN

D O R S O D U R O

ACCADEMIA

Gallerie
dell'Accademia

PONTE
DELL'ACCADEMIA

FONDAMENTA BRAGADIN

CANALE DELLA GIUDECCA

ISOLA DELLA GIUDECCA

1

'... and then my daughter-in-law told me that I should come in and tell you about it. I didn't want to, and my husband told me I was an idiot to get involved with you because it would only lead to trouble, and he's got enough trouble at the moment. He said it would be like the time when his uncle's neighbour tapped into the ENEL line and started to steal his electricity, and he called to report it, and when they came, they told him he had to ...'

'Excuse me, Signora, but could we go back to what happened last month?'

'Of course, of course, but it's just that it ended up costing him three hundred thousand lire.'

'Signora.'

'My daughter-in-law said if I didn't do it, she'd call you herself, and since I'm the one who saw it, it's probably better that *I* come and tell you, isn't it?'

'Certainly.'

'So when the radio said it was going to rain this morning, I put my umbrella and boots by the door, just in case, but then it didn't, did it?'

'No, it didn't, Signora. But you said you wanted to tell me about something unusual that happened in the apartment opposite you?'

'Yes, that girl.'

'Which girl, Signora?'

'The young one, the pregnant one.'

'How young do you think she was, Signora?'

'Oh, maybe seventeen, maybe older, but maybe younger. I have two boys, you know, so I could tell if she was a boy, but she was a girl.'

'And you said she was pregnant, Signora?'

'Yes. And right at the end of it. In fact, that's why I told my daughter-in-law, and that's when she told me I had to come and tell you about it.'

'That she was pregnant?'

'That she had the baby.'

'Where did she have the baby, Signora?'

'Right there, in the *calle* across from my place. Not out in the *calle*, you understand. In the apartment across the *calle*. It's a little way down from my place, opposite the house next door, really, but because the house sticks out a little bit, I can see into the windows, and that's where I saw her.'

'Where is this exactly, Signora?'

'Calle dei Stagneri. You know it. It's near San Bortolo, the *calle* that goes down to Campo de la Fava. I live down on the right side, and she was on the left, on the same side as that pizzeria, only we're both down at the end, near the bridge. The apartment used to belong to an old woman—I never knew her name—but then she died and her son inherited it, and he started to rent it out, you know, the way people do, by the week, to foreigners, or by the month.

'But when I saw the girl in there, and she was pregnant, I thought maybe he'd decided to rent it like a real apartment, you know, with a lease and all. And if she was pregnant, she'd be one of us and not a tourist, right? But I guess there's more money if you rent by the week, especially to foreigners. And then you don't have to pay the . . .'

'Oh, I'm sorry. I suppose that isn't important, is it? As I was saying, she was pregnant, so I thought maybe they were a young couple, but then I realized I never saw a husband in there with her.'

'How long was she there, Signora?'

'Oh, no more than a week, maybe even less. But long enough for me to get to know her habits, sort of.'

'And could you tell me what they were?'

'Her habits?'

'Yes.'

'Well, I never saw too much of her. Only when she walked past the window and went into the kitchen. Not that she ever cooked anything, at least not that I saw. But I don't know anything about the rest of the apartment, so I don't know what she did, really, while she was there. I suppose she was just waiting.'

'Waiting?'

'For the baby to be born. They come when they want.'

'I see. Did she ever notice you, Signora?'

'No. I've got curtains, you see, and that place doesn't. And the *calle*'s so dark that you can't really see into the windows on the other side, but about two years ago, whenever it was, they put one of those new street lamps just across from her place, so it's always light there at night. I don't know how people stand them. We sleep with our shutters closed, but if you didn't have them, I don't know how you'd get a decent night's sleep, do you?'

'Not at all, Signora. You said you never saw her husband, but did you ever see any other people in there with her?'

'Sometimes. But always at night. Well, in the evening, after

3

dinner, not that I ever saw her cook anything. But she must have, mustn't she, or someone must have taken her food? You have to eat when you're pregnant. Why, I ate like a wolf when I was expecting my boys. So I'm sure she must have eaten, only I never saw her cook anything. But you can't just leave a pregnant woman in a place and not feed her, can you?'

'Certainly not, Signora. And who was it you saw in the apartment with her?'

'Sometimes men would come in and sit around the table in the kitchen and talk. They smoked, so they'd open the window.'

'How many men, Signora?'

'Three. They sat in the kitchen, at the table, with the light on, and they talked.'

'In Italian, Signora?'

'Let me think. Yes, they spoke Italian, but they weren't us. I mean they weren't Venetian. I didn't know the dialect, but it wasn't Veneziano.'

'And they just sat at the table and talked?'

'Yes.'

'And the girl?'

'I never saw her, not while they were there. After they left, sometimes she would come out into the kitchen and maybe get a glass of water. At least, I'd see her at the window.'

'But you didn't speak to her?'

'No, as I told you, I never had anything to do with her, or with those men. I just watched her and wished she'd eat something. I was so hungry when I was pregnant with Luca and Pietro. I ate all the time. But I was lucky that I never gained too much . . .'

'Did the men eat, Signora?'

'Eat? Why, no, I don't think they ever did. That's strange,

isn't it, now that you mention it? They didn't drink anything, either. They just sat there and talked, like they were waiting for a vaporetto or something. After they left, sometimes she'd go into the kitchen, but she never turned the light on. That was the funny thing: she never turned the lights on at night, not anywhere in the apartment, at least anywhere I could see. I could see the men sitting there, but I saw her only during the day or, sometimes, when she walked past a window at night.'

'And then what happened?'

'Then one night I heard her calling out, but I didn't know what she was saying. One of the words might have been "*mamma*," but I'm not really sure. And then I heard a baby. You know the noise they make when they're born? Nothing like it in the world. I remember when Luca was born . . .'

'Was anyone else there?'

'What? When?'

'When she had the baby.'

'I didn't see anyone, if that's what you mean, but there must have been someone. You can't just leave a girl to have a baby on her own, can you?'

'At the time, Signora, did you wonder why she was living in the apartment alone?'

'Oh, I don't know. Maybe I thought her husband was away or that she didn't have one, and then the baby came too fast for her to get to the hospital.'

'It's only a few minutes to the hospital from there, Signora, isn't it?'

'I know, I know. But it can happen, you know, that it comes on you very fast. My two boys took a long time, but I've known women who had only a half-hour, or an hour, so I figured that's what happened with her. I heard her, and then I heard the baby, and then I didn't hear anything.'

'And then what happened, Signora?'

'The next day, or maybe it was the day after that—I don't remember—I saw another woman, standing at the open window and talking on the *telefonino*.'

'In Italian, Signora?'

'In Italian? Wait a minute. Yes, yes, it was Italian.'

'What did she say?'

'Something like, "Everything's fine, We'll see one another in Mestre tomorrow."'

'Could you describe this woman, Signora?'

'You mean what she looked like?'

'Yes.'

'Oh, let me think a minute. She was about the same age as my daughter-in-law. She's thirty-eight. Dark hair, cut short. Tall, like my daughter-in-law, but perhaps not as thin as she is. But, as I told you, I saw her only for a minute, when she was talking on the *telefonino*.'

'And then?'

'And then they were gone. The next day, there was no one in the apartment, and I didn't see anyone there for a couple of weeks. They just vanished.'

'Do you know if any of your neighbours noticed any of this, Signora?'

'Only the *spazzino*. I saw him one day, and he said he knew there was someone in there because they left a garbage bag outside the door every morning, but he never saw anyone going in or out.'

'Did any of the neighbours ever say anything to you about it?'

'No, not to me. But I imagine some of them must have noticed that someone was in there, or heard something.'

'Did you speak to anyone about this, Signora?'

'No, not really. To my husband, but he told me not to have anything to do with it, that it wasn't any of our business. If he knew I was here now, I don't know what he'd do. We've never been involved with the police before, and it always leads to trouble . . . oh, I'm sorry. I didn't mean to say that, not really, but you know how it is, I mean, you know how people think.'

'Yes, Signora, I do. Can you remember anything else?'

'No, not really.'

'Do you think you'd recognize the girl again if you saw her?'

'Maybe. But we look so different when we're pregnant, especially at the end like she was. With Pietro, I looked like a . . .'

'Do you think you'd recognize any of the men, Signora?'

'Maybe, maybe I would. But maybe I wouldn't.'

'And the woman?'

'No, probably not. She was there, at the window, for only a minute and she was standing sort of sideways, like she was keeping her eye on something in the apartment. So no, not her.'

'Can you think of anything else that might be important?'

'No, I don't think so.'

'I'd like to thank you for coming to see us, Signora.'

'I wouldn't have if my daughter-in-law hadn't made me. You see, I told her about it while it was going on, how strange it all was, with the men and no lights and all. It was something to talk about, you see. And then when she had the baby and then they all disappeared, well, my daughter-in-law told me I had to come and tell you about it. She said I might get into trouble if anything happened and you found out I saw her there and hadn't come in to tell you. She's like that, you see, my daughter-in-law, always afraid she's going to do something wrong. Or that I will.'

'I understand. I think she told you to do the right thing.'

'Maybe. Yes, it's probably a good thing I told you. Who knows what it's all about, eh?'

'Thank you again for your time, Signora. The Inspector will go downstairs with you and show you the way out.'

'Thank you. Er . . . ?'

'Yes, Signora?'

'My husband won't have to find out that I've been here, will he?'

'Certainly not from us, Signora.'

'Thank you. I don't want you to think anything bad of him, but he just doesn't like us to get mixed up in things.'

'I understand completely, Signora. You can be perfectly sure that he won't find out.'

'Thank you. And good morning.'

'Good morning, Signora. Inspector Vianello, will you take the Signora to the front door?'

2

Gustavo Pedrolli lay on the edge of the sleep of the just, curled round the back of his wife. He was in that cloudy space between waking and sleeping, reluctant to trade his happiness for mere sleep. The day had brought him an emotion different from any he had ever known, and he refused to let himself drift away from the radiance of memory. He tried to remember when he had ever been this happy. Perhaps when Bianca had said she would marry him, or on the actual day of their wedding, the Miracoli filled with white flowers and Bianca stepping up to the landing from the gondola, as he hurried down the steps to take her hand and her into his care for ever.

He had known happiness, certainly—on completing his medical studies and finally becoming *un dottore*, on being appointed assistant chief of paediatrics—but those happinesses were far removed from the flooding joy he had felt just before dinner, when he finished giving Alfredo his bath. He had fastened both sides of the diaper with practised hands and pulled on the flannel bottoms of his son's pyjamas. Then he slipped the duck-covered pyjama top over his head, and when it emerged, had played their usual game of hunting for the child's hands before pulling them one at a time through the sleeves. Alfredo squealed with delight, as surprised as his father at the sight of his tiny fingers as they peeped through the open ends of the sleeves.

Gustavo picked him up by the waist, hefting him up and down as Alfredo waved his arms in the same rhythm. 'And who's a beautiful boy? And who's his father's darling?' Gustavo asked. As always, Alfredo raised one of those clenched marvels, unfurled a finger, and placed it on his own nose. Dark eyes intent on his father's, he pressed his broad nose flat to his face, then lifted his finger away, only to point to himself repeatedly, throwing his arms around and squealing all the while with delight.

'That's right, Alfredo is his *papà*'s darling, *papà*'s darling, *papà*'s darling.' There followed more dangling, more lifting up, more waving. He did not toss the boy into the air: Bianca said the baby became too excited if they played like that before bedtime, so Gustavo merely raised him up and down repeatedly, occasionally drawing him close to kiss the end of his nose.

He took the boy into his bedroom and carried him over to the cot. Above it hung a galaxy of floating, turning shapes and animals; the top of the dresser was a zoo. He hugged the boy to his chest, careful to exert only the gentlest of pressure, well aware of the fragility of those ribs. Alfredo squirmed, and Gustavo buried his face in the soft folds of his son's neck.

He moved his hands down and held the boy at arm's length. 'And who is *Papà*'s darling?' he asked again in a singsong voice; he could not stop himself. Again Alfredo touched his own nose, and Gustavo felt his heart turn. The tiny fingers moved through the air until one of them rested on the tip of Gustavo's nose, and the boy said something that sounded like '*Papà*', waved his arms and gave a goofy, toothless smile.

It was the first time Gustavo had heard the boy say the word, and he was so moved that one of his hands flew to his own heart. Alfredo fell against his shoulder; luckily, Gustavo had the presence of mind, and enough experience with frightened children, to make a joke of it and ask, 'And who is trying to climb into his *papà*'s sweater?' Holding Alfredo against his chest, he pulled at one side of his cardigan and wrapped it around the boy's back, laughing out loud to show what a wonderful new game this was.

'Oh, no, you can't try to hide in there. Not at all. It's time to go to sleep.' He lifted the boy and placed him on his back in the cot. He pulled up the woollen blanket, making sure his son's chest was covered.

'Sweet dreams, my little prince,' he said, as he had said every night since Alfredo had begun to sleep in the cot. At the door he lingered, but only for a moment, so that the boy would not develop the habit of trying to delay his father's exit from the room. He looked back at the tiny lump and found tears in his eyes. Embarrassed at the thought that Bianca would see them, he wiped them away as he turned from the open door.

When he reached the kitchen, Bianca had her back to him, just pouring the penne through the strainer. He opened the refrigerator and took a bottle of Moët from the bottom shelf. He put it on the counter, then took a pair of crystal flutes, from a set of twelve that Bianca's sister had given them as a wedding present.

'Champagne?' she asked, as curious as she was pleased.

'My son called me *Papà*,' he said and peeled the golden foil from the cork. Avoiding her sceptical glance, he said, 'Our son. But just this once, because he called me *Papà*, I want to call him my son for an hour, all right?'

Seeing his expression, she abandoned the steaming pasta and moved to his side. She picked up the glasses and tilted them towards him. 'Fill both of these, please, so we can toast your son.' Then she leaned forward and kissed him on the lips.

As in the first days of their marriage, the pasta grew cold in the sink, and they drank the champagne in bed. Long after it was gone, they went into the kitchen, naked and famished. Ignoring the dry pasta, they ate the tomato sauce on thick slices of bread, standing at the sink and feeding chunks to one another, then washed it down with half a bottle of Pinot Grigio. Then they went back to the bedroom.

He lay suspended in the afterglow of the evening and marvelled that, for some months now, he had feared that Bianca had somehow changed in her . . . in her what? It was natural— he knew this from his practice—for a mother to be distracted by the arrival of a new child and thus to seem less interested in or responsive to the father. But that night, with the two of them behaving like teenagers gone wild at the discovery of sex, had eliminated any uncertainties.

And he had heard that word: his son had called him *Papà*. His heart filled again and he slid himself closer to Bianca, half hoping she would wake and turn to him. But she slept on, and he thought of the morning, and the early train to Padova he had to catch, so he began to will himself towards sleep, ready now to drift off to that gentle land, perhaps to dream of another son, or a daughter, or both.

He became vaguely conscious of a noise beyond the door to the bedroom, and he forced himself to listen, to hear if it was Alfredo calling or crying. But the ringing noise was gone, and so he followed it, his lips curved in memory of that word.

As Doctor Gustavo Pedrolli sank into the first and most profound sleep of the night, the sound came again, but he no longer heard it, nor did his wife, sleeping beside him, naked and exhausted and satisfied. Nor did the child in the other room, sunk in happiness and dreaming, perhaps, of the wonderful new game he had learned that night, hidden and safe under the protection of the man he now knew was *Papà*.

Time passed, and dreams played in the minds of the sleepers. They saw motion and colour; one of them saw something that resembled a tiger; and all of them slept on.

The night exploded. The front door of the apartment burst inward and slammed against the wall: the handle gouged a hole in the plaster. A man leaped into the apartment: he wore a ski mask, something that resembled a camouflage uniform, and heavy boots; and he carried a machine-gun. Another masked man, similarly uniformed, followed him. Behind them came another man in a dark uniform but without a mask. Two more men in the same dark uniform remained outside the house.

The two masked men ran through the living room and down the hall towards the bedrooms. The man without a mask followed more cautiously. One of the masked men opened the first door, and seeing it was a bathroom, left it open and moved down the hallway towards an open door. He saw the cot, the mobiles moving slowly in the draught created by the open door.

'He's here,' the man called out, making no attempt to keep his voice down.

The second masked man went to the door of the bedroom opposite. Still holding his machine-gun, he ran in, the other man close behind him. The two people in the bed sat up, startled by the light from the hallway: the third man had switched on the light before going into the room where the baby slept.

The woman screamed and pulled the covers up over her breasts. Dottor Pedrolli launched himself from the bed so suddenly that the first intruder was taken by surprise. Before he could react, the naked man was on him, one fist crashing down on his head, the other slamming into his nose. The intruder cried out in pain and went down as Pedrolli screamed to his wife, 'Call the police, call the police!'

The second masked figure raised his gun and pointed it at Pedrolli. He said something, but the mask over his mouth distorted the words, and no one in the room could understand them. Pedrolli was beyond hearing him, anyway, and came at him, hands raised to attack. Instinctively, the masked man reacted. Raising the butt of his gun towards the head of the approaching figure, he caught him above the left ear.

The woman screamed, and from the other room the baby sent up an answering wail, that high keening noise of infant panic. She pushed back the covers and, driven by instinct and no longer conscious of her nakedness, ran towards the door.

She stopped abruptly when the man without a mask stepped into the doorway, blocking her escape. She raised her arms to cover her breasts in a gesture she was not conscious of making. Seeing the tableau in the room, he moved quickly to the side of the man with the rifle that pointed at the naked man who lay motionless at his feet. 'You fool,' he said and grabbed at the thick material of the other's jacket. He pulled the man around in a semicircle and pushed him stumbling away. He turned back towards the woman and raised his hands, palms towards her. 'The baby's all right, Signora. Nothing will happen to him.'

She stood, frozen in panic, unable to scream.

The tension was broken by the masked man on the floor, who moaned and then struggled, as if drunkenly, to his feet. He put one gloved hand over his nose, and when he pulled it away he seemed shocked by the sight of his own blood. 'He broke my nose,' he said in a muffled voice, then pulled his mask over his face and let it fall to the floor. Blood continued to drip from his nose on to the front of his jacket. As he turned towards the man who appeared to be in charge, the woman saw the single word spelled out in iridescent letters on the back of his padded jacket.

'"Carabinieri?"' she asked, her voice barely audible over the continued screams of the baby.

'Yes, Signora. Carabinieri,' said the man who had spoken to her. 'Didn't you know we'd come, Signora?' he asked, something close to sympathy in his voice.

3

Guido Brunetti lay just on the edge of the sleep of the just, curled round the back of his wife. He was in that cloudy space between sleeping and waking, reluctant to let go of the happiness of the day. His son had casually mentioned at dinner how stupid one of his classmates was to fool around with drugs and had failed to see the look of relief that passed between his parents. His daughter had apologized to her mother for an angry remark made the previous day, and the words 'Mohammad' and 'mountain' sounded just at the edge of Brunetti's consciousness. And his wife, his sweet wife of more than twenty years, had surprised him with an outburst of amorous need that had inflamed him as though those two decades had never passed.

He drifted, full of contentment and greedy to run each of the events through his mind again. Unsolicited repentance from a teenager: should he alert the press? What caused him to marvel even more was Paola's assurance that this was not an attempt on Chiara's part to achieve some quid pro quo in return for the seemly expression of sentiments proper to her age and station. Surely, Chiara was smart enough to realize how effective a ploy this would be, but Brunetti chose to believe his wife when she said that Chiara was fundamentally too honest to do that.

Was this the greatest delusion, he wondered, our belief in

the honesty of our children? The question, unanswered, slipped away from him, and he drifted into sleep.

The phone rang.

It rang five times before Brunetti, in the thick voice of the drugged or mugged, answered it. '*Sì?*' he muttered, his mind flashing down the hall but instantly comforted by the memory of having wished both of his children goodnight as they went to bed.

'It's Vianello,' the familiar voice said. 'I'm at the hospital. We've got a mess.'

Brunetti sat up and turned on the light. The urgency in Vianello's voice, as much as the message, told him he would have no choice but to join the Inspector at the hospital. 'What sort of mess?'

'There's a doctor here, one of the paediatricians. He's in the emergency room, and the doctors are talking about possible brain damage.' This made no sense to Brunetti, regardless of his fuddled state, but he knew Vianello would get to it quickly, so he said nothing.

'He was attacked in his home,' the Inspector continued. Then, after a long pause, he added, 'By the police.'

'By us?' Brunetti asked, astonished.

'No, the Carabinieri. They broke in and tried to arrest him. The captain who was in charge says he attacked one of them,' Vianello said. Brunetti's eyes narrowed as the Inspector added, 'But he would say that, wouldn't he?'

'How many of them were there?' Brunetti asked.

'Five,' Vianello answered. 'Three in the house and two outside as backup.'

Brunetti got to his feet. 'I'll be there in twenty minutes.' Then he asked, 'Do you know why they were there?'

Vianello hesitated but then answered, 'They went to take his son. He's eighteen months old. They say he adopted the child illegally.'

'Twenty minutes,' Brunetti repeated and put the phone down.

It was only as he was letting himself out of the house that he bothered to check the time. Two-fifteen. He had thought to put on a jacket and was glad of it now, in the first chill of autumn. At the end of the *calle* he turned right and headed towards Rialto. He probably should have asked for a launch, but he never knew how long one would take, while he was sure to the minute how long it would take to walk.

He ignored the city around him. Five men to take an eighteen-month-old baby. Presumably, especially if the man was in the hospital with brain damage, they had not rung the doorbell and politely asked if they could come in. Brunetti himself had taken part in too many early morning raids to have any illusions about the panic they caused. He had seen hardened criminals whose bowels had loosened at the sound and sight of armed men bursting in upon them: imagine the reaction of a doctor, illegally adopted baby or no. And the Carabinieri—Brunetti had encountered too many of them who loved bursting in and imposing their sudden, terrifying authority, as if Mussolini were still in power and no one to say them nay.

At the top of the Rialto, he was too preoccupied with these thoughts to think of looking to either side but hurried down the bridge and into Calle de la Bissa. Why should they need five men and how would they get there? Surely they'd need a boat, and by whose authority were they carrying out an action like this in the city? Who had been informed, and if official notice had been given, why had nothing been said to him about it?

The *portiere* seemed to be asleep behind the window of his office: certainly he did not look up as Brunetti entered the hospital. Blind to the magnificence of the entrance hall though aware of the sudden drop in temperature, Brunetti worked his way right and left and then left again until he arrived at the automatic doors of the emergency room. They slid aside to let him enter. Inside the second set of doors, he pulled out his warrant card and approached the white-jacketed attendant behind the glass partition.

The man, fat and jolly-faced and far more cheerful than either the time or the circumstances warranted, glanced at Brunetti's card, smiled at him and said, 'Down to the left, Signore. Second door on the right. He's in there.'

Brunetti thanked him and followed the directions. At the door, he knocked once and went in. Though Brunetti did not recognize the man in battle fatigues who lay on the examining table, he recognized the uniform of the man standing at the window. A woman in a white lab coat sat beside the man on the table, smoothing a strip of plastic tape across his nose. As Brunetti watched, she cut a second strip and placed it parallel to the other. They anchored a thick cotton bandage to the man's nose; both nostrils were plugged with cotton. Brunetti noticed that there were already dark circles under his eyes.

The second man leaned comfortably against the wall, arms and legs crossed, observing. He wore the three stars of a captain and a pair of high black leather boots more appropriate for riding dressage than a Ducati.

'Good morning, Dottoressa,' Brunetti said when the woman looked up. 'I'm Commissario Guido Brunetti, and I'd be very grateful if you could tell me what's going on.'

Brunetti expected the Captain to interrupt him here, but

was both surprised and disappointed by the man's continued silence. The doctor turned back to her patient, pressing the ends of the tape a few times until they were secure on the man's face. 'Keep this in place for at least two days. The cartilage has been pushed to one side, but it should reattach itself without any trouble. Just be careful with it. Take the cotton out tonight before you go to bed. If the bandage comes loose, or if it starts to bleed again, see a doctor or come back in here. All right?'

'Si,' the man agreed with rather more sibilance than might have been heard in his normal voice.

The doctor extended a hand, and the man took it. She held him steady as he lowered his feet to the ground and stood, his other hand propped on the examining table. He needed a moment to steady himself. The doctor crouched down and looked upwards, at the cotton wadding in the man's nose, but evidently it did not trouble her, so she stood up and stepped back. 'Even if nothing happens, come back in three days, all right, and I'll take another look.' The man gave a very cautious nod, and looked as if he wanted to say something, but she cut him off and added, 'And don't worry. It should be fine.'

The man glanced at the Captain, then turned back to the doctor. 'I'm from Verona, Dottoressa,' he said in a muffled voice.

'In that case,' she said briskly, 'see your own doctor after three days or if it starts to bleed again. All right?'

He nodded and then turned to the Captain. 'And work, sir?'

'I don't think you'd be much use to anyone with that,' the Captain said, pointing at the bandage, then added, 'I'll call your sergeant and explain.' He turned to the doctor and said, 'If you'd give him some sort of letter, Dottoressa, he can go on sick leave for a few days.'

Something, perhaps nothing more than a sense of theatre or the habit of suspicion, made Brunetti wonder if the Captain would have been so gracious had he not been there as witness and if he had not introduced himself as a police officer. The doctor walked to the desk and pulled a pad towards her. She wrote a few lines, tore off the paper, and handed it to the injured man, who thanked her, then saluted the Captain and left the room.

'I was told that another man came in with them, Dottoressa,' Brunetti said. 'Could you tell me where he is?'

She was young, he noticed now, far younger than a doctor had any right to be. She was not beautiful, but she had a pleasant face, the sort that would wear well through life, becoming more attractive as she grew older.

'He's a colleague of mine, the assistant chief of *pediatria*,' she began, emphasizing the title as though offering it as sufficient proof that the Carabinieri had no business being involved with him. 'I didn't like the look of his injuries'—this with a glance towards the Captain—'so I sent him up to *neurologia* and called the assistant *primario* at home.' Brunetti was aware that she had the Captain's attention as well as his own. 'His pupils wouldn't dilate, and he had trouble placing his left foot, so I thought someone from *neurologia* should take a look at him.'

At this, the Captain interrupted from his place against the wall. 'Couldn't it have waited until later, Dottoressa? There's no need to get a doctor out of bed because a man's hit his head, is there?'

She turned her attention to the Captain, and the look she gave him made Brunetti prepare for a barrage. Instead, she said in an entirely neutral voice, 'I thought it wiser, Captain, as he seems to have hit his head against the butt of a rifle.'

So much for you, Captain, Brunetti thought. He caught the look the officer gave her in response and was surprised to see that the young man actually looked embarrassed.

'He said that, Dottoressa?' the Captain asked.

'No. He didn't say anything. Your man did. I asked what had happened to his nose, and he told me.' Her voice remained neutral.

The Captain nodded and pushed himself away from the wall. He approached Brunetti and put out his hand. 'Marvilli,' he said as they shook hands. Then he turned to the doctor and said, 'For what it's worth, Dottoressa, he's not my man. As he told you, he's from the command in Verona. All four of them are.' When neither Brunetti nor the doctor acknowledged this remark, the Captain revealed his youth and his uncertainty by explaining, 'The officer who was supposed to come with them had to replace someone in Milano, so they assigned me to the operation because I'm stationed here.'

'I see,' the doctor said. Brunetti, who had no idea of the extent—even the nature—of the operation, thought it wisest to remain silent.

Marvilli seemed to have run out of things to say, so after a pause, Brunetti said, 'I'd like to see this man, if I may, Dottoressa. The one in *neurologia*.'

'Do you know where it is?'

'Next to *dermatologia*?' Brunetti asked.

'Yes.'

'Then I see no reason why you can't go up,' she said.

Wanting to thank her by name, Brunetti looked at the tag on her jacket. 'Dottoressa Claudia Cardinale,' he read to himself. She'd had to live with that, he supposed, but had some parents no sense at all?

'Thank you, Dottoressa Cardinale,' he said formally and held out his hand. She shook it, then surprised Brunetti by also shaking the Captain's. Then she left them alone in the room.

'Captain,' Brunetti said in a neutral tone, 'would it be possible for me to know what's going on here?'

Marvilli raised his hand in a gesture that was curiously self-effacing. 'I can tell you at least part of it, Commissario.' When Brunetti said nothing, Marvilli went on, 'What happened tonight is part of an investigation that's been going on for some time: almost two years. Dottor Pedrolli,' he said, mentioning what Brunetti could only assume was the name of the man in *neurologia*, 'illegally adopted a baby eighteen months ago. In separate operations, he and a number of other people have been arrested tonight.'

Though curious about the number of people, Brunetti made no rejoinder, and Marvilli obviously thought no further explanation necessary.

'Is that what he's being accused of,' Brunetti asked, 'the illegal adoption of a child?' and by so doing became involved in Gustavo Pedrolli's exposure to the might and majesty of the law.

Marvilli said, 'I imagine he's also likely to be charged with the corruption of a public official, falsification of state documents, kidnapping of a minor, and illegal transfer of funds.' He watched Brunetti's face, and when he saw how sombre his expression grew, the Captain went on. 'As the case continues, there will no doubt be further charges.' With the toe of one of his elegant boots, he prodded at a bloody piece of gauze that lay at his feet, then looked up at Brunetti. 'And I wouldn't be at all surprised if resisting arrest and violence to a public official in performance of his duties were added.'

Brunetti chose to stay silent, aware of how very little he

knew about what was going on. He opened the door and stood back to let Marvilli pass into the corridor. The Captain's accent, though from the Veneto, was not Venetian, so Brunetti doubted he would be familiar with the labyrinth of the hospital. Silently, Brunetti led the other man through the empty corridors, turning left or right with little conscious thought.

They stopped outside the doors to the neurology department. 'Do you have one of your men with him?' Brunetti asked the Captain.

'Yes. The one he didn't attack,' he explained, then, when he realized how this sounded, he corrected this to, 'One of the others from Verona.'

Brunetti pushed open the doors to the ward. A young nurse with long black hair sat at a counter just inside. She looked up, and Brunetti thought she looked both tired and grumpy.

'Yes?' she asked as they came in. 'What do you want?'

Before she could tell them the ward was closed, Brunetti walked towards her, smiling a placatory smile. 'I'm sorry to disturb you, nurse. I'm from the police and I'm here to see Dottor Pedrolli. I think my Inspector might be here, as well.'

At the reference to Vianello, some of the sternness disappeared from her face and she said, 'He was, but I think he's gone downstairs. They brought Dottor Pedrolli in about an hour ago: Dottor Damasco is examining him now.' She turned her attention from the Veneziano-speaking Brunetti to the uniformed Marvilli. 'He's been beaten by the Carabinieri, it seems.'

Brunetti felt Marvilli stiffen and start to move forward, so he stepped in front of him to prevent him. 'Would it be possible for me to see him?' he asked, then turned and gave Marvilli a glance severe enough to stop him from speaking.

'I suppose so,' she said slowly. 'Come with me, please.' She rose from her chair. As they walked past her desk, Brunetti saw that the screen of the computer showed a scene from a historical film, perhaps *Gladiator*, perhaps *Alexander*.

He followed her down the corridor, aware of Marvilli's footsteps behind them. She stopped at a door on the right, knocked, and in response to a noise Brunetti did not hear, opened the door and put her head inside. 'A policeman's here, Dottore,' she said.

'One of them's in here already, damn it,' a man's voice said, with no attempt to disguise his anger. 'That's enough. Tell him to wait.'

The nurse drew her head back and closed the door. 'You heard him,' she said, all pleasantness fled from her voice and from her face.

Marvilli looked at his watch. 'What time does the hospital bar open?' he asked.

'Five,' she answered. Seeing the face he made in response to this, her tone softened and she said, 'There are some coffee machines on the ground floor.' She left them without another word and went back to her film.

Marvilli asked Brunetti if he wanted anything, but Brunetti declined. Saying he would be back soon, the Captain turned away. Brunetti immediately regretted his decision and was about to call after his retreating back, '*Caffè doppio, con due zuc-cheri, per piacere*,' but something restrained him from breaking the silence. He watched Marvilli pass through the swinging doors at the end of the corridor, then went over to a row of orange plastic chairs. Brunetti took a seat and began to wait for someone to emerge from the room.

4

While Brunetti waited, he tried to make some sense of what was going on. If the assistant chief of neurology had been called in at three in the morning, then something serious had been done to this Dottor Pedrolli, despite Marvilli's attempts to downplay the situation. Brunetti could not understand the excessive use of force, though it was possible that a captain who was not part of the men's command unit might not have been able to control the operation as effectively as would someone more familiar with his men. No wonder Marvilli was uneasy.

Could it be that Dottor Pedrolli, as well as having illegally adopted a baby himself, was more deeply involved in whatever traffic was going on? As a paediatrician, he would have access to children and, through them, to their parents, perhaps to parents who wanted other children, or even to those who could be persuaded to part with an unwanted child.

Or he might have access to orphanages: those children must have as much need of a doctor's services—perhaps more—than children living at home with their parents. Vianello, he knew, had been raised with orphans: his mother had taken in the children of a friend, but she had done it to keep them from being sent to an orphanage, that atavistic terror of his parents' generation. Surely things were different now, what with the involvement of the social services, of child psychologists. But Brunetti was forced to admit that he didn't know how many orphanages still existed in the country and, in fact, even where any of them were.

His mind flashed to the early years of his marriage to Paola, when the university had assigned her to teach a class on Dickens, and he, with the solidarity of a new husband, had read the novels along with her. He remembered, with a shudder, the orphanage where Oliver Twist was sent, but then he recalled the passage in *Great Expectations* that had most chilled his blood at the time, Mrs Joe's admonition that children should be 'brought up by hand', a phrase neither he nor Paola could ever decipher but which had nevertheless unsettled them both.

But Dickens had written almost two centuries ago, when families, by today's standards, were enormous: his own parents had each had six siblings. Do we try today to treat children better, now that they are in short supply? he wondered.

Brunetti suddenly raised the fingers of his right hand to his forehead in an involuntary gesture of surprise. No formal charge had been brought against Dottor Pedrolli, Brunetti had seen no evidence, and here he was, assuming the man's guilt, just on the word of some captain in riding boots.

His reverie was broken by Vianello, who appeared at the end of the corridor and came to sit beside him. 'I'm glad you're here,' the Inspector said.

'What's going on?' Brunetti asked, no less relieved to see the Inspector.

Speaking softly, Vianello began to explain. 'I was on night shift with Riverre when the call came in: I couldn't make any sense of it,' he said, then tried and failed to stop himself from yawning.

He slumped forward with his elbows on his knees and turned his head to Brunetti. 'A woman called, saying that there were men with guns in front of a house in San Marco. Over by La Fenice: Calle Venier. Near the old Carive offices. So we sent a patrol over, but by the time they got there, the men were gone, and someone shouted down from a window that it was the Carabinieri and that a man was hurt and they'd taken him to the hospital.'

Vianello glanced at Brunetti to see if he was following, then continued. 'It was the guys on the patrol—our guys—who called and told me all of this and that it was a doctor who was hurt, so I came over here to see what was going on, and that's when some jerk of a captain—wearing riding boots, for God's sake—told me it was their case and none of my business.' Brunetti let his Inspector's contempt for an officer go unremarked.

'That's when I decided to call you,' Vianello said.

The Inspector paused and Brunetti asked, 'What else?'

'After I did—call you, that is—I waited here for a while. I spoke to the neurologist when he got here and tried to tell him what was going on. But then Little Red Riding Boots came out of the room, and the doctor went in to see his patient. So I went down to the boat and talked to one of the Carabinieri who brought him in. He told me the squad making the arrest were from Verona, but the guy with the boots is stationed here. He's from Pordenone or some place like that, but he's been here for six months or so. Anyway, there was trouble when they went in to arrest this doctor. He'd fallen or something when he attacked one of them, and when they couldn't get him back on his feet, his wife started screaming, so they decided to bring him over here to have the doctors take a look.'

'Did he say anything about a baby?' Brunetti asked.

'No. Nothing,' Vianello answered with a confused look. 'The man I spoke to didn't seem to want to say much, and I wasn't sure what to ask. I just wanted to find out what happened to this doctor, how he got hurt.'

Briefly, Brunetti told Vianello what he had learned from Marvilli about the raid, its purpose, and its result. Vianello muttered something; Brunetti thought he heard the word 'attacked'.

'You don't think he fell?' Brunetti asked, remembering what Dottoressa Cardinale had said.

Vianello let out his breath in a sudden noise of disbelief. 'Not unless he tripped over the Captain's spurs when they got him out of bed. He was naked when they brought him in. Or at least that's what one of the nurses downstairs told me. Wrapped in a blanket, but naked.'

'And so?' Brunetti asked.

'Take a man's clothes off him, and he's only half a man,' Vianello said. 'A naked man doesn't attack a man with a gun,' he concluded, incorrectly in this case.

'Two, I think,' Brunetti observed.

'Exactly,' Vianello answered, refusing to abandon his conviction.

'Yes,' Brunetti agreed, and then looked up at the sound of footsteps in the corridor. Marvilli was approaching them.

The Captain noticed Vianello and said, 'I see your sergeant's filling you in on what happened.'

Vianello started to speak, but Brunetti forestalled him by getting to his feet and taking a step towards Marvilli. 'The Inspector's telling me what he's been told, Captain,' Brunetti said with an easy smile, then added, 'That's not necessarily the same thing.'

Seamlessly, Marvilli replied, 'That would depend on whom he's spoken to, I suppose.'

'I'm sure someone will tell us the truth, in the end,' Brunetti countered, wondering if Marvilli was in some sort of caffeine-induced state of agitation.

Marvilli's response was cut off by the opening of the door to Pedrolli's room. A man in middle years, vaguely familiar to Brunetti, stepped into the corridor, looking back at something inside. He wore what seemed to be a Harris tweed jacket over a pale yellow sweater, and jeans.

He raised a hand and pointed into the corridor. 'Out,' he said in a dangerous voice, his eyes still on something or, it now seemed, someone.

A much younger man, dressed in camouflage fatigues and carrying a machine-gun, appeared just in the doorway. He stopped, his face rigid with confusion, and looked down the corridor. He opened his mouth as if to speak.

The Captain waved him to silence and then jerked his head to one side, commanding him from the room. The man with the gun walked out into the corridor and down to Marvilli, but the Captain repeated the gesture, this time angrily, and the young man continued past him. All of them could hear the sound of his disappearing boots.

When silence returned, the doctor closed the door and approached them. He nodded in recognition of Vianello, then asked Marvilli, 'Are you the person in charge?' His voice was openly aggressive.

'Yes, I am,' Marvilli answered, and Brunetti could hear him struggle to keep his voice calm. 'May I ask who you are?' the Captain asked, then added, 'and why you ask?'

'Because I'm a doctor and I've got a patient in there who's been the victim of an assault, and since you're a Carabiniere officer and presumably know what's going on, I'd like to report it and report it as a crime.'

'Assault?' Marvilli asked with feigned curiosity. 'Your patient attacked two of my men and broke the nose of one of them. So if there's any talk of assault, he's the one who is more likely to be charged with it.'

The doctor looked at Marvilli with contempt, and made no effort to keep it out of his voice. 'I have no idea what your rank is, officer, but unless your men decided to take his clothes off him after fracturing his skull, then your men—and I assume they were armed—were assaulted by a naked man.' After a brief pause, he added, 'I don't know where you come from, but in Venice we don't allow the police to beat people up.' He turned away from Marvilli, making it clear that he had said all he wanted to say to him. Addressing Vianello, he said, 'Inspector, could I have a word with you?' Then, as Vianello started to speak, he added, 'Inside.'

'Of course, Dottore,' Vianello said. Indicating Brunetti with his right hand, he said, 'This is my superior, Commissario Brunetti. He's very concerned about what's gone on here.'

'Ah, that's who you are,' the doctor said, extending a hand to Brunetti and giving him an easy smile, as though it were perfectly natural to be introduced at four o'clock in the morning. 'I'd like to speak to you, as well,' he said, as though Marvilli were not standing less than a metre from them.

The doctor stood aside until Brunetti and Vianello had gone in; then he closed the door behind them. 'My name's Damasco,' he said, moving towards the bed. 'Bartolomeo.'

On the bed lay a man, who looked up at them with confused eyes. The overhead light was not on, and the only illumination came from a small lamp on the other side of the bed. Brunetti could make out a shock of light brown hair that fell across the man's forehead and a beard in which there seemed to be a great deal of grey. The skin above the beard was rough and pitted, and the top of his left ear swollen and red.

Pedrolli opened his mouth, but the other doctor bent over him and said, 'Don't worry, Gustavo. These men are here to help. And don't worry about your voice. It'll come back. You just need to rest and give the drugs a chance to work.' He patted the other man on his naked shoulder, then pulled the blanket up to his neck.

The man on the bed stared up at him intently, as if willing him to understand what it was he wanted to say. 'Don't worry, Gustavo. Bianca's fine. Alfredo's fine.'

At the last name, Brunetti noticed the man's face twist in pain. He squeezed his eyes shut to avoid showing whatever emotion it was he felt, then turned his head away, eyes still closed.

'What happened to him?' Brunetti asked.

Damasco shook his head as if wanting to shake away both the question and the reason for it. 'It's your business to find that out, Commissario. My concern is treating the physical consequences.'

Damasco saw how surprised the other two were by his abruptness and led them away from the bed. At the door, he said, 'Dottoressa Cardinale called me at about two this morning. She said that there was a man in the emergency room—she told me who it was, Gustavo Pedrolli, one of our colleagues—who had been brought in by the Carabinieri. He had been hit behind the left ear, by something hard enough to have caused a fracture of the skull. Luckily, the skull is thick there, so it's only a hairline fracture, but still it's a serious injury. Or can be.

'When I got here about twenty minutes later, there were two Carabinieri guarding the door. They told me the injured man had to be kept under guard because he had assaulted one of their colleagues when they tried to arrest him.' Damasco closed his eyes and pressed his lips together in an indication of how credible he found this explanation.

'Soon after that, my colleague in Pronto Soccorso called to tell me that this man, this "assaulted" man, had nothing more than a displaced cartilage in his nose, so I'm not willing to believe he was the victim of a serious assault.'

Curious, Brunetti asked, 'Is Dottor Pedrolli the sort of man who would react like this? So violently?'

Damasco started to speak but appeared to reconsider, then said, 'No. A naked man doesn't attack a man with a machine-gun, does he?' He paused and then added, 'Not unless he's defending his family, he doesn't.' When he saw that he had their attention, he went on, 'They tried to stop me from coming in here to see my patient. Perhaps they thought I'd try to help him escape through a window or something: I have no idea. Or help him concoct some sort of story. I told them I'm a doctor, and when I demanded the name of their commanding officer, they let me in, though the one in charge insisted that the other stay in here with me while I examined Gustavo.' He added, not without pride, 'But then I threw him out. They can't do that here.'

The way Damasco spoke the last word struck a responsive chord in Brunetti. No, not here, and certainly not without asking permission of the local police. Brunetti saw no sense, however, in mentioning this to Damasco and so limited himself to saying, 'The way you spoke to him, Dottore,' Brunetti began, 'made it sound like your patient's unable to speak. Could you tell me more about that?'

Damasco glanced away, as if looking for the answer to this

question on the wall. Finally he said, 'He seems to want to speak, but no words come out.'

'The blow?' Brunetti asked.

Damasco shrugged. 'It could be.' He looked at the two men one by one, as if judging how much he should tell them. 'The brain's a strange thing, and the mind's even stranger. I've been working with the one for thirty years, and I've learned something about the way it works, but the other is still a mystery to me.'

'Is that the case here, Dottore?' Brunetti asked, sensing that the doctor wanted to be asked.

Again, the shrug, and then Damasco said, 'For all I know, the blow isn't the cause of the silence. It could be shock, or it could be that he's decided not to speak until he has a clearer idea of what's going on.' Damasco reached up and rubbed at his face with open palms.

When he lowered his hands, he said, 'I don't know. As I say, I work with the physical brain, the neurons and synapses, and the things that can be tested and measured. All the rest—the non-physical stuff, the mind, if you will—I leave that to other people.'

'But you mention it, Dottore,' Brunetti said, keeping his voice as low as the doctor's.

'Yes, I mention it. I've known Gustavo for a long time, so I know a little about the way he thinks and reacts to things. So I mention it.'

'Would you be willing to expand on that, Dottore?' Brunetti asked.

'About what?'

'About the way your patient thinks and reacts?'

Damasco turned his full attention to Brunetti, and his consideration of the question was as clear as it was serious. 'No, I don't think I can, Commissario, except to say that he is rigorously honest, a quality which, at least professionally, has sometimes worked to his disadvantage,' he said, then paused, as though listening to his own words. Then he added, 'He's my friend, but he's also my patient, and my responsibility is to protect him as best I can.'

'Protect him from what?' Brunetti asked, choosing to ignore for the moment Dottor Damasco's observations about the consequences of his friend's honesty.

Damasco's smile was both natural and good-natured as he said, 'If from nothing else, Commissario, then from the police.' He turned away and walked over to the figure on the bed. Glancing back, he said, 'I'd like to be left alone with my patient, gentlemen, if you don't mind.'

5

As Brunetti and Vianello left the room, they saw that Marvilli was still there, propped against the wall, his arms and legs crossed, as he had been when Brunetti first saw him.

'What did the doctor have to say?' Marvilli asked.

'That his patient can't talk and that it's caused by a blow to his head,' Brunetti said, opting to provide only one of the possibilities the doctor had offered. He allowed the Captain to consider this before asking, 'Do you want to tell me what happened?'

Marvilli's eyes shot up and down the corridor, as if checking for unsympathetic listeners, but there was no one in sight. He uncrossed his legs and unfolded his arms, then pushed up his sleeve and looked at his watch. 'The bar's still not open, is it?' he asked, suddenly sounding more tired than wary. Then he added, 'The machine's broken. And I'd really like a coffee.'

'Sometimes the bar downstairs opens early,' Vianello said.

Nodding by way of thanks, Marvilli started to walk away, not waiting to see if the policemen would follow. He passed through the door into the Department of Dermatology, and Brunetti was too surprised and too slow to call him back. 'Come on,' said Vianello, turning in the opposite direction. 'He'll find it eventually.'

Downstairs, as they approached the open door of the bar, they heard the rasping noise of the coffee grinder and the hiss of the espresso machine. As they walked in, the barman started to object, but when Brunetti identified them as police, he agreed to serve them. The two men stood at the bar, stirring sugar into their coffees, waiting for Marvilli. Two attendants in blue smocks entered and ordered *caffè coretto*, one with a stiff shot of grappa and the other with Fernet-Branca. They drank quickly and left without paying, though Brunetti watched the barman take a notebook wedged beside the cash register, thumb through it, and write in it briefly.

'Good morning, Commissario,' a soft voice said from behind him, and he turned to see Dottor Cardinale.

'Ah, Dottoressa,' Brunetti said, making room for her at the bar. 'May I offer you a coffee?' he asked, making his voice loud enough for the barman to hear.

'And save my life,' she said, smiling. She set her doctor's bag on the floor. 'The last hour is the worst. Usually no one comes in, and by then I've started to think about coffee. I suppose that's what it's like if you're stranded in the desert,' she said. 'All you can think of is that first sip, the first taste of it saving your life.'

Her coffee came and she poured three sugars into it. Seeing the looks on the policemen's faces, she said, 'If I saw my patients doing this, I'd scream at them.' She swirled the cup around a few times, and Brunetti had the feeling she knew exactly how many times to swirl it before it would be cool enough to drink.

With one gulp, she downed the coffee, set the cup back in the saucer, looked at Brunetti and said, 'I am saved. I am human again.'

'Dare you risk another?' Brunetti asked.

'Not if I want to sleep when I get home,' she said, 'but thank you for the offer.'

She bent to pick up her bag and Brunetti said, 'How badly was that policeman hurt, Dottoressa?'

'Aside from his pride, not very much at all, I'd say.' She hefted the bag, adding, 'If he'd been hit really hard, the bone would have been broken or the cartilage knocked entirely out of place. This was nothing more than if he'd walked into a door. That is, if he was standing very near.'

'And Dottor Pedrolli?' Brunetti asked.

She shook her head. 'I told you: *neurologia* is not something I know much about. That's why I called Dottor Damasco.'

Over her shoulder, Brunetti saw Marvilli. The Captain, not bothering to conceal his irritation at having got lost, came up to the bar and ordered a coffee.

Dottoressa Cardinale shifted her bag to her left hand, shook hands with Brunetti and then leaned forward to shake Vianello's. 'Thanks again for the coffee, Commissario,' she said. She smiled at Marvilli and extended her hand. After only a moment's hesitation, he relented and took it.

The doctor went out into the corridor and looked back into the bar. She waited for Marvilli to turn and look at her. With an enormous smile, she said, 'Great boots, Captain,' turned, and was gone.

Brunetti kept his eyes on his coffee, finished it, and set down the cup quietly in its saucer. Seeing that they were the only customers in the bar, he turned to Marvilli. 'Do you think you could tell me a bit more about this operation, Captain?'

Marvilli took a sip and set down his cup before saying, 'As I told you before, Commissario, the investigation has been going on for some time.'

'Since when?' Brunetti asked.

'As I told you: almost two years.'

Vianello set down his cup perhaps a bit too loudly and asked the barman for three more coffees.

'Yes, Captain, you told me that,' answered Brunetti. 'But what I meant was what event triggered the investigation, especially this part of it?'

'I'm not sure I can tell you that, Commissario. But I can say that the action here was only part of a series of actions in other cities that took place last night.' He pushed his cup away and added, 'Beyond that, I'm not sure what I can tell you.'

Brunetti resisted the impulse to point out that one of the 'actions' had put a man in hospital. 'Captain,' he said softly, 'I, however, *am* sure that I'm at liberty to arrest you—or whichever of your men struck Dottor Pedrolli—for assault.' Brunetti smiled and added, 'I'm not going to, of course, but I mention it as an example of how we need not feel ourselves bound by what we are or are not at liberty to do.' He flirted with the idea of suggesting that the Captain's boots were enough to cause him to charge him with impersonating a cavalry officer, but good sense prevailed.

He tore open a packet of sugar and poured it in. Stirring gently and keeping his eyes on his spoon, he continued in an entirely conversational tone, 'In the absence of any information about this operation of yours and thus entirely unsure if your men had any right to carry it out in this city, Captain, I'm left with no choice but to protect the safety of the people of Venice. Which is my duty.' He looked up. 'That's why I would like more information.'

Wearily, Marvilli reached for his second coffee and pushed his empty cup and saucer across the bar. He pushed so hard that they slid off the other side and clattered, without breaking, into the sink below. 'Sorry,' he said automatically. The barman retrieved the cup and saucer.

Marvilli shifted his attention to Brunetti and asked, 'And if all this is only a bluff, Commissario?'

'If that's your response, Captain,' Brunetti said, 'I'm afraid I'll have to lodge an official complaint about the excessive violence used by your men and request an official investigation.' He put down his cup. 'In the absence of a warrant from a judge authorizing your entry into Dottor Pedrolli's home, your men remain guilty of assault.'

'There's a warrant,' Marvilli said.

'Issued by a judge in this city?'

After a long pause, Marvilli said, 'I don't know that the judge is from this city, Commissario. But I know there is a warrant. We would never have done something like this without one—not here and not in the other cities.'

That was certainly likely enough, Brunetti agreed. The times when the police could break in anywhere without a warrant were not upon them, not yet. After all, this was not the United States.

In a voice into which he put all the tiredness of a man woken long before his usual time and out of patience with what had happened since then, Brunetti said, 'If we can both stop being tough guys, Captain, perhaps we could walk back to the Questura together, and you could tell me along the way just what's going on.' He dug out a ten-Euro note and placed it on the bar then turned towards the door.

'Your change, Signore,' the barman called after him.

Brunetti smiled at him. 'You saved the Dottoressa's life, remember? That's beyond price, I'd say.' The barman laughed and thanked him, and Brunetti and Vianello headed down the corridor towards the entrance hall. A thoughtful Marvilli followed.

Outside, Brunetti felt the growing warmth of the day and observed that the pavement was damp in places: he could not remember if it had been raining when he had arrived at the hospital; while inside he had not been aware of rain. There was no sign of it now, and the air had been washed clean, presenting them with one of those pellucid days that early autumn gives the city, perhaps as consolation for having stolen the summer. Brunetti was tempted to walk down to the end of the canal to see if the mountains were visible beyond the *laguna*, but he knew that would most likely provoke Marvilli, so he abandoned the idea. If he waited until the afternoon, smog and gathering humidity would have obscured the mountains again, but perhaps tomorrow they would be visible.

As they crossed the *campo*, Brunetti noticed that the statue of Colleoni was finally free of the scaffolding that had covered it for years: it was wonderful to see the old villain again. He cut right beyond Rosa Salva, still not open, and started down Calle Bressana. At the top of the bridge he waited for Vianello and Marvilli to join him, but Vianello opted to remain at the bottom of the steps, leaning back against the low wall, establishing a distance between Brunetti and himself. Brunetti turned and leaned against the low wall of the bridge. Marvilli, standing beside him but looking in the other direction, started to speak. 'About two years ago, we were informed that a Polish woman, in the country legally, employed as a domestic, unmarried, was about to give birth in a hospital in Vicenza. Some days later, a married couple from Milano, in their late thirties, childless, came out of the same hospital with the baby and a birth certificate with the man's name on it. He claimed that the Polish woman was his lover and that the child was his, and the Polish woman testified that this was true.'

Marvilli rested his forearms on the flat surface of the bridge, gazing off at the buildings at the end of the canal. As if there had been no break in the conversation, he continued, 'What made no sense was that the man, the supposed father, had been working in England at the time the child would have been conceived. She must have been pregnant when she arrived in Italy: her work permit says she entered the country six months before the baby was born. The man claiming to be the father has never been to Poland, and she never left there before she came here.' Before Brunetti could ask, Marvilli said, 'We're sure. Believe me.' He paused and studied Brunetti's face. 'He's not the father.'

'How did you find out about all of this?' Brunetti asked.

His eyes still on the water, Marvilli replied, his voice suddenly grown nervous, as if he were divulging information he was not authorized to provide. 'One of the women in the room with the Polish woman. She had a baby at the same time. She said that all the Polish woman could talk about was her boyfriend and how much she wanted to make him happy. It seemed that the way she was going to make him happy was by taking a lot of money back to Poland, which is what she told him every time she phoned him.'

'I see,' said Brunetti. 'And this other woman in the room with her called you?'

'No, she told her husband, who works for the social services, and he called the command in Vicenza.'

Brunetti turned and stared off in the same direction as Marvilli, his attention drawn by an approaching taxi, and said, 'How wonderfully convenient, Captain. How very lucky indeed are the forces of order to be graced by such fortunate coincidences. The other woman just happened to speak enough Polish to understand what she told her boyfriend.' Brunetti glanced sideways at the Captain. 'Not to mention the convenient fact that her husband just happened to work for the social services and that he was conscientious enough to think of alerting the Carabinieri.' His look was long, and he made no attempt to disguise his anger.

Marvilli hesitated for a long time before he said, 'All right, Commissario.' He raised his hands in surrender. 'We knew about it before, from another source, and she was already planted in the room when the Polish woman got there.'

'And the concerned call you received from the man from social services?'

'These operations are secret,' said an irritated Marvilli.

'Go on, Captain,' Brunetti said, slipping open the buttons on his jacket as the morning light advanced and the temperature rose.

Marvilli turned to him abruptly. 'May I speak honestly, Commissario?' As the light increased, Brunetti noticed that Marvilli looked younger.

'I shouldn't bother to point this out, Captain, but your question suggests that you haven't been so far; but, yes, you may speak honestly,' Brunetti said in a voice grown suddenly gentle.

Marvilli blinked, not sure whether to respond to Brunetti's words or to his tone. He rose up on his toes and stretched backwards, saying, 'God, I hate these early morning things. We didn't even bother to sleep.'

'Another coffee?' Brunetti suggested.

For the first time, Marvilli smiled, and it made him look still younger. 'You told the barman the coffee saved that doctor's life. It'll probably save mine, too.'

'Vianello,' Brunetti called to the Inspector, who was still at the bottom of the steps, pretending to admire the façade of the building to his left. 'What's open around here?'

Vianello looked at his watch. 'Ponte dei Greci,' he said and started up the steps towards them.

When they reached the bar, the metal grille that protected the door and front windows was raised a few centimetres, enough to suggest that coffee was available inside. Brunetti tapped on the grille, calling out, 'Sergio, you in there?' He tapped again, and after a moment four hirsute fingers appeared at the bottom of the grille, and it slowly began to rise. Marvilli surprised them by squatting down and helping to lift the grille until it slid into place above the door and Sergio stood before them: thick, dark, hairy and as welcome a sight as Brunetti could imagine.

'Don't you guys ever sleep?' Sergio asked, more bark than bite. He retreated into the bar and went behind the counter.

'Three?' he asked, not bothering to specify: the sight of them was enough.

Brunetti nodded and led the others to a booth by the front window.

He heard the hiss of the coffee machine, and a banging at the door; he looked up to see a tall African in a light blue jellaba and woollen jacket carrying a paper-covered tray of fresh pastries. Sergio called out, 'Take it over to the men at the table, Bambola, would you?'

The African turned towards them, and when he saw Marvilli's uniform jacket gave an instinctive jerk of recognition and fear. He stopped and pulled the tray defensively closer to his chest.

Vianello made a casual gesture. 'It's before work,' he called. Bambola looked from Vianello to the other two, and they nodded in agreement. His face relaxed and he walked over to their table and set the tray down; then, like a magician, he whipped back the paper, filling the space between them with the aromas of cream, eggs, sugar, raisins, and fresh baked dough.

'Just leave it,' Marvilli said, then added, 'please.'

The African went over to the counter and said something to Sergio, then left the bar.

Each of them chose a pastry, and then Sergio was there with three coffees on a tray and a plate on to which he placed several of the pastries. He picked up the remainder and carried them behind the counter, where he began to place them on a Plexiglas tray.

As if in silent acknowledgement that it is difficult to discuss police business while eating cream-filled brioche, the three men remained silent until the coffees and the pastries were gone. Brunetti felt the rush of caffeine and sugar, and saw that the others were looking more alert.

'Then, after this couple from Milano took the Polish woman's baby home, what happened?' Brunetti asked. In the hospital, the Captain had said that the Pedrolli operation was 'separate,' but Brunetti was certain that he could, sooner or later, be led to explain this.

Tossing his paper napkin on to the plate, Marvilli said, 'A judge issued an order allowing them to be kept under surveillance.'

'Which means?' Brunetti asked, as though he didn't already know.

'Their home phone and fax and email were tapped, so were their *telefonini*. Their mail was opened, and they were followed occasionally,' Marvilli answered.

'And was the same true for Dottor Pedrolli and his wife?' Brunetti asked.

'No, they were different,' said Marvilli.

'In what way?'

Marvilli's lips flattened into a straight line and he said, 'I can't say more than that we received the information about them from a different source.'

'Can't or won't?' Brunetti asked.

'Can't,' Marvilli said, sounding displeased. Brunetti was unsure whether this resulted from being asked the question or from not being able to answer it.

He decided to risk one more question. 'Did you know about them from the beginning, too?'

Marvilli shook his head but said nothing.

Brunetti accepted Marvilli's response with apparent resignation, intrigued by the repeated suggestion that Pedrolli's situation was somehow different and in some way separate from the long-planned action. He sensed that Vianello wanted to say something and decided to let him. It would serve as a graceful way to move the subject away from the anomalous case of the Pedrollis. He turned to Vianello and, careful to use his first name, asked, 'What is it, Lorenzo?'

'Captain,' Vianello began, 'if your superiors knew what these people had done, why weren't they simply arrested?'

'The middle man, the person behind the arrangements. That's who we wanted,' Marvilli explained. He turned to Brunetti and said, 'You realize by now that it's not just the people who were arrested last night that we're interested in, no?'

Brunetti nodded.

'These aren't isolated cases,' Marvilli continued. 'This is going on all over the country. We probably don't have any idea of how common it is.'

He turned back to Vianello. 'That's why we need the middle man, so we can find out who was providing the documents, the birth certificates, in one case even false medical papers, claiming that a woman had given birth to a child that wasn't hers.' He folded his hands on the table like an obedient schoolboy.

Brunetti waited a few moments before saying, 'We've had a few cases here, in the Veneto, but as far as I know, this is the first time anyone's been arrested in the city.'

Marvilli acknowledged this and Brunetti asked, 'Does anyone have any idea . . . well, of the whole picture?'

'I can't answer that, either, Commissario. I was assigned this case only last night, and I was briefed about it then.' It seemed to Brunetti that the Captain had certainly learned a great deal in a very short time.

Instead of commenting on this, Brunetti asked, 'And do you know if this man you call the middle man was arrested?'

Marvilli shrugged, leading Brunetti to assume that the answer was no. 'What I do know is that two of the couples who were to be arrested last night had visited the same clinic in Verona,' the Captain finally said.

The surprise Brunetti felt at the name of a city in the economic heart of the country forced him to accept how automatic was his assumption that crime was somehow the natural heritage of the South. But why should the willingness to go to criminal lengths to have a child be more prevalent there than in the comfortable, rich North?

He tuned back in to hear Marvilli say, ' . . . Dottor Pedrolli and his wife.'

'Sorry, Captain, could you say that again? I was thinking about something else.'

Marvilli pleased Brunetti by showing no irritation that his listener's attention had drifted away. 'As I said, two of the other couples had been to the same clinic in Verona, a clinic that specializes in fertility problems. People are referred there from all over the country.' He watched them register this and added, 'About two years ago, the Pedrollis went to the same clinic for a joint exam.' Brunetti had no idea how many clinics in the Veneto specialized in fertility problems and wondered whether this need be anything more than coincidence.

'And?' Brunetti asked, curious as to how deeply and for how long the police might have concerned themselves with the clinic and with the lives of the people who went there as patients.

'And nothing,' Marvilli said angrily. 'Nothing. They had an appointment, and that's all we know.'

Brunetti forbore to ask whether the Carabinieri had kept both the Pedrollis and the clinic under surveillance and if so, to what extent. He wondered how, in fact, the Carabinieri had learned of their visit, and by what right, but the voice of patience whispered into his ear a list of the secrets open to the not inconsiderable skills of Signorina Elettra Zorzi, his superior's secretary, and so he held close to his bosom his sense of righteous indignation at the thought of the invasion of a citizen's privacy. He asked, 'And did you find any connection to this clinic?'

Marvilli pushed the plate away. 'We're working on it,' he said evasively.

Brunetti stretched his legs out under the table, careful not to nudge Marvilli's. He slumped down slightly on the bench and folded his arms across his chest. 'Let me think out loud, Captain, if I may.' The glance Marvilli gave Brunetti was wary. 'Hundreds of people must consult this clinic every year.'

When Marvilli did not answer, Brunetti asked, 'Am I right, Captain?'

'Yes.'

'Good,' Brunetti said and smiled as though Marvilli had confirmed in advance whatever theory he was about to propose. 'Then the Pedrollis are among hundreds of people with similar problems.' He smiled again at Marvilli, as though trying to encourage enthusiasm in a favourite pupil. 'So how is it, I wonder, that the Carabinieri decided that Dottor Pedrolli—out of all the people who went for a consultation at this clinic—also adopted a child illegally? That is, if this middle man has not been arrested.'

Marvilli hesitated too long before answering, 'I wasn't told.'

After another pause, the Captain added, 'I think that's something you should discuss with Dottor Pedrolli.'

A more brutal man than Brunetti, or a more unforgiving one, would have reminded Marvilli that Pedrolli was incapable of discussion in his current state. Instead, he surprised Marvilli by saying, 'I shouldn't have asked you that.' Deciding to change the subject, Brunetti continued, 'And the children? What'll happen to them?'

'The same thing as to all of them,' Marvilli said.

'Which is?' Brunetti asked.

'They'll be sent to an orphanage.'

6

Brunetti gave no sign of the effect Marvilli's words had had on him and resisted the desire to exchange glances with Vianello. He hoped the Inspector would follow his example and say nothing that would lessen, or spoil, the easy communication they seemed to have established with the Captain.

'And then what?' Brunetti asked professionally. 'What happens to the children?'

Marvilli could not disguise his confusion. 'I told you, Commissario. We see that they're taken to an orphanage, and then it's the duty of the social services and the Children's Court to see that they're taken care of.'

Brunetti chose to let this lie and continued, 'I see. So in each case, you...' Brunetti tried to think what word he was supposed to use here Repossessed? Confiscated? Stole?—'got the baby and handed it over to social services.'

'That was our responsibility,' agreed Marvilli simply.

Brunetti asked, 'And Pedrolli? What will happen to him?'

Marvilli considered before answering, 'That will depend on the examining magistrate, I suppose. If Pedrolli decides to cooperate, then the charges will be minor.'

'Cooperate how?' Brunetti asked. From Marvilli's silence, Brunetti realized that he had asked the wrong question, but before he could ask another, Marvilli shot back his cuff and looked at his watch. 'I think I have to get back to headquarters,

Signori.' He moved sideways and out of the booth. When he was standing, he asked, 'Will you let me pay for this?'

'Thanks, Captain, but no,' Brunetti answered with a smile. 'I'd like to be able to save two lives in one day.'

Marvilli laughed. He offered his hand to Brunetti and then, with a polite, 'Goodbye, Inspector,' leaned across the table and shook Vianello's hand as well.

If Brunetti expected him to make some remark about keeping the local police informed, perhaps to ask them to share with the Carabinieri any information they might obtain, he was disappointed. The Captain thanked Brunetti again for the coffee, turned and left the bar.

Brunetti looked at the plates and discarded napkins. 'If I have another coffee, I'll be able to fly back to the Questura.'

'Same here,' muttered Vianello, then asked, 'Where do we start?'

'With Pedrolli, I think, and then perhaps we should find this clinic in Verona,' Brunetti answered. 'And I'd like very much to know how the Carabinieri found out about Pedrolli.'

Vianello gestured towards the place where Marvilli had been sitting. 'Yes, he was very coy about that, wasn't he?'

Neither proposed a solution, and finally, after a contemplative silence, Vianello said, 'The wife's probably at the hospital. You want to go and talk to her?'

Brunetti nodded. He got to his feet and went over to the bar.

'Ten Euros, Commissario,' said Sergio.

Brunetti placed the bill on the counter then half turned to the door, where Vianello was already waiting for him. Over his shoulder, Brunetti asked, 'Bambola?'

Sergio smiled. 'I saw his real name on his work permit, and

there was no way I was going to be able to pronounce it. So he suggested I call him Bambola, since it's as close as anyone can get to his real name in Italian.'

'Work permit?' Brunetti asked.

'At that *pasticceria* in Barbaria delle Tolle,' Sergio said, pronouncing the name of the *calle* in Veneziano, something Brunetti had never heard a foreigner succeed in doing. 'He actually has one.'

Vianello and Brunetti left the bar, heading back to the Questura. It was not yet seven, so they went to the squad room, where there was an ancient black and white television on which they could watch the early morning news. They sat through the interminable political reports, as ministers and politicians were filmed speaking into microphones while a voiceover explained what they had supposedly said. Then a car bomb. Government denials that inflation was rising. Three new saints.

Gradually, other officers drifted in and joined them. The programme moved on to a badly focused film of a blue Carabinieri sedan pulling up at the Questura in Brescia. A man with his face buried in his handcuffed hands emerged from the car. The voiceover explained that the Carabinieri had effected night-time raids in Brescia, Verona, and Venice to close up a ring of baby-traffickers. Five people had been arrested and three babies consigned to the care of the state.

'Poor things,' Vianello muttered, and it was clear that he was speaking about the children.

'But what else to do with them?' Brunetti responded.

Alvise, who had come in unnoticed and now stood near them, interrupted loudly, as though speaking to the television but in reality addressing Brunetti, 'What else? Leave them with their parents, for the love of God.'

'Their parents didn't want them,' Brunetti observed drily. 'That's why all this is happening.'

Alvise threw his right hand into the air. 'I don't mean the people they were born to: I mean their parents, the people who raised them, who had them for—' he raised his voice further— 'some of them had them for eighteen months. That's a year and a half. They're walking by then, talking. You can't just go in and take them away and put them in an orphanage. *Porco Giuda*, these are children, not shipments of cocaine we can sequester and put in a closet.' Alvise slammed his hand down on a table and gave his superior a red-faced look. 'What sort of country is this, anyway, where something like this can happen?'

Brunetti could only agree. Alvise's question was perfectly fair. What sort of country, indeed?

The screen was filled with soccer players, either on strike or being arrested, Brunetti could not tell and did not care, so he turned away from the television and left the room, followed by Vianello.

As they climbed the stairs, the Inspector said, 'He's right, you know. Alvise.'

Brunetti did not answer, so Vianello added, 'It might be the first time in recorded history that he *has* been right, but he's right.'

Brunetti waited at the top of the stairs, and when Vianello reached him, said, 'The law is a heartless beast, Lorenzo.'

'What's that supposed to mean?'

'It means,' Brunetti said, stopping just inside the door to his office, 'that if these people are allowed to keep the babies, it establishes a precedent: people can buy babies or get them any way they want and from anywhere they want, and for any purpose they want, and it's completely legal for them to do so.'

'What other purpose could there be than to raise them and love them?' asked an outraged Vianello.

From the first time he had heard them, Brunetti had decided to treat all rumours of the buying of babies and children for use as involuntary organ donors as an urban myth. But, over the years, the rumours had grown in frequency and moved geographically from the Third World to the First, and now, though he still refused to believe them, hearing them unsettled him. Logic suggested that an operation as complicated as a transplant required a number of people and a controlled and well-staffed medical environment where at least one of the patients could recover. The chances that this could happen and that all of those involved would keep quiet were odds Brunetti was not willing to give. This, at least, surely held true in Italy. Beyond its borders, Brunetti no longer dared to speculate.

He still remembered reading—it must have been more than a decade ago—the agonized, and agonizing, letter in *La Repubblica*, from a woman who admitted that she had broken what she knew to be the law and taken her twelve-year-old daughter to India for a kidney transplant. The letter recounted the diagnosis, the assigning of her daughter's name to a ranking so low on the health service waiting list for transplants as to amount to a sentence of death.

The woman wrote that she was fully aware that some person, some other child, perhaps, would be constrained by poverty to sell a piece of their living flesh. She knew, further, that the donor's health would afterwards be permanently compromised, regardless of what they were paid and regardless of what they did with the money. But when she measured her daughter's life against the increased risk for some stranger, she had opted to accept that guilt. So she had taken her daughter to

India with one badly functioning kidney and had brought her back to Italy with a healthy one.

One of the things Brunetti had always secretly admired about some of the ancients—and he had to admit that it was one of the reasons he read them so relentlessly—was the apparent ease with which they made ethical decisions. Right and wrong; white and black. Ah, what easy times they seemed.

But along came science to stick a rod between the spinning wheels of ethical decision while the rules tried to catch up with science and technology. Conception could be achieved any which way, the dead were no longer entirely dead, the living not necessarily fully alive, and maybe there did exist a place where hearts and livers were for sale.

He wanted to express this in his answer to Vianello, but could find no way to compress or phrase it so that it made any sense. Instead, he turned to Vianello and put a hand on his shoulder. 'I don't have any big answers, only small ideas.'

'What does that mean?'

'It means,' he said, though the idea came to him only as he spoke, 'that because we didn't arrest him, maybe we can try to protect him.'

'I'm not sure I understand,' said Vianello.

'I'm not sure I do, either, Lorenzo, but I think he's a man who might need protection.'

'From Marvilli?'

'No, not from him. But from the sort of men Marvilli works for.'

Vianello sat down in one of the chairs in Brunetti's office. 'Have you dealt with them before?' he asked.

Brunetti, still feeling the buzz of the caffeine and sugar and too restless to sit, leaned against his desk. 'No, not with the men in Verona. I suppose I meant the type.'

'Men who'd give the babies to an orphanage?' Vianello asked, unable to evade the hold that thought had taken on him.

'Yes,' Brunetti agreed, 'I suppose you could refer to them that way.'

Vianello acknowledged this concept with a shake of his head. 'How can we protect him?'

'The first way would be to find out if he has a lawyer and, if so, who that is,' Brunetti answered.

With a wry smile, Vianello said, 'Sounds like you want to stack the deck against us.'

'If they're going to charge him with the list Marvilli gave us, then he needs a good one.'

'Donatini?' Vianello suggested, pronouncing the name as though it were a dirty word.

Brunetti raised his hands in feigned horror. 'No, I'd draw the line short of that. He'll need someone as good as Donatini, but honest.'

More because it was expected of him than because he fully meant it, Vianello repeated, 'Honest? A lawyer?'

'There are some, you know,' Brunetti said. 'There's Rosato, though I don't know how much criminal work she does. And Barasciutti, and Leonardi...' His voice wound down and stopped.

Without feeling it necessary to mention that they had been working among criminal lawyers for close to half a century between them and had come up with the names of only three honest ones, Vianello said, 'Instead of honest, we could settle for effective.' They chose to overlook the fact that this would place Donatini's name back at the top of the list.

Brunetti glanced at his watch. 'When I see his wife, I'll ask her if she knows one.' He pushed himself away from his desk, walked around behind it and sat down.

He noticed some papers that had not been there when he left the previous day but barely glanced at them. 'There's one thing we have to find out,' he said.

'Who authorized it?' Vianello asked.

'Exactly. There's no way a squad of Carabinieri would come into the city and break into a home without having permission from a judge and without having informed us.'

'Patta?' Vianello asked. 'Could he have known?'

The Vice-Questore's name had been the first to come to Brunetti's mind, but the more he considered this, the less likely it seemed. 'Possibly. But then we would have heard.' He did not mention that the inevitable source of that information would not have been the Vice-Questore himself but his secretary, Signorina Elettra.

'Then who?' Vianello asked.

After some time, Brunetti said, 'It could have been Scarpa.'

'But he belongs to Patta,' Vianello said, making no attempt to disguise his distaste for the Lieutenant.

'He's mishandled a few things recently. He could have taken it straight to the Questore as a way of trying to bolster his position.'

'But when Patta hears about it?' Vianello asked. 'He's not going to like having been hopped over by Scarpa.'

It was not the first time that Brunetti had considered the symbiosis between those two gentlemen from the South, Vice-Questore Patta and his watchdog, Lieutenant Scarpa. He had always assumed that Scarpa's sights were set on the Vice-Questore's patronage. Could it be, however, that the Lieutenant saw his liaison with Patta as nothing more than a flirtation, a stepping stone on the way to the realization of a higher ambition and that his real target was the Questore himself?

Over the years, Brunetti had learned that he underestimated Scarpa to his cost, so perhaps it was best to admit this possibility and bear it in mind in his future dealings with the Lieutenant. Patta might be a fool and much given to indolence and personal vanity, but Brunetti had seen no evidence that he was corrupt in anything beyond the trivial nor that he was in the hands of the Mafia.

He glanced away from Vianello to follow this train of thought. Have we arrived, then, he wondered, at the point where the absence of a vice equals the presence of its opposite? Have we all gone mad?

Vianello, accustomed to Brunetti's habits, waited until his superior's attention returned and asked, 'Shall we ask her to find out?'

'I think she'd enjoy that,' Brunetti answered immediately, though he suspected he should not give even this much encouragement to Signorina Elettra's habit of undermining the system of police security.

'Do you remember that woman who came in about six months ago, the one who told us about the pregnant girl?' Brunetti asked.

Vianello nodded and asked, 'Why?'

Brunetti cast his mind back to the woman he had interviewed. Short, older than sixty, with much-permed blonde hair, and very worried that her husband would somehow become aware that she had been to see the police. But someone had told her to come. A daughter or a daughter-in-law, he remembered, was mixed up in it somehow.

'I'd like you to check if there was a transcript made of the interview. I don't remember whether I asked for one, and I don't remember her name. It was in the spring some time, wasn't it?'

'I think so,' Vianello answered. 'I'll see if I can track it down.'

'It might not have anything to do with this, but I'd like to read what she said, maybe talk to her again.'

'If there is a transcript, I'll find it,' Vianello said.

Brunetti looked at his watch. 'I'm going over to the hospital to see what his wife will tell me,' he said to Vianello. 'And do ask Signorina Elettra if she can find out who was informed about the Carabinieri... operation.' He wanted to use a stronger word—attack, raid—but he restrained himself.

'I'll speak to her when she comes in this afternoon,' said the Inspector.

'Afternoon?' asked a puzzled Brunetti.

'It's Tuesday,' Vianello said by way of explanation, as if to say, 'Food stores close on Wednesday afternoon, fish restaurants don't open on Monday, and Signorina Elettra doesn't work on Tuesday mornings.'

'Ah, yes, of course.'

7

She was strong. Had Brunetti been asked to explain why this word came to him when he first saw Pedrolli's wife, he would have been hard-pressed to answer, but the word came to his mind when he saw her and remained with him for as long as he dealt with her. She stood at the side of her husband's bed and gave Brunetti a startled look when he came in, even though he had knocked. Perhaps she expected someone else, someone in a white doctor's coat.

She was beautiful: that was the second thing that struck Brunetti: tall and slender with a mane of dark brown curls. She had high cheekbones and light eyes that might have been green or might have been grey, and a long, thin nose that tipped up at the end. Her mouth was large, disproportionately so below her nose, but the full lips seemed somehow to suit her face perfectly. Though she must have been in her early forties, her face was still unwrinkled, the skin taut. She looked at least a decade younger than the man in the bed, though the circumstances prevented that from being a fair comparison.

When she registered that Brunetti was not whoever she was expecting, she turned back to her husband, who appeared to be asleep. Brunetti could see Pedrolli's forehead and nose and chin, and the long shape of his body under the blanket.

She kept her eyes on her husband, and Brunetti kept his on her. She was wearing a dark green woollen skirt and a beige sweater. Brown shoes, expensive shoes, made for standing, and not for walking.

'Signora?' said Brunetti, remaining by the door.

'Yes?' she said, glancing at him quickly but then turning back to her husband.

'I'm from the police,' he said.

Her rage was instantaneous and caught him off guard. Her voice took on a threatening sibilance that sounded one remove from physical violence. 'You do this to us, and you dare to come into this room? You beat him unconscious and leave him lying there, speechless, and you come in here and you dare to talk to me?'

Fists clenched, she took two steps towards Brunetti, who could not stop himself from raising his hands, palms outward, in a gesture more suited to warding off evil spirits than the threat of physical violence. 'I had nothing to do with what happened last night, Signora. I'm here to investigate the attack on your husband.'

'Liar,' she spat, but she came no nearer.

'Signora,' Brunetti said, intentionally keeping his voice low, 'I was called at home at two o'clock this morning and came down here because the Questura had received a report that a man had been attacked and taken to the hospital.' It was an elaboration—one might even have called it a lie—but the essence was true. 'If you wish, you can ask the doctors or the nurses if this is so.'

He paused and watched her consider. 'What's your name?' she demanded.

'Guido Brunetti, Commissario of Police. The operation in which your husband was injured . . .' He watched her begin to object, but he continued '. . . was a Carabinieri operation, not ours. To the best of my knowledge, we were not informed of it in advance.' Perhaps he should not have told her this, but he did so in an attempt to deflect her wrath and induce her to speak to him.

The attempt failed, for she immediately returned to the attack, though no matter how forceful her words, her voice never grew louder than a whisper. 'You mean these gorillas are free to come into the city whenever they want and break into our homes and kidnap our children and leave a man lying there like that?' She turned and pointed to her husband, and the gesture, as well as the words, struck Brunetti as intentionally dramatic. However sympathetic he might be towards Pedrolli and his wife, Brunetti did not allow himself to forget, as she seemed capable of doing, that they were accused of illegally adopting a child and that her husband was under arrest.

'Signora, I don't want to disturb your husband.' She seemed to soften, so he continued. 'If I can find a nurse who will stay in the room with him, will you come into the corridor and talk to me?'

'If you can find a nurse in this place, you're better than I. I haven't seen anyone since they brought me in here,' she said, still angry, but less so now. 'They're quite happy just to leave him lying there.'

Good sense told Brunetti not to respond. He held up his hand in a calming gesture. The uniformed Carabiniere still sat in the corridor though he didn't so much as glance up when Brunetti left the room. At the end of the corridor, the day shift was just coming on duty, two women of middle years dressed in today's nursing uniform: jeans and sweaters worn under long white jackets. The taller of the two wore red shoes; the other had white hair.

He took his warrant card from his wallet and showed it to them. 'I'm here for Dottor Pedrolli,' he said.

'What for?' the tall one demanded. 'Don't you think you've done enough?'

The older one put a restraining hand on her colleague's arm, as if she feared she and Brunetti were about to get into a fist-fight. She tugged at her colleague's arm, not gently, and said, 'Be careful, Gina,' then, to Brunetti, 'What is it you want?' Her tone, though milder, still seemed to accuse Brunetti of complicity in the blow that had put Dottor Pedrolli in the room half-way down the corridor.

Unwilling to relent, the one called Gina snorted, but at least she was listening to him, so Brunetti continued. 'I was here at three this morning to visit someone I thought was the victim of an attack. My men were not involved in it.'

The older one at least seemed willing to believe him, and that appeared to lessen the tension. 'Do you know him?' he asked, directing the question only at her.

She nodded. 'I used to work in paediatrics, until about two years ago, and there was no one better. Believe me, he's the best. Sometimes I'd think he was the only one who really cared about the kids: he was certainly the only one who ever acted like it was important to listen to them and talk to them. He spent most of his time here; he'd come in for almost anything. We all knew he was the one to call if anything happened during the night. He never made you feel you shouldn't have called him.'

Brunetti smiled at this description and turned to her colleague. 'Do you know him, too, nurse?'

She shook her head. The older woman gave her arm a squeeze and said, 'Come on, Gina. You know you do,' and re-leased her hold.

Gina spoke to her friend. 'I never worked with him, Sandra. But, yes,' she said, and now she turned her attention to Brunetti. 'I've seen him around sometimes, in the bar or in the corridors, but I don't think we've ever spoken—well, not more than to say good morning or something like that.' At Brunetti's nod, she continued. 'But I've heard about him: I suppose everyone does, sooner or later. He's a good man.'

'And a good doctor,' Sandra added. Neither Brunetti nor Gina seemed willing to speak, and so she changed the subject. 'I read the chart. They don't know what it is. Damasco wants to take more X-rays and do a CAT scan later this morning: that's what he wrote before he went home.'

Brunetti knew he would be able to get the medical information later, so he turned to Gina. 'Do you know his wife?'

The question surprised her, and she grew suddenly formal. 'No. That is, I never met her. But I've spoken to her on the phone a few times.' She glanced at the door to Pedrolli's room. 'She's in there with him, isn't she?'

'Yes,' Brunetti answered. 'And I'd like one of you to stay with him while I talk to her out here, if that's possible.'

The two women exchanged a glance and Sandra said, 'I'll do it.'

'All right,' said Gina, leaving Brunetti with her colleague.

He led the way to the door, knocked, and entered. Pedrolli's wife was where he had left her, by the bed, looking at her husband.

She glanced in their direction and, seeing the nurse's white jacket, asked her, 'Do you know when a doctor will come to see him?' Though the words were neutral enough, her tone suggested that she feared there might be days to wait, or longer.

'Rounds begin at ten, Signora,' the nurse answered dispassionately.

Pedrolli's wife looked at her watch, drew her lips together, and addressed Brunetti. 'There's plenty of time for us to talk, then.' She touched the back of her husband's right hand and turned away from the bed.

Brunetti stepped back to allow her to precede him, then pulled the door shut. She glanced at the Carabiniere and back at Brunetti with a look that suggested he was responsible for the other man's presence, but said nothing. The corridor ended at a large window that looked down on a courtyard and a scrawny pine tree leaning so sharply to one side that it appeared to grow horizontally, some branches touching the ground.

Reaching the window, he said, 'My name is Guido Brunetti, Signora.' He did not offer his hand.

'Bianca Marcolini,' she said, half turned away from him and gazing through the window at the tree.

As if he had not recognized the surname, Brunetti said, 'I'd like to speak to you about last night, Signora, if I may.'

'I'm not sure there's much to say, Commissario. Two masked men broke into our home along with another man. They were armed. They beat my husband insensible and left him like that,' she said, pointing angrily back towards his room. Then she added, her voice rough, 'And they took our child.'

Brunetti had no idea whether she was trying to provoke him by continuing to act as though he had been responsible, but he simply asked, 'Would you tell me what you remember of what happened, Signora?'

'I just told you what happened,' she said. 'Weren't you listening, Commissario?'

'Yes,' he agreed. 'You did tell me. But I need a clearer picture, Signora. I need to know what was said, and whether the men who came into your house announced themselves as Carabinieri and whether they attacked your husband without provocation.' Brunetti wondered why the Carabinieri had worn masks: usually they did that only when there was some danger that they would be photographed and thus identified. In the case of the arrest of a paediatrician, that hardly seemed the case.

'Of course they didn't tell us who they were,' she said, raising her voice. 'Do you think my husband would have tried to fight them if they had?' He watched as she cast her thoughts back to the scene in her bedroom. 'He told me to call the police, for God's sake.'

Making no attempt to correct her for confusing the Carabinieri with the police, Brunetti asked, 'Did he, or you, have any reason to expect them to come, Signora?'

'I don't know what you mean,' she said angrily, perhaps trying to deflect the question with her tone.

'Let me try to make my question clearer, then, if I might. Is there any reason why you, or your husband, thought the police or the Carabinieri might be interested in you or might approach you?' Even as he said it, Brunetti knew he had chosen the wrong word, one that was sure to inflame her.

He was not wrong. ' "Approach" us,' she gasped, driven beyond her powers of restraint. She took a step away from the window and raised her hand. She shot a finger out at him and said, her voice tight with rage she could no longer contain, 'Might *approach* us. That was no approach, Signore: it was an attack, an assault, a raid.' She stopped, and Brunetti saw that the flesh around her mouth stood out white in the sudden redness of her face. She took a step towards him but then faltered. She braced a hand against the windowsill, locking her elbow to keep herself from falling.

Brunetti was immediately beside her, supporting her until she half leaned, half sat on the windowsill. He kept his hold on her arm. She closed her eyes and leaned forward, hands propped on her knees, head hanging limply.

Halfway down the corridor, Sandra put her head out of the door to Pedrolli's room, but Brunetti raised a calming hand and she moved back inside. The woman beside him took a number of deep, rasping breaths, her head still lowered.

A man in a white lab coat came into view at the end of the corridor, but his attention was on a sheet of paper in his hand: he ignored, or didn't see, Brunetti and the woman. He disappeared into one of the rooms without knocking.

Time passed, until finally Signora Marcolini pushed herself up and stood, but did not open her eyes. Brunetti released her arm.

'Thank you,' she said, still breathing heavily. Eyes still closed, she said, 'It was terrible. The noise woke me up. Men shouting, and when I looked, I saw a man hit Gustavo with something, and then he was on the ground, and then Alfredo started to scream, and I thought they were there to hurt us.'

She opened her eyes and looked at Brunetti. 'I think we must have been a little crazy. From the fear.'

'Fear of what, Signora?' Brunetti asked softly, hoping his question would not propel her into rage again.

'That they'd arrest us,' she said.

'Because of the baby?'

She lowered her head, but he heard her answer, 'Yes.'

8

'Would you like to tell me about it, Signora?' Brunetti asked. He glanced along the corridor and saw the man in the white lab coat leave the room on the left and head back towards the double glass doors at the end of the corridor. The man went through the doors, turned, and disappeared.

Experience told Brunetti to remain as still as he could until his presence became an almost imperceptible part of the woman's surroundings. A minute passed, and then another. Intensely aware of the woman beside him, he continued to gaze off down the corridor.

Finally she said, in a softer voice, 'We couldn't have children. And we couldn't adopt.' Another pause, and then she added, 'Or, if we could have, by the time our papers were processed and we were approved, the only children we could have would be . . . well, would be older. But we wanted,' she said, and Brunetti prepared himself to hear what she would say, '. . . a baby.' She spoke calmly, as though entirely unconscious of the pathos of what she had said, and Brunetti found an even greater pathos in that.

He still did not look at her; he permitted himself to nod in acknowledgement, but still he said nothing.

'My sister isn't married, but Gustavo's sister has three children,' she said. 'And his brother has two.' She glanced at him as if to register his response to this evidence of their failure, and went on. 'Then someone here at the hospital—I think it was one of his colleagues, or one of his patients—well, someone told Gustavo about a private clinic.' He waited for her to continue, and she added. 'We went and we had tests, and there were... there were problems.' The fact that Brunetti knew about the nature of the visit embarrassed him as much as if he had been caught reading someone else's mail.

Idly, she rubbed the toe of her shoe against a long scratch in the floor tiles that had been left by a cart or some heavy object. Still looking down, she added, 'We both had problems. If it had been just one of us, it might have been possible. But with both of us...' Brunetti let the pause stretch out until she added, 'He saw the results. He didn't want to tell me, but I made him.'

Brunetti's profession had made him a master of pauses: he could distinguish them the way a concert-master could distinguish the tones of the various strings. There was the absolute, almost belligerent pause, after which nothing would come unless in response to questions or threats. There was the attentive pause, after which the speaker measured the effect on the listener of what had just been said. And there was the exhausted pause, after which the speaker needed to be left undisturbed until emotional control returned.

Judging that he was listening to the third, Brunetti remained silent, certain that she would eventually continue. A sound came down the corridor: a moan or the cry of a sleeping person. When it stopped, the silence seemed to expand to fill its place.

Brunetti glanced at her then and nodded, a gesture that could be read as agreement or as encouragement to continue. She apparently took it as both and went on, 'After we had the results, we had no choice but to resign ourselves. To not having a baby. But then Gustavo—it must have been a few months after we went to the clinic—he said that he was examining the possibility of private adoption.'

It sounded to Brunetti as if she were repeating a statement she had prepared in advance. 'I see,' he said neutrally. 'What sort of possibility?'

She shook her head and said, her voice barely above a whisper, 'He didn't say.'

Though Brunetti doubted this, he gave no indication and merely asked, 'Did he mention the clinic?'

She gave him a puzzled glance, and Brunetti explained, 'The clinic where you had the tests.'

She shook her head. 'No, he never mentioned the clinic, only that there was a possibility that we could have a baby.'

'Signora,' Brunetti said, 'I can't force you to tell me these things.' In a certain sense this was true, but sooner or later someone *would* have the authority to force her to do so.

She must have realized this, for she continued, 'He didn't say from where, said he didn't want me to get my hopes up, but that it was something he thought he could arrange. I assumed it was because of his work or because of people he knew.' She looked through the window, then at Brunetti. 'If I have to tell the truth, I suppose I didn't want to know. He said that everything would be *in regola* and that it would be legal. He said he had to claim that the child was his, but it wouldn't be: he told me that.'

Had he been questioning a suspect, Brunetti would have asked, voice pumped full of scepticism, 'And you *believed* him?' Instead, in the voice of concerned friendship, he asked, 'But he didn't tell you how this would happen, Signora?' He allowed three beats to pass and added, 'Or did you think to ask him?'

She shook the question away. 'No. I think I didn't want to know. I just wanted it to happen. I wanted a baby.'

Brunetti gave her a moment to recover from what she had said, then asked, 'Did he tell you anything about the woman?'

'Woman?' she asked, genuinely confused.

'Whose baby it was.'

She hesitated but then tightened her lips. 'No. Nothing.' Brunetti had the strange sensation that she had aged during this conversation, that the lines formerly confined to her neck had migrated up to the sides of her mouth and eyes.

'I see,' Brunetti said. 'And you never learned any more?' Surely, thought Brunetti, the man must have told her something; she must have wanted to know.

He saw that her eyes in fact were light grey and not green. 'No,' she said, lowering her head. 'I never discussed it with Gustavo: I didn't want to. He thought—Gustavo, that is—well, I suppose he thought it would upset me to know. He told me he wanted me to think from the very beginning that the baby was ours, and . . .' She stopped herself, and Brunetti had the feeling that she had forced herself not to add some vital final phrase.

'Of course,' Brunetti muttered when he realized she was not going to end the sentence. He had no idea how much more he could induce her to tell him, and he did not want to continue to question her if, by displaying curiosity rather than concern, he weakened the confidence she appeared to have developed in him.

Sandra opened the door to the room down the corridor and gestured to Signora Marcolini.

'Your husband's very agitated, Signora. Perhaps you could come and speak to him.' Her concern was evident, and Pedrolli's wife responded to it instantly by joining her at the door, then closing it after them.

Assuming that she would be some time in the room with her

husband, Brunetti decided to try to find Dottor Damasco and ask if there had been any change in Pedrolli's condition. He knew the way to *neurologia*, and when he got there he started down the corridor toward where he knew the doctors had their offices.

He found the door, but when he knocked, a male nurse who was passing told him that the doctor was just finishing his rounds and usually came back to his office after that. When he added that this should be within the next ten minutes or so, Brunetti said he would wait. When the nurse was gone, he sat in one of the now-familiar, and familiarly uncomfortable, orange chairs. Without anything to read, Brunetti leaned his head back against the wall and closed his eyes, the better to consider what he might ask Dottor Damasco.

'Signore? Signore?' was the next thing he heard. He opened his eyes and saw the male nurse. 'Are you all right, Signore?' the young man asked.

'Yes, yes,' Brunetti said, pushing himself to his feet. It all came back, and he asked, 'Is the doctor free now?'

The nurse gave a nervous smile. 'I'm sorry, Signore, but he's gone. He went home as soon as he finished his rounds. I didn't know he'd gone, and when someone mentioned it, I came down here to tell you. I'm sorry,' he repeated, sounding as if he were responsible for Dottor Damasco's disappearance.

Brunetti looked at his watch and saw that more than half an hour had passed. 'It's all right,' he said, suddenly aware of just how tired he was. He wished that, like Dottor Damasco, he could just finish his rounds and go home.

Instead, making a pretence of being fully awake, he thanked the young man and started back towards the reception desk. Passing the nurses' station, he approached the glass doors that led to the ward. He was stunned to see, halfway down the corridor, a few paces from the closed door of Pedrolli's room, the unmistakable back of his superior, Vice-Questore Giuseppe Patta. Brunetti recognized the broad shoulders in the cashmere overcoat and the thick head of silver hair. What he did not recognize was the attentive, posture of the Vice-Questore, who was leaning towards a man, all of whom save an outline was blocked from view by Patta's body. Patta raised his right hand and patted at the air between them in a conciliatory manner, then lowered it to his side and moved back a step as if to allow more room for the man's response.

Beta dog deferring to alpha dog, was Brunetti's instant thought, and he retreated until he was partly hidden behind the chest-high counter of the nurses' station. Should Patta start to turn towards him, he would have time to back away and out of sight while he decided if he wanted his superior to discover him; he could take a few steps down the corridor, turn, then give vent to the very real surprise he felt at seeing his superior here at this hour.

The other man, most of his considerable bulk still obscured by Patta's body, raised both hands in what could be exasperation or surprise, then jabbed an angry finger repeatedly towards the closed door of Pedrolli's room. In response, Patta's head shook from side to side, then nodded up and down, much in the manner of a toy dog in the back of a car that had just hit a rough patch.

Suddenly the other man wheeled away from Patta and started down the corridor away from him. All Brunetti saw before he ducked behind the counter was the man's back: neck almost as thick as his head, short buzz-cut white hair, a body almost as wide as it was tall. When Brunetti looked again, he saw that Patta had made no motion to follow the man. As Brunetti watched, the man reached the doors at the end of the corridor and shoved them open, slamming the right one back against the wall with a crack that reverberated down the corridor.

Brunetti's impulse was to approach Patta and feign surprise, but good sense propelled him backwards, down a corridor, then through another set of doors. He waited there a full five minutes, and when he returned to *neurologia*, there was no sign of Patta.

9

Brunetti went back to the corridor outside Pedrolli's room, waiting for Signora Marcolini to emerge so that he could slip back into his role of sympathetic listener. He reached into his jacket pocket for his *telefonino* but discovered that he had left it at home. He did not want to miss Signora Marcolini when she emerged, but he did want to call Paola and tell her he would not be home for lunch and had no idea when he would be.

He sat in the plastic chair and stared into space, careful to keep his head forward and away from the temptation of the wall behind him. After less than a minute, he went to the end of the corridor and read the list of instructions for evacuation in case of fire, then the list of doctors working on the ward. Gina came through the door on the other side of the desk.

'Signora Gina, excuse me, but could I use the phone?'

She gave him a very small smile and said, 'Dial nine first.' He picked up the phone behind the nurses' desk and dialled his home number.

'*Sì?*' he heard Paola answer.

'Still too tired to talk?' he couldn't resist asking.

'Of course not,' she answered. Then, 'Where are you?'

'At the hospital.'

'Trouble?'

'The Carabinieri over-reacted making an arrest, it seems,

and the man is here. He's a doctor, so at least he's assured of good care.'

'The Carabinieri attacked a doctor?' she said, incapable of keeping the shock from her voice.

'I didn't say they attacked him, Paola,' he said, though what she said was true enough. 'I said they over-reacted.'

'And what does that mean, that they drove their boats too fast taking him to the hospital? Or made too much noise and disturbed the neighbours when they were kicking in his door?'

Though Brunetti tended to share Paola's scepticism about the overall competence of the Carabinieri, he did not, in his caffeine-and-sugar-induced state, want to have to listen to her voice it. 'It means he resisted arrest and broke the nose of one of the men who were sent to get him.'

She was on to him like a hawk. 'One of the men? How many were there?'

'Two,' Brunetti chose to lie, marvelling at how quickly he had been manoeuvred into defending the men who had assaulted Pedrolli.

'*Armed* men?' she asked.

Suddenly tired of this, Brunetti said, 'Paola, I'll tell you everything when I see you, all right?'

'Of course,' she answered. 'Do you know him?'

'No.' Having heard enough about the doctor to have formed a favourable opinion of him did not count as knowing him, Brunetti told himself.

'Why did they arrest him?' she asked.

'He adopted a baby a year and a half ago, and it seems now that he did it illegally.'

'What happened to the baby?' Paola asked.

'They took him away,' Brunetti said in a neutral voice.

'Took him away?' Paola asked with all of her former bellig-
erence. 'What's that supposed to mean?'

'He was taken into care.'

'Into care as in given back to his real mother, or into care as
in put in an orphanage?'

'The latter, I'm afraid,' Brunetti admitted.

There was a long pause, after which Paola said, as if to herself, 'A year and a half,' and then she added, 'God, what heartless
bastards they are, eh?'

Betray the state by agreeing with her or betray humanity by
demurring: Brunetti considered the options open to him and
gave the only response he could. 'Yes.'

'We'll talk about it when you get home, all right?' said a
suddenly accommodating Paola.

'Yes,' Brunetti said and replaced the phone.

Brunetti was relieved he had not told Paola about the other
people, the ones who had been kept under surveillance for almost two years. Alvise—even Brunetti himself—had focused
on that number, that year and a half that a knowing authority
had allowed the new parents to keep the child. That's when a
man becomes a father, Brunetti knew, or at least he remembered that it was during that first year and a half that his own
children had been soldered into his heart. Had either of them
been taken from him, for any reason, after that time, he would
have gone through life with some essential part of himself ir-
reparably damaged. Before that conviction could fully take
shape in his mind, Brunetti realized that, had either child been
taken from him at any time after he first saw them, his suffering
would have been no different than if he had had them for
eighteen months, or eighteen years.

Back in his chair, he resumed his consideration of the wall

and of the strange fact of Patta's presence, and after another twenty minutes, Signora Marcolini let herself out into the hallway and walked over to him. She looked far more tired than when she had gone back into the room.

'You're still here?' she said. 'I'm sorry, but I've forgotten your name.'

'Brunetti, Signora. Guido,' he said as he got to his feet. He smiled again but did not extend his hand. 'I've spoken to the nurses here, and it seems your husband is very well regarded. I'm sure he'll be well taken care of.'

He expected a sharp response, and she did not disappoint. 'That could begin by keeping the Carabinieri away from him.'

'Of course. I'll see what I can do about arranging that,' Brunetti said, though he wondered if this would be possible. Changing the subject, he asked, 'Can your husband understand what you say, Signora?'

'Yes.'

'Good.' Brunetti's grasp of the workings of the brain was rudimentary, but it seemed to him that, if the man could understand language, then there might be some likelihood of his being able to regain speech. Was there some way that Pedrolli's powers could be tested? Without language, what were we?

'. . . away from the media,' he heard her say.

'I beg your pardon, Signora. I didn't hear that: I was thinking about your husband.'

'Is there any way that all of this can be kept out of the media?' she repeated.

Presumably, she meant the accusations of false adoption that would be brought against them, but Brunetti's mind flashed to the Carabinieri's brutal tactics: surely it was in the best interests of the state that those be kept from the press. But in the event that the arrests became public knowledge—and the memory of that morning's television news interrupted to tell him that they already had—then it was in the best interests of the Pedrollis that their treatment at the hands of the Carabinieri became so, too.

'If I were in your place, Signora, I'd wait to see how they choose to present this.'

'What do you mean?' she asked.

'You and your husband have erred out of love, it seems to me,' Brunetti began, aware that he was coaching a witness, even aiding a suspect. But so long as he confined himself to discussing the behaviour of the media, he saw nothing improper in anything he might say or any warning he might offer. 'So they might decide to treat you sympathetically.'

'Not if the Carabinieri talk to them first,' she said, displaying a remarkable clear-sightedness about the ways of the world. 'All they've got to do is mention the wounded officer, and they'll be all over us.'

'Perhaps not, Signora, once they learn about your husband's treatment—and yours, of course.'

At times, Brunetti worried about the growing ferocity of his contempt for the media. All a criminal had to do, it seemed to him at times, was present himself as a victim, and the howl would be heard in Rome. Plant a bomb, rob a bank, cut a throat: it hardly mattered. Once the media decided that the accused had been subjected to ill-treatment or injustice, of any sort and however long ago, then he or she was destined to become the subject of long articles, editorials, even interviews. And here he was, all but coaching a suspect to present herself in just this way.

Brunetti hauled himself from these ideas and returned his attention to Signora Marcolini. '. . . back to my husband,' he heard her say.

'Of course. Would it be possible for me to speak to you again, Signora?' he asked, knowing that he had the authority to take her down to the Questura and keep her there for hours, should he choose to.

'I want to see a lawyer first,' she said, raising herself in Brunetti's estimation. Knowing the name of the family that was likely to surround and protect her, Brunetti had no doubt that her legal representation would be the best available.

Brunetti considered asking her about the man who had so clearly dominated Patta in the brief scene outside her husband's room, but thought it might be better to keep his knowledge of that to himself. 'Of course, Signora,' he said, taking one of his cards from his wallet and giving it to her. 'If there's any way in which I can help you, please call me.'

She took the card, slipped it into the pocket of her skirt without looking at it, and nodded before re-entering her husband's room.

Brunetti walked away from the ward and then from the hospital, heading back toward the Questura, musing on his last exchange with Signora Marcolini. Her concern for her husband seemed genuine, he told himself. His thoughts turned to Solomon and the story of the two women who claimed to be the mother of the same baby. The real mother, for love of her son, renounced all claim to him when faced with Solomon's decision to cut the baby in half so that each claimant could have a part, while the false claimant made no objection. The story had of course been told endlessly and had thus become one of the set pieces that had entered into the common memory.

Why, then, had Signora Marcolini displayed no curiosity about the fate of the baby?

10

As soon as Brunetti got back to the Questura, he decided to stop and see if Patta had returned, but when he went upstairs, he was surprised to find Signorina Elettra at work behind her desk. She looked, at first glance, like a rainforest scene: her silk shirt was wildly patterned with leaves and violently coloured birds; a pair of tiny monkey legs peeked out from under her collar. Her scarf was the red of a baboon's buttocks, contributing to the tropical effect.

'But it's Tuesday,' Brunetti said when he saw her.

She smiled and raised her hands in a gesture acknowledging human weakness. 'I know, I know, but the Vice-Questore called me at home and said he was in the hospital. I offered to come in because he didn't know how long he'd be.'

Then, in a voice in which Brunetti detected real concern, she asked, 'There's nothing wrong with him, is there?'

Brunetti smiled. 'Ah, Signorina, you ask me a question that my sense of good taste and fair play prevent me from answering.'

'Of course,' she said, smiling herself. 'I fear I must use that lovely expression that American politicians use when they're caught lying: "I misspoke."' Though her pronunciation was excellent, the word sounded dreadful to Brunetti. 'I meant to ask why he was in the hospital when he phoned me.'

'I saw him there about an hour ago,' Brunetti supplied. 'He was

outside the room of a man—a paediatrician named Pedrolli—
who was hurt during a Carabinieri raid on his home.'

'Why would the Carabinieri want to arrest a paediatrician?'
she asked, and he watched as various possibilities played across
her face.

'It would seem that he and his wife adopted a baby boy illegally. About a year and a half ago,' Brunetti explained and went
on, 'The Carabinieri raided homes in a number of cities last
night: one of them was his. They must have been informed
about the baby.' As he said this, Brunetti realized that it was an
inference drawn from what Marvilli—who had been singularly
evasive on the subject—had said rather than a piece of information the Captain had given him.

'What happened to the baby?' she demanded.

'I'm afraid they took him.'

'What? Who took him?'

'The Carabinieri,' Brunetti answered. 'At least that's what
the one I spoke to told me.'

'Why would they do that?' Her voice had risen, demanding
a response from Brunetti, as if he were responsible for the fate
of the child. When Brunetti failed to answer, she insisted,
'Took him where?'

'To an orphanage,' was the only answer Brunetti could give.
'I suppose it's where they place a child until the real parents are
found or the court decides what will happen to him.'

'No, I'm not talking about that. How could they take away a
child after more than a year?'

Brunetti again found himself attempting to justify what he
thought unjustifiable. 'The doctor and his wife came by the
child illegally, it seems. She as much as admitted that to me
when I spoke to her. The Carabinieri are interested in finding

the person who organized it—the sale, whatever it was. The captain I spoke to said they're looking for a middle man who's involved in some of the cases.' He did not tell her that Marvilli had not in fact mentioned this middle man in connection with the Pedrollis.

Signorina Elettra put her elbows on her desk and lowered her head into her outspread palms, effectively hiding her face. 'I've heard people tell Carabinieri jokes all my life, but it would never occur to me that they could be this stupid,' she said.

'They're not stupid,' Brunetti asserted quickly but with little conviction.

She opened her hands and looked at him. 'Then they're heartless, and that's worse.' She took a deep breath and Brunetti thought that she was summoning up a more professional manner. After a moment, she asked, 'So what do we do?'

'Pedrolli and his wife apparently went to a clinic—I assume it's a private clinic—in Verona. A fertility clinic, or at least one that works with problems of fertility. I'd like you to see if you can find one in Verona that specializes in fertility problems. Two of the other couples who adopted illegally were patients there.'

She said, calmer now that she had a task to focus on, 'I suppose it shouldn't be difficult to find. After all, how many fertility clinics can there be in Verona?' He left her to it and went upstairs.

It was more than an hour later when she came to his office. He saw that she wore a green skirt that fell to mid-calf. Below it were a pair of boots that put Marvilli's to shame.

'Yes, Signorina?' he asked when he had finished examining the boots.

'Who would have believed it, sir?' she asked, apparently having forgiven him for his attempt to defend the Carabinieri.

'Believed what?'

'That there are three fertility clinics, or private clinics with specialist departments for fertility problems, in or near Verona?'

'And the public hospital?'

'I checked. They handle them through the obstetrical unit.'

'So that makes four,' Brunetti observed. 'In Verona.'

'Extraordinary, isn't it?'

He nodded. A broad reader, Brunetti had been aware for years of the sharp decline in sperm counts among European men, and he had also followed with distress the publicity campaign that had helped defeat a referendum that would have aided fertility research. The positions many politicians had taken—former Fascists in favour of artificial insemination; former Communists following the lead of the Church—had left Brunetti battered both in spirit and in mind.

'If you're sure they went to a clinic there, then all I'll have to do is find their medical service numbers: they'd have to give them, even for a private clinic.'

When Signorina Elettra had first arrived at the Questura, such a statement would have impelled Brunetti into an impromptu lecture on a citizen's right to privacy, in this case the sacred privacy that must exist between a doctor and his patient, followed by a few words about the inviolability of access to a person's medical history. 'Yes,' he answered simply.

He saw that she wanted to add something and raised his chin questioningly.

'It would probably be easier to check their phone records and see what numbers they called in Verona,' she suggested. Brunetti no longer enquired as to how she would go about obtaining those.

He watched as she wrote down Pedrolli's name, then she

looked at him and asked, 'Does his wife use his name or her own?'

'Her own. It's Marcolini: first name Bianca.'

She glanced at him and made a small noise of either affirmation or surprise. 'Marcolini,' she repeated softly and then, 'I'll see what I can find out,' and left.

After she was gone, Brunetti thought about who might be able to provide him with the names of the other people the Carabinieri had arrested. Quicker, perhaps, to try the existing bureaucratic channels and simply ask the Carabinieri themselves.

He started by calling the central command at Riva degli Schiavoni and asking for Marvilli, only to learn that the Captain was out on duty and not available by telephone. Forty minutes later, Brunetti had spoken to Marvilli's commander as well as to those in Verona and Brescia, but each of them said he was not at liberty to divulge the names of the people who had been arrested. Even when Brunetti claimed that he was calling at the order of his superior, the Questore of Venice, no information was forthcoming. When he requested that the guard be removed from in front of Dottor Pedrolli's room, Brunetti was told that his request had been recorded.

Changing tactics, Brunetti dialled the office number of Elio Pelusso, a friend who worked as a journalist for *Il Gazzettino*. Within a few minutes, he had the names, professions, ages, and addresses of the people who had been arrested, as well as the name of the clinic in Verona where many of those arrested had sought treatment.

He took this information down to Signorina Elettra and repeated what Signora Marcolini had told him about their attempts to have a child. She nodded as she wrote this down, then said, 'There's a book about this, you know.'

'Excuse me?'

'A novel, by an English writer, I forget who. About when there are no more babies and what people will do to get them.'

'A rather anti-Malthusian idea, isn't it?' Brunetti asked.

'Yes. It's almost as if we're living in two worlds,' she said. 'There's the world where people have too many children, and they get sick and starve and die, and our world, where people want to have them and can't.'

'And will do anything to get them?' he asked.

She tapped a finger on the papers in front of her and said, 'So it seems.'

Back in his office, Brunetti called his home number. When Paola answered with the laconic *sì* that suggested he had taken her away from a particularly riveting passage of whatever it was she was reading, Brunetti said, 'Can I hire you as an Internet researcher?'

'That depends on the subject.'

'Treatments for infertility.'

There was a long pause, after which she said, 'Because of this case?'

'Yes.'

'Why me?'

'Because you know how to do research.'

After an overly loud sigh, Paola said, 'I could easily teach you how, you know.'

'You've been telling me that for years,' Brunetti replied.

'As have Signorina Elettra and Vianello, and your own children.'

'Yes.'

'Does it make any difference?'

'No, not really.'

There unfolded yet another long silence, after which Paola said, 'All right. I'll give you two hours of my time and print out whatever seems interesting.'

'Thank you, Paola.'

'What do I get in return?'

'Undying devotion.'

'I thought I had that already.'

'Undying devotion and I'll bring you coffee in bed for a week.'

'You were called out of bed at two this morning,' she reminded him.

'I'll think of something,' he said, conscious of how lame that sounded.

'You better,' she said. 'All right, two hours, but I can't begin until tomorrow.'

'Why?'

'I have to finish this book.'

'What book?'

'*The Ambassadors*,' she answered.

'Haven't you read it already?'

'Yes. Four times.'

A man less familiar with the ways of scholars, the ways of marriage, and the ways of wisdom might have raised some objection here. Brunetti caved in, said, 'All right,' and hung up.

As he put the phone down, Brunetti realized he could have asked Vianello, or Pucetti, or, for all he knew, any one of the other officers downstairs. He had grown up reading printed pages, at school had learned from printed pages, and he still had the habit of belief in the printed page. The few times he had allowed someone to try to teach him how to use the Internet to search for information, he had found himself flooded with ads for all manner of rubbish and had even stumbled on to a pornographic website. Since then, on the few occasions when he had placed his trembling feelers on the web, he had quickly drawn them back in confusion and defeat. He felt incapable of understanding the links by which things were connected.

That thought reverberated in his mind. Links. Specifically, what was the link between the Questura of Venice and the Carabinieri command in Verona, and how had permission been obtained to raid Dottor Pedrolli's home?

Had any of the other commissari given permission for such a thing, surely he would have heard, but there had been no mention of such an order, either before or after the raid. Brunetti considered for a moment the possibility that the Carabinieri had mounted the raid without informing the Venice police and that the magistrate who had authorized the raid had told them it was acceptable not to do so. But he considered this only to dismiss it instantly: there had been too many well-publicized shoot-outs between different police powers operating in ignorance of each other's plans, and few judges would now risk another such incident.

He was left, then, with an obvious possibility: incompetence. How easily it could have happened: an email sent to the wrong address; a fax read and then lost or misfiled; a phone message not written down and passed on. The explanation which most easily accounts for all the facts is usually the correct one. Though he would be among the last to deny that deceit and double-dealing played their part in the normal business of the Questura, he knew that simple incompetence was far more common. He marvelled at himself for finding this explanation so comforting.

11

Brunetti waited until almost two for Signorina Elettra to bring him whatever she had discovered about the people arrested the previous night: when she did not appear, he went to her. From behind the door to Patta's office, he heard the Vice-Questore's voice: the long pauses meant he was talking on the phone. There was no sign of Signorina Elettra, so Brunetti assumed she had decided to make up for her lost morning's freedom and would return to the office when she chose to.

It was by then too late to go home for lunch, and most of the restaurants in the area would no longer be serving, so Brunetti went down to the officers' squad room, looking for Vianello, to see if he wanted to go to the bar at the bridge and have a panino. Neither the Inspector nor Pucetti was there, only Alvise, who gave Brunetti his usual affable smile.

'You seen Vianello, Alvise?' Brunetti asked.

Brunetti observed the officer process the question: with Alvise, the process of thinking always had a visible component. First he considered the question, then he considered the person who had asked it and the consequences of the answer he might give. His eyes shot around the room, perhaps to check if it were still as empty as when Brunetti had come in, perhaps to see if he had somehow overlooked Vianello lying under one of the desks. Seeing that no one was there to help him answer, Alvise finally said, 'No, sir.' His nervousness provided Brunetti with the key: Vianello was out of the Questura for his own purposes but had told Alvise where he was going.

The bait was too strong for Brunetti to resist. 'I'm going down to the corner for a panino. Would you like to join me?'

Alvise grabbed a stack of papers from his desk and showed them to Brunetti. 'No, sir, I've got to read through these. But thank you. It's as if I had accepted.' He turned his attention to the first page and Brunetti left the room, amused but at the same time feeling obscurely cheapened by his teasing.

Vianello was in the bar, reading the paper at the counter, when Brunetti arrived. A half-full glass of white wine stood in front of him.

Food first, then talk. Brunetti pointed to a few of the *tramezzini* and asked Sergio for a glass of Pinot Grigio, then went over to stand beside Vianello. 'Anything?' he asked, gesturing towards the paper.

His eyes on the headlines, which blared news of the latest in-fighting among the various political parties as they attempted to butt one another aside in their frenzy to keep their trotters in the trough, Vianello said, 'You know, I always used to think it was all right to buy this, so long as I didn't read it. As though buying it was a venial sin and reading it a mortal.' He looked at Brunetti, then again at the headlines. 'But now I think I might have got it the wrong way round and it's a mortal sin to buy because it encourages them to keep on printing it. And reading it's only a venial sin because it really doesn't make any impression on you.' Vianello raised his glass and drank the rest of his wine.

'You'll have to talk to Sergio about that,' Brunetti said, nodding his thanks to the approaching barman for his plate of *tramezzini* and glass of wine, more interested in quelling his hunger than in listening to Vianello's vilification of the press.

'Talk to me about what?' Sergio asked.

'About how good the wine is,' Vianello said. 'So good I better have another.'

Vianello set the paper aside. Brunetti took one of the *tramezzini* and bit into it. 'Too much mayonnaise,' he said, then finished the sandwich and drank half a glass of wine.

'The wife tell you anything?' Vianello asked after Sergio brought his wine.

'Usual stuff. She left everything about the adoption to her husband and didn't want to know that it was illegal.' Brunetti's words were neutral, his tone sceptical. 'The other people who were arrested were couples. So I guess they didn't get this middle man.'

'Any chance the Carabinieri will tell us what comes out of their questioning?' Vianello asked.

'They wouldn't even tell me the names of the people they arrested,' Brunetti answered. 'I had to go to Pelusso for that.'

'They're usually more cooperative.'

Brunetti was not convinced of this. He had often encountered individual Carabinieri who were, but the overall organization had never struck him as willing to share its information, or its successes, with other police agencies.

'What did you make of Zorro?' Vianello asked.

'Zorro?' asked Brunetti absently, his attention focused on his second *tramezzino*.

'The guy with the cowboy boots.'

'Ah,' Brunetti said and finished his wine. He signalled to Sergio for another, and as he waited he weighed his opinion of the young officer. 'He's young to have reached captain, so it's unlikely he has much experience in leading this sort of raid. His men got out of control, so there's going to be trouble: that means he's worried about his career. The victim was a doctor, after all.'

'Yes, And his wife's a Marcolini,' added Vianello.

'Yes. His wife's a Marcolini.' In the Veneto that could count for considerably more than her husband's profession.

'But what about the Captain?' Vianello asked.

'He's young, as I said, so he could go either way.'

'Meaning?'

'Meaning he could turn out to be a good officer: he was a bit high-handed with his own man, but he *was* there with him in the hospital and he made sure he got a few days off,' Brunetti said. 'Eventually he might stop wearing the boots.'

'Or?'

'Or he could turn into a complete bastard and cause everyone a lot of trouble.' Sergio set down the second glass of wine; Brunetti thanked him and began his third *tramezzino*: tuna with egg. 'What about you?' Brunetti asked.

Without a moment's hesitation, Vianello answered, 'I think he might be all right.'

'Why?'

'Because he helped Sergio lift up the grating and because he said please to the black guy.'

Brunetti sipped at his wine and considered this. 'Yes, he did, didn't he?' To Brunetti, it seemed as good an indication of character as any he could come up with. 'Let's hope you're right.'

It was well past three when they returned to the Questura; the rest of the day brought nothing new. Signorina Elettra neither returned nor called to explain her absence, at least not to Brunetti; none of the Carabinieri commands he had contacted called to volunteer information. He tried the station at Riva degli Schiavoni and asked for Marvilli, but he was still not there: Brunetti did not leave his name, nor did he bother to renew his request that the guard in the hospital be removed.

He dialled the number of the neurology ward a little before five and asked to speak to Signora Sandra. She recognized his name and said that Dottor Pedrolli, so far as she knew, had still not spoken, though he seemed aware of what was going on around him. Yes, his wife was still in the room with him. Sandra said she had followed her instincts and kept the Carabinieri from talking to Dottor Pedrolli, though one was now sitting in the corridor, apparently to prevent anyone except doctors and nurses from entering the room.

Brunetti thanked her and replaced the phone. So much for cooperation between the forces of order. Pissing contest, turf war, escalation: call it whatever he wanted, Brunetti knew what was coming. But he preferred not to think about it until the following day.

Brunetti usually disliked eating the same thing for lunch and dinner, but the tuna steaks Paola had simmered in a sauce of capers, olives, and tomatoes could hardly be said to have originated on the same planet as the tuna *tramezzini* he had eaten for lunch. Tact and good sense prevented his making any reference to the latter, since comparison even with such paltry opposition might offend. He and his son Raffi shared the last piece of fish, and Brunetti spooned the remainder of the sauce on to his own second helping of rice.

'Dessert?' Chiara asked her mother, and Brunetti realized that he had managed to save space for something sweet.

'There's fig ice-cream,' Paola said, filling Brunetti with a flush of anticipation.

'Fig?' Raffi asked.

'From that place over by San Giacomo dell'Orio,' Paola explained.

'He's the one who does all the weird flavours, isn't he?' Brunetti asked.

'Yes. But the fig's sensational. He said these are the last of the season.'

Sensational it was, and after the four of them had managed to knock off an entire kilo, Brunetti and Paola repaired to the living room, each with a small glass of grappa, just what Brunetti's Uncle Ludovico had always prescribed to counteract the effects of a heavy meal.

When they were sitting side by side, watching the dim remnants of light they thought could still be seen in the west, Paola said, 'When the clocks go back, it'll be dark even before we eat. It's what I hate most about the winter, how dark it gets, how soon and for how long.'

'Good thing we don't live in Helsinki, then,' he said and took a sip of grappa.

Paola squirmed around until she found a more comfortable position and said, 'I think you could name any city in the world, and I'd agree that it's a good thing we don't live there.'

'Rome?' he offered, and she nodded. 'Paris?' and she nodded more forcefully. 'Los Angeles?' he ventured.

'Are you out of your mind?'

'Why this sudden devotion to *patria*?' he asked.

'No, not to *patria*, not to the whole country, just to this part of it.'

'But why, all of a sudden?'

She finished her grappa and turned aside to set the glass on the table. 'Because I took a walk over towards San Basilio this morning. For no reason, not because I had to go anywhere or do anything. Like a tourist, I suppose. It was still early, before nine, and there weren't a lot of people around. I stopped in a *pasticceria*, a place I've never been in before, and I had a brioche that was made of air and a cappuccino that tasted like heaven, and the barman talked about the weather with everyone who came in, and everyone spoke Veneziano, and it was like I was a kid again and this was just a sleepy little provincial town.'

'It still is,' Brunetti observed.

'I know, I know, but like it was before millions of people started coming here.'

'All in search of that brioche that's made of air and the cappuccino that's like heaven?'

'Exactly. And the inexpensive little trattoria where only the locals eat.'

Brunetti finished his grappa and rested his head against the back of the sofa, his glass cradled in his hands. 'Do you know Bianca Marcolini? She's married to the paediatrician, Gustavo Pedrolli.'

She glanced at him and said, 'I've heard the name. Works in a bank. Does social things, I think: you know, Lions Club and Save Venice and things like that.' She paused and Brunetti could almost hear the pages of her mind flipping over. 'If she's the one I think she is—that is, if it's the Marcolini family I think it is—then my father knows hers.'

'Personally or professionally?'

She smiled at this. 'Only professionally. Marcolini is not the sort of man my father would acknowledge socially.' She saw the expression with which Brunetti greeted this and added, 'I know what you think of my father's politics, Guido, but I can assure you that even he finds Marcolini's politics repellent.'

'For what specific reason?' Brunetti asked, though he was

not surprised. Count Orazio Falier was a man as likely to despise politicians of the Right as those of the Left. Had a Centre existed in Italy, he would no doubt have found cause to despise them, as well.

'My father has been heard to call his ideas Fascistic.'

'In public?' enquired Brunetti.

This caused Paola to smile again. 'Have you ever known my father to make a political remark in public?'

'I stand corrected,' Brunetti admitted, though he found it difficult to imagine a political position which someone like the Count would consider Fascistic.

'Have you finished *The Ambassadors*?' Brunetti asked, thinking this more polite than asking if she had had time to begin her research on infertility.

'No.'

'Good, then don't bother with the research I asked you to do.'

'On infertility?'

'Yes.'

She was evidently relieved. 'But I would like you to keep your shell-like ears open for anything you might hear about Bianca Marcolini or her family.'

'Including the dreadful father and his even more dreadful politics?

'Yes. Please.'

'Are the police going to pay me for this or is it supposed to be one of my duties as a citizen of the state?'

Brunetti pushed himself to his feet. 'The police will get you another grappa.'

12

Brunetti slept until almost nine, after which he dawdled in the kitchen to read the papers Paola had gone out and got before leaving for the university. All of the articles named the the people arrested in the Carabinieri round-up: only *Il Corriere*'s account mentioned that the Carabinieri were still searching for the man believed to have organized the trafficking. None of the articles discussed the fate of the children, though *La Repubblica* did say that they varied in age from one to three years.

Brunetti paused after reading this: if simply hearing that a baby had been taken from his parents at eighteen months could incite someone as unimaginative as Alvise to rage, imagine what the reality would be for the parents of a three-year-old. Brunetti could not bring himself to think of the people who had adopted the children as anything other than their parents: not as illegal parents, not as adoptive parents: only as parents.

He went directly to his office and found some papers on his desk—routine things—staffing, promotions, new regulations concerning the registering of firearms. There was also, and more interestingly, a note from Vianello. The Inspector wrote that he had gone to meet someone to talk about 'his doctors'. Not with, but about, which was enough to tell Brunetti that the Inspector was continuing with what had become his all-but-private investigation of the connection he suspected existed between three specialists at the Ospedale Civile and at least one local pharmacist, possibly more.

Vianello's interest had first been piqued some weeks before, when one of his informants—a man whose identity Vianello was unwilling to reveal—had suggested that the Inspector might be interested in the frequency with which certain pharmacists who were authorized to schedule specialist appointments referred their clients to these three doctors. Vianello had mentioned the suggestion to Signorina Elettra, who found it as intriguing as he did. Together they had turned it into a kind of school science project, competing with one another to discover just how these three doctors might have earned the attention of Vianello's source.

Illumination had been provided by Signorina Elettra's sister Barbara, herself a doctor, who had explained to them a recent bureaucratic innovation which permitted pharmacists access to the central computer of the city health service so as to enable them to schedule specialist appointments for their patients when these visits were recommended by their regular doctors. The patient would thus be saved the time spent in hospital queues waiting to schedule an appointment, and the pharmacist would be paid a fee for performing the service.

Signorina Elettra had seen one possibility immediately, as had Vianello: all an enterprising pharmacist needed was a specialist, or more than one, willing to accept appointments for what were effectively phantom patients. And how much easier to create need for those appointments than for that same pharmacist to add a single line, recommending a specialist visit, to the bottom of an ordinary prescription? The health service, ULSS, was not known for the efficiency of its bookkeeping, so it was unlikely that the handwriting on these prescriptions would be examined closely: all that had to be in order were the patient's name and health service registration number. Patients almost never saw their own computer records, so there was little chance that they would learn that these phantom appointments had been made in their names: the health system would thus have no reason to question the doctor's charge for having seen the patient, nor the pharmacist's fee for having scheduled the appointment. And whatever arrangement the pharmacist and doctor might come to between themselves would certainly remain private, though 25–75 would seem an equitable division. If a specialist visit cost between 150 and 200 Euros, happy the pharmacist who managed to schedule four or five a week, and happy the doctors who could increase their income without having to increase their workload.

Presumably, then, Vianello was that morning again somewhere in the city talking to the man who had first mentioned the arrangement to him or to one of the other people who kept him supplied with information the police might find useful. What Vianello gave in exchange for this information Brunetti had no idea and did not choose to ask, just as he hoped no one would ask how he managed to repay his own sources for the information they provided him.

Knowing he would learn more when Vianello returned, Brunetti dialled the number of *neurologia* and asked to speak to Signora Sandra.

'It's Commissario Brunetti, Signora,' he said when she came to the phone.

'He's fine,' she offered, avoiding pleasantries to save them both time.

'Is he talking?' Brunetti asked.

'Not to me and not to anyone on the staff, at least not that I know about,' she said.

'To his wife?'

'I don't know, Commissario. She went home, about half an hour ago, but she said she'd be back by lunchtime. Dottor Damasco came on to the ward about an hour ago and is in with him now.'

'If I were to come over there, could I speak to him?'

'To whom? Dottor Damasco or Dottor Pedrolli?'

'Either. Both.'

Her voice softened to a whisper. 'The Carabiniere is still outside his room. They don't let anyone in except his wife and the medical staff.'

'Then I suppose I'd like to speak to Dottor Damasco,' Brunetti said.

After a long pause, the nurse said, 'Come over now, and perhaps you could talk to them both.'

'I beg your pardon.'

'Come to the desk. If I'm not there, wait for me. There'll be a stethoscope in the right-hand drawer.' She hung up.

Brunetti left without telling anyone where he was going, walked to the hospital, and went directly to the neurology ward. No one was behind the desk. Brunetti felt a moment's nervousness, looked down the corridor to be sure it was empty, then stepped behind the desk and opened the top drawer on the right. He slipped the stethoscope around his neck and returned to the other side of the desk. He took two sheets of paper from the wastepaper basket and attached them to a clipboard, then bent over the papers and began to read.

A moment later, Signora Sandra, today in black jeans and black tennis shoes, joined him. Another nurse Brunetti did not recognize came up behind them and Sandra said, addressing Brunetti, 'Ah, Dottore, I'm glad you could come. Dottor Damasco is waiting for you.' Then, to the other nurse, 'Maria Grazia, would you take Dottor Costantini down to 307, please? Dottor Damasco is waiting for him.'

He wondered if Sandra wanted to keep herself entirely out of her subterfuge, should there be trouble later, but then it occurred to him that her protective manner towards Dottor Pedrolli might well already have made the guards suspicious of her.

Keeping one eye on the papers, copies of lab reports that made no sense to him at all, Brunetti followed the nurse towards the room. A uniformed Carabiniere sat outside. He looked at the nurse, then at Brunetti, as they approached.

'Dottor Costantini,' the nurse explained to the officer, indicating Brunetti. 'He's here for a consultation with Dottor Damasco.'

The guard nodded and went back to the magazine spread on his lap. The nurse opened the door, announced the arrival of Dottor Costantini, and allowed Brunetti to enter the room without joining him. She closed the door.

Damasco looked in his direction and nodded. 'Ah, yes, Sandra told me you wanted to see us.' He then looked at Pedrolli, whose eyes were on Brunetti, and said, 'Gustavo, this is the man I told you was here before.'

Pedrolli kept his attention on Brunetti.

'He's a policeman, Gustavo. I told you that.'

Pedrolli raised his right hand and moved it back and forth above his chest, in the place where the stethoscope lay against Brunetti's. 'The Carabinieri have a guard outside. The only way he could get in here to talk to you was by pretending to be a doctor,' Damasco explained.

Pedrolli's face softened: his beard disguised the hollows in his cheeks, which Brunetti thought had deepened overnight. He lay flat on the bed, a blanket pulled to his waist; above it Brunetti saw a blue and white pyjama jacket. Pedrolli's hair had once been light brown but was now, like his beard, mixed with equal portions of grey. He had the light skin and eyes that often accompany fair hair. A black bruise ran down from behind his left ear and disappeared into his beard.

Brunetti remained silent, waiting to see if Pedrolli would, or could, say anything. As he set the chart on the table next to the doctor's bed, his arm brushed across the stethoscope, making him feel foolish in his impersonation.

A minute passed, and none of the men spoke. Finally Damasco said, making no attempt to disguise his displeasure, 'All right, Gustavo. If you insist, we'll continue to play guessing games.' To Brunetti he said, 'If he raises one finger, the answer is yes. Two means no.'

When Brunetti said nothing, Damasco prodded him, 'Go ahead, Commissario. It's time-consuming and probably unnecessary, but if this is the way Gustavo's decided to protect himself, then that's the way we'll play it.' Damasco reached out and grabbed one of Pedrolli's blanketed feet; he gave it an affectionate shake, as if to contradict the exasperation in his words.

When Brunetti still did not speak, Damasco said, 'I haven't asked him anything about what happened. Well, except if he remembers being hit, which he says he doesn't. As his doctor, that's my only concern.'

'And as his friend?' Brunetti asked.

'As his friend,' he began and considered for a moment. 'As his friend I went along with Sandra's harebrained idea to have you come and talk to him.'

Pedrolli appeared to have followed their conversation; at least his eyes had shifted back and forth as the two men spoke. As Damasco finished, Pedrolli's gaze moved to Brunetti, waiting for him to respond.

'As your friend told you,' Brunetti said, speaking to the man in the bed, 'I'm a police officer. One of my staff called me early yesterday morning and said an assaulted man was in the hospital, and I came down here to see what had happened. My concern then was the same as it is now: an armed assault on a citizen of this city, not the reason for it and not your response to it. As far as I've learned, you acted as would any citizen who was attacked in his home: you attempted to defend your family and yourself.'

He paused and looked at Pedrolli. The doctor raised one finger.

'I have no idea how the Carabinieri are going to proceed with this case nor how they will present the information, and I don't know what accusations may be brought against you, Dottore,' Brunetti said, deciding it was best to stay as close as possible to the truth. 'I do know that there is a long list of charges they believe they can bring against you.'

Here, Pedrolli held up his right hand and fluttered it back and forth in the air.

'The officer I spoke to mentioned corruption of a public official, falsification of state documents, resisting arrest, and the assault of a public official in the performance of his duties. That last is the officer you hit.'

Again, the interrogatively raised hand.

'No, he wasn't hurt. His nose wasn't even broken. A lot of blood, but no real damage.'

Pedrolli closed his eyes in what could have been relief. Then he looked again at Brunetti and, with the fingers of his right hand, took his left hand and slid his wedding ring up and down his finger.

'Your wife is fine, Dottore,' Brunetti answered, wondering at Pedrolli's concern, for the woman had only recently left the room.

Pedrolli shook his head and repeated the gesture with the ring, then to make things clearer, pressed his wrists together as though they were tied. Or handcuffed.

Brunetti raised both hands as if to ward off the idea. 'No charges have been brought against her, Dottore. And the captain I spoke to said that there probably would not be.'

At this, Pedrolli pointed the index finger of his right hand at his heart, and Brunetti said, 'Yes, only against you, Dottore.'

Pedrolli tipped his head to one side and shrugged the other shoulder, as if consigning himself to his fate.

For what it was worth, Brunetti added, economical with the truth, 'I'm in no way involved in that investigation, Dottore. It will be conducted by the Carabinieri, not by us.' He paused, then continued, 'It's a jurisdictional thing. Because they made the original arrest, the case belongs to them.' He waited for some sign that Pedrolli understood or believed this, then added, 'My concern is with you as an injured person, the victim of an assault, if not a crime.' Brunetti smiled and turned to Dottor Damasco. 'I don't want to tire your friend, Dottore.' Careful of his phrasing, he added, 'If things change, would you let me know?'

Before Damasco could answer, Pedrolli reached out and seized Brunetti's wrist. He tugged at it with some force, pulling him closer to the bed. His mouth moved, but no sound emerged. Seeing Brunetti's evident confusion, Pedrolli made a cradling gesture with both arms and rocked them back and forth over his chest.

'Alfredo?' Brunetti asked.

Pedrolli nodded.

Brunetti patted the back of Pedrolli's right hand, saying, 'He's fine, Dottore. Don't worry about him, please. He's fine.'

Pedrolli's eyes widened, and Brunetti saw the tears gather. He looked away, pretending Damasco had said something, and when he looked back, Pedrolli's eyes were closed.

Damasco stepped forward, saying, 'I'll call you if anything happens, Commissario.'

Brunetti nodded his thanks, retrieved the clipboard, and left the room. The Carabiniere guard was still seated outside the door, but he barely glanced at Brunetti. At the nurses' desk, Brunetti saw no one, nor was there anyone in the corridor. He unclipped the papers and tossed them back into the waste basket, then set the clipboard on the desk. He removed the stethoscope, put it back in the drawer, and left the ward.

13

Brunetti took his time returning to the Questura, his mind occupied by the things he had failed to ask and the lingering unknowns of the Pedrolli . . . he didn't even know what to call it: Case? Situation? Dilemma? Mess?

Without information about the other adoptions, and in the face of Pedrolli's continuing silence, Brunetti knew as little about the details of the acquisition of the doctor's baby as he did of the others. He had no idea if the mothers were Italian or where they had given birth to their babies, how or where they took physical possession of the babies, what the going rate was. This last phrase appalled him. There was also the bureaucratic issue: just how much paperwork was needed to give evidence of paternity? In an orange metal box that had once contained Christmas biscuits, he and Paola kept the children's birth certificates, inoculation and health records, certificates of baptism and first communion, and some school records. The box stood, if memory served, on the top shelf of the wardrobe in their room, while their passports were in a drawer in Paola's study. He had no memory of how they had managed to get passports for the children: surely they must have been asked to provide birth certificates, and those certificates must also have been necessary to enrol the kids in school.

All official information about Venetian births and deaths, as well as changes in official place of residence, is kept at the Ufficio Anagrafe. As Brunetti left the hospital he decided to pass by the office: no time better than the present to speak to someone there about the bureaucratic process that led to the creation of legal identity.

He followed a slow-moving snake of tourists across Ponte del Lovo, down past the theatre and around the corner, but when Brunetti arrived at the Ufficio Anagrafe, tucked into the warren of city offices on Calle Loredan, his plan was to be frustrated by the most banal of reasons: city employees were on strike that day to protest about delays in the signing of their contract, which had expired seventeen months before. Brunetti wondered if the police—city employees, after all—were allowed to strike, and deciding that they were, he went into Rosa Salva for a coffee and then over to Tarantola to see what new books had come in. Nothing caught his fancy: biographies of Mao, Stalin, and Lenin would surely lead him to despair. He had read an unpleasant review of a new translation of Pausanias and so left it unbought. Because he made it a rule never to leave a bookstore without buying something, he settled for a long out-of-print translation of the Marquis de Custine's 1839 travels in Russia, printed in Torino in 1977: *Lettere dalla Russia*. The period was closer to the present than ordinarily would have interested him, but it was the only book that appealed, and he was in a hurry, strike or not.

Brunetti was conscious of how very virtuous he felt in proceeding to the Questura to go back to work, now that he knew about the strike and the possibility it offered him of going home to start on the book. Instead, buoyed by pride in his self-restraint, he set the book on his desk and picked up the papers that had accumulated there. Try as he might to concentrate on lists and recommendations, Brunetti felt his attention drawn towards the unanswered questions surrounding Pedrolli. Why had Marvilli refused to divulge more information? Who had authorized the Carabinieri raid on the home of a Venetian citizen? What power had summoned the Vice-Questore to Pedrolli's hospital room not half a day after he arrived there? And how was it, anyway, that the Carabinieri had learned about Pedrolli's baby?

His reflections were interrupted by the ringing of his phone. 'Brunetti.'

'Come down here now.' And then Patta's voice was gone.

As he stood, Brunetti's eye was caught by the copy on the back cover of the book he had just bought, ' ... the arbitrary imposition of power which characterized . . .'

'Ah, M. le Marquis,' he said out loud, 'if you knew the half of it.'

Downstairs, he found no sign of Signorina Elettra. He knocked and entered Patta's office without waiting to be told to do so. Patta was at his desk, the papers of the overworked public official spread before him; even his summer tan had begun to fade, contributing to the total effect of tireless dedication to the many obligations of office.

Before Brunetti moved towards Patta's desk, the Vice-Questore asked, 'What are you working on, Brunetti.'

'The baggage handlers at the airport, sir, and the Casinò,' he answered, much as he might inform a dermatologist about the foot fungus he kept picking up at work.

'All that can wait,' Patta said, a sentiment in which Brunetti most heartily joined. Then, when Brunetti stood in front of him, Patta asked, 'You've heard about this mix-up with the Carabinieri, I assume?'

Mix-up, was it? 'Yes, sir.'

'Good, then. Sit down, Brunetti. You make me nervous standing there.'

Brunetti did as he was told.

'The Carabinieri over-reacted, and they'll be lucky if the man in the hospital doesn't bring charges against them.' Patta's remark raised Brunetti's estimation of the man who had stood with the Vice-Questore outside Pedrolli's door. After a moment's reflection, Patta tempered his opinion and said, 'But I doubt that he will. No one wants that sort of legal trouble.' Indeed. Brunetti was tempted to ask if the white-haired man at the hospital would be involved in whatever legal mess were to ensue, but good sense suggested that he keep his knowledge of Patta's meeting to himself and so he asked, 'What would you like me to do, sir?'

'There seems to be some uncertainty about the nature of the communications that took place between the Carabinieri and us,' Patta began. He peered across at Brunetti, as if to enquire whether he were receiving the coded message and knew what to do with it.

'I see, sir,' Brunetti said. So the Carabinieri could produce evidence that they had informed the police of the projected raid, but the police could find no evidence that they had received it. Brunetti's mind cast back to the rules of logic he had studied with such interest, decades ago now, at university. There had been something about the difficulty—or was it the impossibility?—of proving a negative. This meant that Patta was thrashing about, trying to decide which would be less risky: to blame the Carabinieri for their excessive use of force or to find someone at the Questura to take the rap for the failure to transmit the Carabinieri's message?

'In light of what's happened to this doctor, I'd like you to keep an eye on things and see that he's treated decently. So that nothing more happens.'

Brunetti prevented himself from completing the Vice-Questore's sentence by adding, '. . . that would lead to trouble for me'.

'Of course, Vice-Questore. Would it be all right if I spoke to him, perhaps to his wife?'

'Yes,' Patta said. 'Do whatever you want. Just see that this doesn't get out of control and cause trouble.'

'Of course, Vice-Questore,' Brunetti said.

Patta, with responsibility effectively transferred to someone else, directed his attention to the papers on his desk.

'I'll keep you informed, sir,' Brunetti said and got to his feet.

Clearly too busy with the cares of office to respond, Patta waved a hand at him, and Brunetti left.

Because Paola had agreed to help him by asking around about Bianca Marcolini, Brunetti steeled himself and went down to the computer in the officers' room, where he managed to surprise his colleagues by the ease with which he connected to the Internet and then typed in the letters for '*infertilità*', having to go back to correct only two typing errors.

For the next hour, Brunetti was the centre of what became a team effort on the part of the uniformed branch to help the research along. Though none of the younger men actually pushed him aside, the occasional hand did slip in below his to type in a word or two; Brunetti, however, never quite relinquished possession of the keyboard or mouse. The fact that he insisted on printing out everything that was of interest to him gave him the sense, however spurious, that he was engaged in the same sort of research he used to conduct in the university library.

When he was finished and went to the printer to pick up the stack of papers that had accumulated, he was struck by two thoughts: it was all so fast, virtually instant, but he had no idea how true any of it was. What made one website more reliable than another, and what, in heaven's name, was 'Il Centro per le Ricerche sull'Uomo'? Or 'Istituto della Demografia'? For all Brunetti knew, either the Catholic Church or the Hemlock Society could be behind all of the sources he had consulted.

He had long accepted that most of what he read in books and newspapers and magazines was only an approximation of the truth, always slanted to Left or Right. But at least he was aware of the prejudices of most journalists and had thus, over the decades, learned to read aggressively, and so he could almost always find some kernel of fact—he entertained no illusions of finding the truth—in what he read. But with the Internet, he was so ignorant of context that all of the sources carried equal weight with him. Brunetti was adrift in what could well be a sea of Internet lies and distortions and utterly without the compass he had learned to use in the more familiar sea of journalistic lies.

When he finally returned to his office and began to read what he had printed out, he was surprised at the consistency across the various websites. Though the numbers and percentages differed minimally, there was no doubt as to the steep decline in birth rates in most Western countries, at least among the native populations. Immigrants had more children. He knew there was some politically correct manner in which this essential statistical truth was meant to be phrased: 'cultural variation', 'differing cultural expectations'. Phrase it as you chose: poor people had more children than rich people, just as poor people had always had more children than rich people. In the past, more of them had died, carried off by disease and poverty. But now, at home in the West, far more of them survived.

At the same time that the number of children born to immigrants was increasing all over Europe, their hosts were having difficulty even in reproducing themselves. European women were older now when they had their first child than they had been a generation ago. Fewer people bothered to get married. The cost of housing had risen dramatically, limiting the chance that young working people could easily set up a household of their own. And who today could afford to have a baby on only one salary?

All of those things, Brunetti knew, merely created options which people could choose to exercise, not physical impediments which could not be overcome. The steady decline in the number of viable sperm, however, was not a matter of choice. Pollution? Some genetic change? An undetected disease? Repeatedly, the websites made mention of a group of substances called phthalates, present in all manner of common products, including deodorants and food packaging: it would seem that there existed an inverse proportion between their presence in a man's blood and a lowered sperm count. Though the clear implication that these substances were responsible for a half-century of decreasing sperm counts was common, none of the articles dared to name them as a direct cause. Brunetti had always been of a mind that rising economic expectations must have exerted as strong an influence on the birth rate as falling sperm counts. After all, if there had been millions of sperm in the past, there were still half that number, and that should surely suffice.

One report stated that the sperm counts of immigrant men began to decline after they had lived in Europe for a few years, which would certainly lend credence to the theory that pollution or environmental contamination was the cause. Wasn't it the lead water pipes that were said to have contributed to the decline in health and fertility among the population of Imperial Rome? Not that it made any difference now, but at least the Romans had had no idea of that possible connection: it fell to later ages to discover the probable cause, and then do nothing to moderate their behaviour.

Historical reflection was cut short by the arrival of Vianello. As he came in, smiling broadly and holding up a few sheets of paper, the Inspector said, 'I used to hate white collar crime. But the more I learn, the more I like it.' He placed the papers on Brunetti's desk and took a seat.

Brunetti wondered if Vianello were planning a career move; not for a moment did he doubt the involvement of Signorina Elettra in whatever change had taken place in Vianello's assessment.

'"Like it"?' Brunetti asked, indicating the papers, as though they were the instruments of Vianello's conversion.

'Well,' Vianello tempered, aware of Brunetti's amusement, 'in the sense that you don't have to go chasing after them or lurk in the rain outside their doors for hours, waiting for them to come out, so that you can follow them.'

At Brunetti's continued silence, the Inspector continued. 'I used to think it was boring, sitting around, reading through tax and financial declarations, checking credit card statements and bank records.'

Brunetti stopped himself from observing that, since most of these activities were illegal unless performed with an order from a judge, it was perhaps better that a policeman, at the very least, find them boring.

113

'And now?' Brunetti enquired mildly.

Vianello shrugged and smiled at the same time. 'And now I seem to be developing a taste for it.' He needed no prompting from Brunetti to explain: 'I suppose it's the thrill of the chase. You get a scent of what they might be up to: figures that don't add up or that are too big or too small, and then you begin to hunt through other records or you find their names in some other place where you didn't expect to find them or where they shouldn't be. And then the numbers keep coming in and they get stranger and stranger, and then you see what it is they're up to and how to keep an eye on them or trace them into other places.'

Without his realizing it, Vianello's voice had grown louder, more impassioned. 'And you just sit there, at your desk, and soon you know everything they're doing because you've learned how to trace them, and so everything they do comes back to you.' Vianello paused and smiled. 'I suppose this is how a spider must feel. The flies don't know the web is there, can't see it or sense it, so they just buzz around and do whatever it is flies do, and you just sit there, waiting for them to land.'

'And then you snap them up?' Brunetti asked.

'You could put it that way, I suppose,' Vianello answered, looking equally pleased both with himself and with his extended metaphor.

'More specifically?' Brunetti asked, looking in the general direction of the papers. 'Your doctors and their accommodating pharmacists?'

Vianello nodded. 'I've had a look at the bank records of the doctors my, er, my contact mentioned. Going back six years.' Even in the face of the patent illegality of Vianello's offhand, 'had a look', Brunetti remained a Sphinx.

'They live very well, of course: they're specialists.' They

would, then, earn a great deal of their income in cash: did there exist the specialist who would provide a receipt for a private visit? 'One of them opened a bank account in Liechtenstein four years ago.'

'Is that when the appointments started?' Brunetti asked.

'I'm not sure, but my contact told me it's been going on a number of years.'

'And the pharmacists?'

'That's the strange thing,' Vianello said. 'There are only five pharmacies in the city that are authorized to make the appointments: I think it has to do with their computer capacity. I've started to look into their records.' Again, Brunetti left that alone.

'None of the ones I've checked has increased his average bank savings or credit card spending during this time,' said a disappointed Vianello. Then, as if to encourage himself, he added, 'But that doesn't necessarily exclude them.'

'How many of them have you checked?' Brunetti asked.

'Two.'

'Hmm,' Brunetti said. 'How long will it take you to check the others?'

'A couple of days.'

'There's no doubt about the existence of these fake appointments?'

'None. I just don't know yet which pharmacists are involved.'

Brunetti ran quickly over the possibilities. 'Sex, drugs, and gambling. Those are usually the reasons people are willing to take illegal risks to make money.'

'Well, if those were the only reasons, then the ones I've already checked would be excluded,' Vianello said, sounding unconvinced.

'Why?'

'Because one of them is seventy-six, and the other lives at home with his mother.'

Brunetti, who was of the opinion that neither of these things necessarily excluded a man from interest in sex, drugs, or gambling, asked, 'Who are they?'

'The old one's Gabetti. Heart condition, goes into the pharmacy only twice a week, no children, only a nephew in Torino he's going to leave it all to.'

'So you exclude him?' Brunetti asked.

'Some people might, but I certainly don't,' Vianello said with sudden heat. 'He's one of those classic misers. Took over the pharmacy from his father about forty years ago. Hasn't done a thing to it since then: I'm told that if you look in the back rooms, you'd think you were in Albania or some place like that. And I'm told you don't want to see the toilet he has there. Never married, never lived with anyone: all he does is make money and invest it and watch it grow. It's his only joy in life: money.'

'And you think he'd do something like this?' Brunetti asked, not attempting to disguise his scepticism.

'Most of the appointments made for the three doctors by a pharmacy come from Gabetti's.'

'I see,' Brunetti said, letting the information filter into his mind. 'What about the other one?'

Vianello's face changed and he gave an involuntary nod, as if expressing agreement with Brunetti's theory. 'This one's very religious; still lives with his mother, to whom he seems to be devoted. There's not much gossip about him, certainly nothing that says he's particularly interested in money. I can't find anything in his bank records.'

116

'There's usually something, especially if they're religious,' said Brunetti: if Vianello could be suspicious of a greedy man, then he could reserve for himself the right to have doubts about a religious one. 'If he's not interested in sex and drugs, what is he interested in?'

'The Church: I told you,' Vianello said, amused by Brunetti's surprise. 'He's a member of one of those Catechumeni groups: prayer meetings twice a week, no alcohol, not even wine with meals, no . . . no anything, it would seem.'

'How'd you learn all this?' Brunetti asked.

'I've asked a number of people about him,' Vianello said obliquely. 'But believe me, there's nothing to find out about this guy. He lives for his mother and for the Church.' Vianello paused for some time, 'And for priding himself, from what I've heard, on leading a virtuous life and lamenting the fact that other people do not. Though he'd probably be the one who gets to define virtue.'

'Why do you say that?'

'Because he refuses to sell condoms in his pharmacy.'

'What?'

'He can't refuse to sell prescription drugs, like contraceptive pills or the morning-after pill, but he has the right to refuse to sell rubbers, and that's his choice.'

'In the third millennium?' Brunetti asked and buried his face in his hands for a moment.

'As I said, he's the one who gets to define virtue.'

Brunetti removed his hands from his face. 'And the others, the ones you haven't looked into yet?'

'I know one of them, Andrea at San Bortolo, and he'd never do something like this.'

'Are you still going to check them all?' asked Brunetti.

'Of course,' Vianello said, sounding wounded at the question.

To change the subject, Brunetti asked, 'But how did you manage to find out the appointments came from these pharmacies?'

Vianello made no attempt to disguise the pride he took in being able to explain. 'The hospital files can be arranged to list appointments by date or patient or doctor or by who made them. We simply arranged all of the specialist appointments for the last year,' he said—not bothering to explain who 'we' were nor how they came by those records—'by who made them and then drew up a list of the ones that were made by those pharmacies. Then we made a list of appointments made in the last two weeks and called all of those patients and said we were running a survey of client satisfaction with ULSS.' He waited to see what degree of astonishment Brunetti would demonstrate at the unlikelihood of this, and when his superior said nothing, he went on. 'Most of them had in fact been seen by the doctor they had an appointment with, but nine of them said they didn't know anything about an appointment. We said immediately that it must have been a computer error—we even pretended to check and then sounded embarrassed when we had to admit it was an error—and apologized for having disturbed them.' He smiled, and said, 'All of the appointments were made by Gabetti.'

'Weren't you afraid one of them would mention your call at the pharmacy?' Brunetti asked.

Vianello waved away the suggestion. 'That's the genius of it,' he said, not without admiration. 'None of these people would have any idea what sort of mix-up could have taken place, and I think they all believed us when we said it was an error in the computer system.'

Brunetti let the possibilities run through his imagination for a moment and then asked, 'But what if one of them really got sick and they had to schedule the same examination, and the computer showed they'd already had it performed?' he asked.

'Then I imagine they'd do what any one of us would do: insist they'd never had the exam and blame it on the computer. And since the person they'd be dealing with would be some paper-pusher at ULSS, they'd probably believe it.'

'And then the appointment would be scheduled?'

'Probably,' Vianello said easily. 'Besides, the possibility that anyone would get suspicious about this is virtually non-existent.'

'And if they did, it's state money that's being wasted, anyway, isn't it?'

'I'm afraid so,' Vianello said. 'It would just be another case of civil servants who make a mistake.'

Neither man spoke for some time, and then Brunetti asked, 'But you still haven't found a pharmacist with the money.'

'It's got to be somewhere,' Vianello insisted. 'We can start taking a closer look tomorrow.'

'It sounds as if nothing will persuade you away from believing this,' Brunetti said with a certain measure of asperity.

'Perhaps,' Vianello answered quickly, almost defensively. 'But the idea is too good for someone not to make use of it. ULSS is a sitting duck.'

'And if you're wrong?' Brunetti asked with some force.

'Then I'm wrong. But I'll still have learned a lot about new ways to find things with the computer,' Vianello said, and good will slipped back into the room.

14

Brunetti went back downstairs with Vianello, then continued to Signorina Elettra's office, where he found her busy on the phone. She beckoned him into the room, signalled that he was not to leave, and continued what appeared to be a series of monosyllabic responses to a flood of verbosity from the other end of the line. 'Yes. No. Of course. Yes. Yes,' she said, each response interrupted by a long pause, during some of which she busied herself with jotting things down. 'I understand,' she said, 'Signor Brunini is very eager to see the doctor and, yes, he and his companion would come as private patients.' Again, there ensued a silence that seemed even longer now that Brunetti had heard the name and wondered what she was up to.

'Yes, I realize, of course. Yes, I'll wait.' She held the phone away and rubbed at her ear, then drew the receiver back at the sound of a female voice. 'Oh, really? So soon? Ah, Signora, you're wonderful. Signor Brunini will be very pleased. Yes, I have it. Three-thirty on Friday. I'll call him right now. And thank you.'

Signorina Elettra put the phone down and glanced at Brunetti, then wrote a few words on the paper in front of her.

'Dare I ask?' Brunetti said.

'The Villa Colonna Clinic. In Verona,' she said. 'Where they went.'

Though the transmission was somewhat semaphoric, Brunetti had no difficulty understanding it.

'And that led you to . . .' Brunetti began, then realized that he was lacking an adequate verb. 'To speculate?' he concluded.

'Yes, you could say that,' she answered, obviously pleased by his choice of word. 'About all manner of things. But chiefly about the coincidence that a number of people who were examined at this clinic were put in contact with the person or persons who had a baby to sell'—one could only admire her directness.

'You putting your money on the clinic?'

The arc of her eyebrow rose no more than a millimetre, but the motion spoke of endless possibility.

Brunetti returned to even more uncertain territory. 'Signor Brunini?' he enquired.

'Ah, yes,' she said. 'Signor Brunini.' Brunetti waited until finally she continued. 'I thought it might be interesting to present the clinic with another couple desperate to have a child and rich enough to pay anything to have one.'

'Signor Brunini?' he asked, recalling that crime films always advised impostors to select a name close enough to their own to allow them to respond to it automatically.

'Even so.'

'And Signora Brunini?' he asked. 'Did you have someone in mind for the role?'

'I thought someone familiar with the investigation should accompany you so that there would be two people able to form an opinion of the place.'

'Go along with *me*?' Brunetti asked, though the emphasis was hardly necessary.

'Friday at three-thirty,' she said. 'There's a Eurocity to Munich that leaves at 1:29. That means it will get to Verona at three.'

'And would this person who goes along with me be Signora Brunini?'

She hesitated a moment, considering this question, though Brunetti knew her well enough to believe she had already answered it. 'I thought perhaps the desire for a child would appear more urgent for Signor Brunini if she were his, er, his companion. Younger, and very much in want of a child.'

Brunetti grasped at the first straw that floated past him. 'What about medical records? Wouldn't a doctor at this clinic want to examine them before he saw . . . them?'

'Oh, those,' she said, as if already bored with mere details. 'Dottor Rizzardi has asked a friend at the Ospedale to prepare them.'

'For Signor Brunini and his, er, his companion?'

'Exactly. They should be ready, and Dottor Rizzardi's friend has only to fax them to Verona.'

Did he have a choice? The question was absurd.

Little happened over the day and a half before Brunetti had to take up the role of Signor Brunini. The couples who had been arrested in Verona and Brescia were sent home, and the police request that they be kept under house arrest was rejected by magistrates in both cities. The children, two articles stated, had been given into the care of the social services. Dottor Pedrolli, too, was told by the Venetian magistrate assigned the case that he could return to his home and to his work, but following the advice of Dottor Damasco, he chose to remain in the hospital. The Carabinieri had decided to bring against him only charges having to do with the false adoption of the baby: mention was no longer made of resisting arrest or injuring a police officer in performance of his duties. Neither he nor his wife made any attempt to contact Brunetti, who was careful to request a written report from the Carabinieri, though there was precious little to report.

Thus, urged by the restless desire to force something, anything, to happen, Brunetti arrived at the station on Friday afternoon on time to catch the 1:29 Eurocity to Munich, scheduled to stop at Verona at 2:54.

'You know, we can stop this if you'd like,' Brunetti said as the train pulled into the Verona station.

Signorina Elettra looked up from her copy of *Il Manifesto*, smiled, and responded, 'But then I'd have to go back to the office, wouldn't I, Commissario?' Her smile was warm, but it did not linger as she shut the paper and got to her feet. She set the newspaper on the seat, took her coat and put it over her arm.

She went into the corridor, and Brunetti picked up the paper, calling after her. 'You've forgotten this.'

'No, better leave it there. I doubt that patients at this clinic read anything other than *Il Giornale*. I'd hardly want to trigger alarms by walking in with a Communist newspaper.'

'One does tend to forget that they eat babies,' Brunetti said conversationally as they made their way to the end of the carriage.

'Communists?' she asked, turning to him at the top of the steps.

'So my Aunt Anna believed,' Brunetti said, then added, 'Probably still does.' He followed her down the steps, and together they walked to the stairway that led to the lower level and the station exit.

A few taxis stood in line; Brunetti opened the back door of

the first and waited as Signorina Elettra got in. He closed it and walked around to the other side. He gave the driver, who appeared to be either Indian or Pakistani, the name and address of the Villa Colonna, and the man nodded as though they were familiar.

Neither Brunetti nor Signorina Elettra spoke as the taxi pulled into traffic, turning left in front of the station and moving off towards what Brunetti calculated must be the west. He was amazed, as he so often was, at how many cars crowded the roads, at how loud it all was, even through the closed windows of the taxi. Cars appeared to come at them from all directions, some sounding their horns, a noise Brunetti had always found particularly aggressive. The driver muttered under his breath in a language that was not Italian, braking and surging ahead in response to spaces that closed or opened ahead of them. Try as he might, Brunetti never quite managed to understand the cause and effect relationship between what a driver saw and what he did: perhaps there was none.

He sat back and studied the endless rows of new buildings to his left, all low, all ugly, and all apparently selling something.

Voice low, Signorina Elettra said, 'Shall we go ahead with what we planned?'

'I think so,' he replied, though it was she who had planned their roles, not they together, and surely not he. 'It will make me look more than a little desperate, and it suggests that I'm willing to do anything at all to keep you happy.'

'And it gives me an interesting role to play.'

Before he could respond, the taxi came to a sharp halt, pitching them forward, forcing them to brace their hands against the seats in front to avoid crashing into them. The driver swore and banged his fist repeatedly against the dashboard as he continued to mutter to himself. In front of them stood a square-backed truck, its red brake lights glaring. As they sat and watched, black fumes poured from beneath the truck. Within seconds, the taxi was trapped in a black cloud, and the inside began to fill with the acrid smell of burning oil.

'Is that truck going to explode?' Brunetti asked the driver, not bothering to ask himself how the man would know.

'No, sir.'

Strangely comforted, Brunetti sat back and glanced at Signorina Elettra, who had her hand over her mouth and nose.

Brunetti was pulling out his handkerchief to hand to her when the taxi suddenly jerked forward and slid around the truck. Then they moved off at a speed that pressed them against the backs of their seats. When Brunetti looked, there was no sign of the truck.

'My God,' Signorina Elettra said, 'how can people live like this?'

'I've no idea,' Brunetti answered.

They lapsed into silence and before long the taxi slowed and turned into an oval driveway in front of a three-storey building, all gleaming metal and glass.

'Twelve Euro, fifty,' the driver said as they drew to a halt.

Brunetti gave him a ten and a five and told him to keep the change. 'Would you like a receipt, sir?' the driver asked. 'I can make it for any amount you like.'

Brunetti thanked him and said it wasn't necessary, got out and went around to open the door for Signorina Elettra. She swung both feet out and stood, then took his arm and leaned towards him. 'It's show time, Commissario,' she said and gave him a broad smile that ended in a wink.

The automatic doors opened into a reception area that might

have served for an advertising agency, perhaps even a television studio. Money was in evidence. It did not shout and it did not whistle, nor did it try in any vulgar way to call attention to itself. But it was there, evident in the parquet, the Persian miniatures on the walls, and in the pale leather chairs and sofa that sat around three sides of a square marble table on which rested a bouquet of flowers more splendid than anything Signorina Elettra had to date thought of ordering for the Questura.

A young woman quite as beautiful as the flowers, if somewhat more restrained in colour choice, sat at a glass-topped table. No papers and nothing to write with could be seen, only a flat-screen computer and a keyboard. Through the surface of the desk, Brunetti saw that she sat with her feet neatly together, a pair of brown shoes peeping out from the bottom of what looked like black silk slacks.

She smiled as they approached, revealing dimples on either side of a perfect mouth. Her hair appeared to be naturally blonde, though Brunetti had abandoned the idea that he could any longer tell, and her eyes were green, though one seemed to be just minimally larger than the other. 'May I help you?' she asked, making it sound as if this were her single goal in life.

'My name is Brunini,' he said. 'I have a three-thirty appointment with Dottor Calamandri.'

Again that smile. 'One moment and I'll check.' She turned aside and typed a few letters into the computer, tapping them out carefully with the tips of her blunt-cut fingernails. She waited a second, glanced back at them and said, 'If you'll take seats over there, the dottore will see you in five minutes.'

Brunetti nodded and started to turn away. The young woman came around her desk to lead them to the seats, almost as if she doubted they could make the two-metre trip unaided.

'Would either of you like something to drink?' she asked, her smile refusing to fade.

Signorina Elettra shook her head, not bothering to say thank you. She was, after all, the spoiled companion of a wealthy man, and such women did not smile at their inferiors. Nor did they smile at women who were younger than they, especially when they were in the company of a man.

They sat down and the young woman returned to her desk, where she busied herself at her computer, the screen of which Brunetti could not see. He looked at the magazines lying beneath the flowers: *AD*, *Vogue*, *Focus*. Nothing so vulgar as *Gente* or *Oggi*, or *Chi*, the sort of magazine one looked forward to being able to read in the doctor's waiting room.

He picked up *Architectural Digest* but tossed it down before opening it, remembering that the reason he was there was to be attentive to the wishes of his companion. He leaned towards her and asked, 'Are you all right?'

'As soon as this is over, I will be,' she said, looking up at him and trying to smile.

Neither spoke for some time, and Brunetti's attention wandered back to the covers of the magazines. He heard a door open and looked up to see another woman, older than the one at the desk and less attractive, approaching them. Her brown hair was parted in the middle and cut to just below her ears, falling forward on both sides of her face. She wore a white lab jacket over a grey wool skirt. Her legs were fine and well-muscled, the legs of a woman who played tennis or ran, but no less beautiful for that.

Brunetti stood. The woman extended her hand, saying, 'Good afternoon, Signor Brunini.' Brunetti expressed his pleasure in meeting her. He noticed the reason for the hair style: a thick layer of makeup attempted—and failed—to cover the rough pitting left by acne or some other skin disease. The scars, confined to the sides of her cheeks, were almost completely hidden by her hair. 'I'm Dottoressa Fontana, Dottor Calamandri's assistant. I'll take you to him.'

Signorina Elettra, secure in the presence of far less competition than that offered by the woman at the desk, could afford a gracious smile. She took Brunetti's arm, suggesting that she might need his help to make whatever distance it was to Dottor Calamandri's office.

Dottor Fontana led them down a corridor where the elegance of the waiting room gave way to the practical sense of a medical institution: the floor was made of square grey tiles, and the prints on the walls were black and white city prospects. The doctor's legs looked as good from the back as from the front.

Dottor Fontana stopped at a door on the right, knocked, and opened it. Allowing Brunetti and Signorina Elettra to precede her into the room, she followed them in and closed the door.

A man somewhat older than Brunetti sat behind a desk the surface of which made no pretence to anything other than chaos. Stacks of files and loose papers lay everywhere, brochures, magazines, boxes of prescription drugs, pencils, pens, a Swiss Army knife, medical reviews abandoned as though the reader had been called away.

The same disorder was evident in the doctor himself, whose loosened tie showed at the top of his lab coat. Pencils and what might be a thermometer stuck up from the breast pocket of the jacket; his name was stitched into the top of the pocket. He had a faintly distracted air, as if he were not quite sure how this mess had accumulated before him. Clean-shaven and round-faced, he glanced up and smiled, reminding Brunetti of the doctors of his youth, men willing to be called out at night to visit people in their homes, men to whom the health of their patients was worth any time or effort.

Brunetti gave the room a quick glance and saw the usual: framed medical degrees on the walls, glass-fronted cabinets filled with boxes of pharmaceuticals, and the end of a paper-sheeted examining table emerging from behind a portable screen.

Calamandri got to his feet and leaned across his desk to offer his hand, first to Signorina Elettra and then to Brunetti. He said good afternoon and indicated two of the chairs in front of his desk. Dottor Fontana took the remaining seat to their right.

'I have your file here,' Calamandri said in a businesslike voice. From a pile of folders, with unerring aim, he pulled out a brown manila one. He pushed papers to one side to clear a space and opened the file. He placed his right palm, fingers spread, on the contents and looked at them. 'I've seen the results of all of your tests and exams, and I think the best thing I can do is tell you the truth.' Signorina Elettra raised a hand halfway to her mouth. Calamandri went on, 'I realize this will not be the news you came here hoping for, but it's the most honest information I can give you.'

Signorina Elettra let out a small sigh as her hand fell to her lap, where it joined the other in grasping at her handbag. Brunetti glanced at her and put a comforting hand on her arm.

Calamandri waited for her to speak, or Brunetti, but when neither did, he went on, 'I could suggest that you have the tests done again.'

Signorina Elettra cut him off with a violent shake of her head. 'No. No more tests,' she said in a harsh voice. Turning to

Brunetti, she said, voice grown softer, 'I can't do that again, Guido.'

Calamandri raised a comforting hand and said, addressing Brunetti, 'I'm afraid I agree with your, er...' Failing to find the word to describe her connection with Brunini, Calamandri turned his attention to Signorina Elettra directly and repeated, 'I'm afraid I agree with you, Signora.' She responded with a small, pained smile.

Glancing back and forth between Brunetti and Signorina Elettra to show that what he had to say now was intended for both of them, Calamandri added, 'The tests you've had, both of you, are definitive. You've had them twice, so there is really no purpose in your bothering with them again.' He looked at the papers in front of him, then towards Brunetti. 'In the second test, the count is even lower.'

Brunetti thought of lowering his head in shame at this blow to his masculinity but refused the temptation and continued to meet the doctor's eye, but he did so nervously.

To Signorina Elettra, Calamandri said, 'I don't know what the other doctors have told you, Signora, but from what I read here, I'd say that there is almost no likelihood of conception.' He turned a page, glanced at whatever had been concocted there by Rizzardi and his friend at the lab, then back at her. 'How old were you when this happened?' he asked.

'Eighteen,' she answered, meeting his glance.

'If I might ask, why did you wait so long to have the infection treated?' he asked, managing to keep any sign of reproach out of his voice.

'I was younger then,' she answered and gave a small shrug, as if to distance herself from that younger person.

Calamandri said nothing, and his silence eventually prodded her into self-justification. 'I thought it was something else. You know, a bladder infection or something like that; one of those fungus things you get.' She turned to Brunetti and took his hand. 'But by the time I went to a doctor, the infection had spread.'

Brunetti was careful to keep his eyes on her face, gazing at her as though she were reciting a sonnet or singing a lullaby to the child they could not have, instead of referring to a bout of venereal disease. He hoped Calamandri had enough experience to recognize a man gone stupid through love. Or lust. Brunetti had seen enough of both to believe the signs were identical.

'Did they tell you then what the consequences of the infection were likely to be, Signora?' Calamandri asked: 'that you probably would not be able to have children?'

'I told you,' she said, making no attempt to disguise the anger that underlay her embarrassment, 'I was younger then.' She shook her head a few times and pulled her hand back from Brunetti's to wipe at her eyes. Then she looked at Brunetti and said, with an intensity that suggested no one was in the room with them, 'That was before I met you, *caro*, before I wanted to have a baby. Our baby.'

'I see,' the doctor said, and closed the file. He folded his hands and placed them very sombrely on top of it. He glanced at his colleague and said, 'Do you have anything to add, Dottoressa?'

She leaned forward and spoke to Brunetti, who sat on the other side of Signorina Elettra. 'Before I looked at the file, I thought assisted conception might be possible, but after seeing the X-rays and reading the report from the doctors at the Ospedale Civile, I no longer think that's feasible.'

Signorina Elettra burst out, 'Don't blame me.'

As if she had not spoken, Dottoressa Fontana continued, turning her attention to her colleague, 'As you say, Dottore, the sperm count is too low, so I don't think it's likely that conception could take place in the normal fashion in any case, regardless of the Signora's condition.' She turned to Signorina Elettra and said coolly, 'We're doctors, Signora. We don't blame people; we simply try to treat them.'

'So what does that mean?' Brunetti asked before Signorina Elettra had a chance to speak.

'I'm afraid it means,' said Calamandri with a small tightening of his lips, 'that we can't help you.'

'But that's not what I was told,' Brunetti blustered.

'By whom, Signore?' Calamandri inquired.

'By my doctor in Venice. He said you worked miracles.'

Calamandri smiled and shook his head. 'I'm afraid only *il Signore* can work miracles, Signor Brunini. And even He had to have something to work with: the bread and fishes or the water at the wedding.' He glanced at their faces and saw that the reference, which Brunetti acknowledged with a nod, was lost on his companion.

'But I have the money,' Brunetti said. 'There's got to be something you can do.'

'I'm afraid the only thing I can do, Signore,' Calamandri said with a very conspicuous glance at his watch, 'is to suggest that you and your wife consider the possibility of adoption. The process is a long one and perhaps not the easiest, but in your circumstances, it's the only route I can see that might be open to you.'

How did she manage to blush, Brunetti wondered? How on earth did Signorina Elettra manage to have her entire face, even her ears, flush a bright red and remain that way for long seconds as she looked down into her lap and began to snap open and closed the hinge on her bag?

'We're not married,' Brunetti said in order to end the silence, something no one else in the room seemed willing or able to do. 'I'm separated from my wife. Well, not legally, that is. And Elettra and I have been together now for more than a year.' His wife, the joy of his life, was in Venice and he was in Verona, so he was indeed separated from her. There existed no legal separation between them and, please heaven, let that possibility remain always as absurd as it was at this moment. And Signorina Elettra had been working at the Questura for a decade now, so he and she had been together, surely, for more than a year. Whatever their profound deceit, then, all of his statements were quite literally true.

He glanced aside at Signorina Elettra and saw that she was still staring at her lap, though her hands were quiet now, and her face had grown a deathly white. 'So, you see,' he said, looking back at Calamandri, 'we can't adopt. That's why we hoped to be able to have a baby. Together.'

After quite a long time, Calamandri said, 'I see.' He closed Brunetti's file and slid it to his right. He glanced at Dottoressa Fontana, but she had nothing to say. Calamandri got to his feet. Dottoressa Fontana followed suit, as did Brunetti. When Signorina Elettra remained in her seat, Brunetti bent down and placed a hand on her shoulder. 'Come on, *cara*. There's nothing more we can do here.'

She turned a tear-streaked face to him and said, voice pleading, 'But you said we'd have a baby. You said you'd do anything.'

Kneeling at her side and pulling her weeping face into his shoulder, Brunetti said softly, but not so softly that the other two would not hear, 'I did promise. I promise on my mother's head. I'll do anything.' He looked at Calamandri and Fontana, but they were already leaving.

When they had closed the door behind them, Brunetti helped Signorina Elettra to her feet and placed his arm around her shoulders. 'Come on, Elettra, we'll go home now. There's nothing else here for us.'

'But you promise, you promise you'll do something?' she pleaded.

'Anything,' Brunetti repeated, and led the weeping woman towards the door.

15

They remained in role until they were on the train back to Venice, sitting across from one another in the all but empty first-class carriage of the Eurocity from Milano. They had not spoken while they waited in the clinic for the taxi the receptionist called, nor in the taxi itself. But in the train, with no remaining chance that they would be seen or overheard, Signorina Elettra sat back in her seat and took a deep breath. Brunetti thought he saw her real persona return to take possession of her, but since he was never quite sure just what that persona was, he was not certain that this had actually taken place.

'Well?' Brunetti asked her.

'No, not yet,' she said. 'I'm still exhausted from all those tears.'

'How did you do it?' Brunetti asked.

'What? Cry?'

'Yes.' In over a decade, he had seen her cry only once, and then it had been for real. Many of the tales of human misery and malice that unfolded at the Questura were such as to cause a stone to weep, but she had always maintained a professional distance from them, even when many others, including the impenetrably unimaginative Alvise, were moved.

'I thought about the *masegni*,' she said with a small smile.

She had made odd remarks in the past, but to suggest that she could cry at the thought of paving stones was not something he was prepared for. 'I beg your pardon,' he said, all thought of Dottor Calamandri momentarily forgotten, 'why do you cry at the thought of the *masegni*?'

'Because I'm Venetian,' she answered, aiding understanding no further.

The conductor passed by at that moment, and when he was finished checking their tickets and had moved down the compartment, Brunetti said, 'Could you explain?'

'They're gone, you know? Or hadn't you noticed?' she asked.

Where would paving stones go? Brunetti wondered. And how? Perhaps the stress of the last hour had . . .

'During the repaving of the streets,' she continued, preventing him from completing the thought. 'When they raised the sidewalks against *acqua alta*,' she added, raising her eyebrows in silent comment on the folly of that attempt. 'They dug up all the *masegni*, the ones that had been there for centuries.' Hearing her, he remembered the months he had spent watching the workmen, as *campi* and *calli* were torn up, pipes and phone wires installed or renewed, then everything put back again.

'And what did they replace them with?' she asked. Brunetti tried never to encourage the asking of rhetorical questions by dignifying them with an answer, and so he remained silent.

'They replaced them with machine-cut, perfectly rectangular stones, every one a living example of just how perfect four right angles can be.'

Brunetti remembered now being struck by how well the new stones did fit together, unlike the old ones with their rough edges and irregular surfaces.

'And where did the old ones go, I wonder?' she asked, raising her right index finger in the air in a ritual gesture of interrogation. When Brunetti still made no answer, she said, 'Friends of mine saw them, stacked up neatly in a field in Marghera.' She smiled, and went on: 'carefully bound in wire, as if ready for shipment to somewhere else. They even photographed them. And there has been talk of a piazza somewhere in Japan where they were used.'

Brunetti made no attempt to disguise his confusion. 'Japan?' he asked.

'That's just talk, sir,' she said. 'Since I haven't seen them myself, only the photographs, I suppose all of this could be nothing more than urban myth. And there's no proof, well, no proof aside from the fact that they were there, thousands of them, centuries-old stones, when the work started, and now most of them *aren't* there. So unless they decided to turn themselves into lemmings and jump into the *laguna* one night when no one was watching, someone took them and didn't bring them back.'

Brunetti was busy calculating the sheer volume of stone. There would have been boatloads, truckfuls, whole acres of the things. Too many of them to hide, enormously expensive to transport, how could anyone organize such a thing? And for what purpose?

Almost as if he had posed the questions out loud, she said, 'To sell them, Commissario. To dig them up and take them away at the city's expense—hand-cut, centuries-old volcanic rock paving stones—and sell them. That's why.' He thought she had finished but she added, 'Even the French and the Austrians, when they invaded—and God knows they stripped us clean— at least they left us the paving stones. Just thinking about it is enough to make me weep.'

As it would, Brunetti realized, any Venetian. He found his

imagination working, wondering who might have organized this, who would have had to be complicit in order for it to have been done, and he liked none of the possibilities that occurred to him. From nowhere, the memory arose of an expression his mother had often used, that Neapolitans 'would steal the shoes from your feet while you were walking'. Well, how much more clever we Venetians, for some of us manage to steal the paving stones from under our own feet.

'As to Dottor Calamandri,' she said, reeling in Brunetti's wandering attention, 'he seemed like a very busy doctor who wanted to be honest with his patients. He at least wanted them not to have any illusions about the possibilities that were open to them. And to discourage false illusions.' She gave that time to register and then asked, 'And you?'

'Pretty much the same. He could very easily have recommended that we have the whole series of tests done again. At his clinic. In his lab.'

'But he didn't,' she agreed. 'Which is a sign of an honest man.'

'Or one who wants to appear to be honest,' Brunetti suggested.

'Those would have been my next words,' she said with a smile. The train began to slow as it approached the Mestre station. On their left, people hurried into and out of the station, into and out of McDonald's. They watched the people on the platform and in the other train to their right, and then the doors slammed shut and they were moving again.

They talked idly, discussing Dottoressa Fontana's chilly manner and agreeing that the only thing now was to wait to see if Brunini would receive a phone call from someone saying they worked with the clinic. Failing that, perhaps either Pedrolli or his wife would be more forthcoming, or Signorina Elettra would find a way to worm her way into the records of the ongoing Carabinieri investigation.

A few minutes later, the smokestacks of Marghera came into view on their right, and Brunetti wondered what sort of comment Signorina Elettra would have to make about them today. But it seemed that her ration of indignation had been used up by the *masegni*, for she remained silent, and soon the train drew into Santa Lucia.

As they walked towards the exit, Brunetti looked up at the clock and saw that it was thirteen minutes after six. He could easily catch the Number One that left at six-sixteen: like a baby penguin that has imprinted the image of his mother in his memory, Brunetti had known for more than a generation that the Number One left from in front of the station at ten-minute intervals, starting at six minutes after the hour.

'I think I'll walk,' she said as they started down the steps, threading their way through the mass of people rushing for their trains. Neither of them discussed the possibility, or the duty, of going back to the Questura.

At the bottom, they paused, she poised to move off to the left and he towards the *imbarcadero* on the right. 'Thank you,' Brunetti said, smiling.

'You're more than welcome, Commissario. It's far better than spending the afternoon working on staff projections for next month.' She raised a hand in farewell, and disappeared into the streams of people walking from the station. He watched her for a moment, but then he heard the vaporetto reversing its engines as it pulled up to the *imbarcadero*, and he hurried to his boat and home.

*

'You're early tonight,' Paola called from the living room as he let himself into the apartment. She made it sound as if his unexpected arrival was the most pleasant thing that had happened to her in some time.

'I had to leave the city to go and talk to someone, and when I got back it was too late to bother going back to work,' he called while he hung up his jacket. He chose to leave it all very vague, this trip out of the city; if she asked he would tell her, but there was no reason to burden her with the details of his work. He loosened his tie: why in God's name do we still wear them? Worse, why did he still feel undressed without one?

He went into the living room and found her, as he expected to, supine on the sofa, a book dropped open on her chest. He walked over to her and bent to squeeze one of her feet.

'Twenty years ago, you would have bent down and kissed me,' she said.

'Twenty years ago, my back would not have hurt when I did,' he answered, then bent down and kissed her. When he stood, he pressed a melodramatic hand to his lower back and staggered, a broken man, towards the kitchen. 'Only wine can save me,' he gasped.

In the kitchen, the mingled aromas of baking pastry and something both sweet and sharp greeted him. With no effort and no protest, he bent to look through the glass door of the oven and saw the deep glass baking tray Paola always used for *crespelle*: this time with zucchini and what looked like *peperoni gialli*: that explained both aromas.

He opened the refrigerator and had a look. No, with the cooler weather Brunetti suddenly wanted a red. From the cabinet he took a bottle of something called Masetto Nero and studied the label, uncertain where it had come from.

He walked back to the door of the living room. 'What's Masetto Nero and where did it come from?'

'If it's from a vineyard called Endrizzi, it's something my father sent over,' she said, her eyes not leaving the page.

This explanation left Brunetti more than a little confused, for he could not determine the dimensions of 'sent over' when Count Orazio Falier was the person doing the sending. Sent his boat over with a dozen cases? Sent one of his employees over with a single bottle for them to taste? Had bought the vineyard and sent over a few bottles to ask what they thought of it?

He went back to the kitchen counter and opened the wine. He sniffed at the cork after he pulled it out, though he never quite knew what he was meant to smell there. It smelled like a cork from a wine bottle: most of them did. He poured two glasses and carried them back to the living room.

He set her glass down beside her, then sat in the space she created by pulling her feet back. He sipped. And hoped the Count had bought the vineyard. 'What are you reading?' he asked, seeing that she had returned to the book, though the glass was in her other hand and she seemed pleased with what she tasted.

'Luke.'

In all these years, she had never dared to refer even to her beloved Henry James with anything but his full name, nor had Jane Austen been exposed to the affront of unsolicited familiarity. 'Luke who?'

'Luke the Evangelist.'

'As in the New Testament?' he asked, though he could think of nothing else that Luke might have written.

'Even so.'

'What about?'

'All that stuff about doing to others what you would have them do unto you.'

'Does that mean you'll get up to get the next bottle?' he asked.

She allowed the book to fall to her chest, he thought a little bit melodramatically. She sipped at her wine and raised her eyebrows in appreciation. 'It's fabulous, but I think one bottle might tide us through until dinner, Guido.' She sipped again.

'Yes, it's very good, isn't it?' he asked.

She nodded and took another sip.

After some time, he asked, curious to learn why someone like Paola was reading Luke. 'And what particular reflections did that text encourage in you?'

'I love it when you try to sweet-talk me with sarcasm,' she said and replaced her glass on the table. She closed the book and placed it beside her glass. 'I was talking to Marina Canziani today. I ran into her at the Marciana.'

'And?'

'And she started talking about her aunt, the one who raised her.'

'And?'

'And the woman's suddenly—I think she's about ninety—got old, old and feeble. It happened to her the way it happens to very old people: one day they're fine, and then two weeks later they've collapsed into the ruin of old age.'

Marina's aunt—he thought her name was Italia: at any rate, something mastodontic like that—had been at the back of Marina's life for as long as Brunetti and Paola had known her, and that had been for decades. The aunt had taken her in when her parents were killed in a road accident, had raised her with rigorous, inflexible rectitude, seen that she went to university and did well, but had never given her even the most minimal demonstration of affection or approval in all the years Marina was in her charge. She had been an astute administrator of Marina's inheritance and had turned her into a very wealthy woman, and she had been a stern opponent of the marriage that had turned Marina into a very happy woman.

No further information was forthcoming. Brunetti thought about Marina's aunt, sipped at his wine, and finally said, 'I'm not sure I see the connection to Saint Luke.'

Paola smiled, showing, he thought, an excess of teeth. 'She begged Marina to take her into her home and let her live there, with them. She offered to pay rent and said she'd pay for someone to come in to be with her every day and to stay there at night to take care of her.'

'And Marina?' Brunetti asked.

'Told her she was willing either to arrange for *una badante* to come and live with her in her own home and take care of her or for her to go to a private nursing home on the Lido.'

Brunetti still failed to grasp the connection to scripture. 'And?' he repeated.

'And it occurred to me that perhaps what Christ was doing was actually giving some very sensible investment advice. That is, maybe we shouldn't read it as some sort of moral imperative always to do good to people, but more as an observation about what happens when we don't. If people are going to pay us back, as it were, in kind, then charity is a wise investment.'

'And Marina's aunt made a bad investment?'

'Exactly.'

He finished his wine and leaned forward to set the glass on the table. 'Interesting interpretation,' he said. 'This the sort of thing you scholarly people talk about when you're at work?'

She took her glass, finished the wine, and said, 'When we're not demonstrating our superiority to our students.'

'One would assume that hardly needs demonstration,' Brunetti said, then, 'What's after the *crespelle*?'

'*Coniglio in umido*,' she said, then posed her own question. 'Why is it that you always assume I have nothing better to do with my time but to cook dinner? I'm a university professor, you know. I have a job. I have a professional life.'

He picked up her sentence at the bounce and continued it '...and I ought not to be relegated to the position of kitchen slave by a husband who, in typical male fashion, assumes that it's my job to cook, while it's his to carry the slaughtered beast home on his back,' he said, then went into the kitchen and came back with the bottle.

He poured some into her glass then filled his own and sat down again beside her feet. He saluted her with his glass and took another sip. 'Really wonderful. How much did he "send over"?'

'Three cases, and you're ignoring my question.'

'No, I'm not ignoring it: I'm trying to figure out how seriously I'm meant to take it. Given the fact that you teach about four hours a week and spend far less time than that talking to students, my conscience is clear on the imbalance of time we spend in the kitchen.' She started to speak, but he ignored her and kept talking. 'And if you're going to say you have to spend so much time reading, I'd say that you'd probably go mad if you couldn't spend all your free time reading.' After a long swallow of wine, he took one of her feet and shook it gently.

She smiled and said, 'So much for my attempt at legitimate protest.'

He closed his eyes and rested his head against the back of the sofa.

'Well, protest,' she admitted, after some time had passed.

After even more had passed, he said, eyes still closed, 'I went out to that clinic in Verona today.'

'The fertility clinic?'

'Yes.'

After she had said nothing for a long time, he opened his eyes and glanced in her direction. 'What is it?' he asked, sensing that she had something she wanted to say.

'It seems I can't read a magazine or a newspaper without coming on an article about overpopulation,' Paola said. 'Six billion, seven, eight, dire warnings about the population bomb and the lack of sufficient natural resources to support us all. And at the same time, people are going to fertility clinics . . .'

'In order to add to the population?' he asked.

'No,' she answered instantly. 'Hardly. In order to satisfy a real human urge.'

'Not a human need?' he asked.

'Guido,' she began in a voice she forced to sound tired, 'we've been here before, trying to define "need". You know what I think it means: if you don't get it—like food or water—you die.'

'And I keep thinking it's more: that it's those things that make us different from the other animals.'

He saw her nod, but then she said, 'I think I don't want to pursue this now. Besides, I know that, even if you badger me with logic and good sense, and even if you argue from the personal about our own children, you still won't get me to agree that it's a need, having children. So let me save us both time and energy by not talking about it, all right?'

He leaned forward to pick up the bottle, then decided against it and set it back on the table. 'I went to Verona with Signorina Elettra,' he said, surprising himself with the revelation. 'We were a couple desperate to have a child. I wanted to see if the clinic is involved with these adoptions.'

'Did they believe you? At the clinic?' she asked, though to Brunetti the more important matter was whether the clinic was in fact involved in the false adoptions.

'I think so,' he said, considering it better not to attempt to explain why this might be so.

Paola shifted her feet on to the floor and sat up. She placed her glass on the table, then turned to Brunetti and picked a long dark hair from the front of his shirt. She let it drop to the carpet and got to her feet. Saying nothing, she went into the kitchen to prepare the rest of dinner.

16

As the days passed, the Pedrolli case, and to a lesser degree the cases of illegal adoption in other cities, disappeared from the news. Brunetti continued to interest himself in a semiofficial way. Vianello managed to find the transcript of the conversation Brunetti had had with the woman who lived near Rialto. When the Inspector went to speak to her, she could remember nothing further, save that the woman who made the phone call had worn glasses. The apartment opposite, where the pregnant woman had spent those days, turned out to be owned by a man in Torino and was rented out by the week or month. When questioned, the managing agent found only an indication that a Signor Giulio D'Alessio, who had not given an address and had preferred to pay with cash, had rented the apartment during the period when the young woman had been there. No, the agent had no clear memory of Signor Rossi. The trail, if indeed it had been a trail, ended there.

Marvilli did not return either of the calls Brunetti made to his office, and the other contacts he had at the Carabinieri failed to divulge any information other than what had been given to the press: the children were in the care of social services and the investigation was proceeding. He did learn, however, that a fax had been sent by the Carabinieri to the Questura the day before the raid, informing the Venice police of the planned raid and giving Pedrolli's name and address.

The absence of reply from the police had been taken by the Carabinieri to signify assent. In response to Brunetti's request, the Carabinieri sent a copy of the fax, along with the receipt for its successful transmission to the appropriate number at the Questura.

Brunetti's reports to the Vice-Questore had included this information, as well as a note of the failure of all attempts to locate the missing fax. In response, Patta suggested that Brunetti return to his other cases and let the Carabinieri get on with Dottor Pedrolli.

Brunetti could not understand the media's apparent lack of interest in the story: he assumed that the veil of official or bureaucratic privacy would have descended to cover the children, their names and their whereabouts, but the parents and the lengths to which they had gone in order to obtain children would surely still be of interest to readers and viewers alike. In a country where the presence of a child in a criminal case, whether as the victim of murder or the survivor of an attempt—or, even better, as the perpetrator—was sure to keep media coverage of a case percolating for days, perhaps weeks, it was strange that these people had so swiftly disappeared from public view.

Years after her arrest for the murder of her child, an interview with 'la madre di Cogne'—even simply an article about her—was a sure-fire way to raise viewer or reader numbers. Even a Ukrainian who tossed her newborn into a skip was bound to get headlines for three days. But the local press dropped Pedrolli after two days, though *La Repubblica* kept the story going for another three before it was superseded by the death of a young Carabiniere, shot by a convicted murderer out of prison on a weekend pass. It was the speed with which the

Pedrolli story vanished from *Il Gazzettino* and *La Nuova*, however, that aroused Brunetti's curiosity, so on the second morning when there was no mention of the case in the papers, he called his friend Pelusso at his office. The journalist explained that the word at *Il Gazzettino* was that the story had not appealed to someone, and so it had been dropped.

Brunetti, a dedicated reader of that newspaper, knew who the chief advertisers were, and Signorina Elettra had discovered that Signora Marcolini belonged to the plumbing supply branch of the family. Thus Brunetti observed 'To say toilet is to say Marcolini.'

'Indeed,' agreed Pelusso, but then quickly added, as though driven to it by whatever remnant of respect for accuracy had managed to survive his decades of journalistic employment, 'He's the likely suspect, because of his daughter, but no one here mentioned his name directly.'

'You think it's necessary to mention it?' Brunetti asked. 'After all, as you said, she's his daughter, and this sort of publicity can't work to anyone's good.'

'Don't be so certain about that, Guido,' the journalist answered. 'The Carabinieri broke in: the husband might still be in the hospital for all anyone knows. And they took the baby. That's got to be enough to earn the two of them a great deal of sympathy, regardless of how they got the baby in the first place.'

This presented an interesting possibility to Brunetti, and he said, 'The Carabinieri, then.'

'Why would they squelch a story like this?'

'Well, first, to dispose of something that presents them in a bad light, but also maybe to lead the people they think are behind all of this to believe it's safe to begin coming out of the woodwork,' Brunetti suggested. When Pelusso said nothing,

Brunetti continued, forming his ideas as he continued to speak. 'If this is some sort of ring, it means whoever's organizing it knows a number of people who want babies and are willing to pay for them, and that means there have got to be other women who have agreed to give them up after they're born.'

'Obviously.'

'But you can't postpone that, can you?' Brunetti asked. 'If a woman's going to have a baby, then she's going to have it when the baby is ready to come, not when some middle man tells her it's time.'

'And if there's as much money in this as I've heard there is,' Pelusso continued slowly, adding his own reasoning to Brunetti's, 'then they'll get back in touch with their buyers.'

Immediately alert, Brunetti asked, 'Do you hear much about this sort of thing?'

'I think a lot of it's urban myth,' Pelusso answered. 'You know, like the Chinese who never die because there's never a funeral. But a lot of people do talk about this business of buying and selling babies.'

'You ever hear anyone mention a price?' Brunetti asked, hoping that Pelusso would not ask him why the police didn't already have this information.

There followed a longish pause, as though Pelusso were entertaining that same thought, but when he spoke, it was merely to answer Brunetti's question. 'No, not with any certainty. I've heard rumours, but as I told you, Guido, people talk about it the way they talk about everything: "I heard this from someone who knows." "My friend knows all about this." "My neighbour has a cousin who has a friend who ..." There's no way to know whether we're being told the truth or not.'

Brunetti stopped himself from observing that this uncertainty was a common phenomenon and hardly limited to Pelusso's experience as a member of the press. Brunetti had no way of knowing if Italians were more gullible than other people, or whether they were simply less informed. He had heard rumours of countries where there existed an independent press that provided accurate information and where the television was not all controlled by one man; indeed, his own wife had expressed belief in the existence of these marvels.

Pelusso's voice summoned him back from these meanderings. 'Is there anything else?' the journalist asked.

'Yes. If you do hear anything definite about who wanted the stories dropped, I'd appreciate it if you'd give me a call,' Brunetti said.

'I'll let you know,' Pelusso said and was gone.

Brunetti replaced the phone, his imagination drawn, by some route he could not identify, to poems Paola had read to him, years ago. They had been written by an Elizabethan poet about the deaths of his two children, a boy and a girl. Brunetti remembered her indignation that the poet was far more disturbed by the death of his son than that of his daughter, but Brunetti recalled only the shattered man's wish that he 'could lose all father now'. How profound would suffering have to be for a man to wish he had never been a father? Two of their friends had seen their children die, and neither had ever come back from that pain. By force of will, he pressed his attention towards the people who might be able to provide him with information about this business in babies, and he recalled his unsuccessful visit to the Ufficio Anagrafe.

Brunetti decided to phone them and within minutes had the information. If a man and the woman of a newborn child came into their office and signed a declaration that the man was the father of the child, that, in essence, was the end of it. Of course, they were required to present their identity cards and proof of the birth; if they chose, they could even do it at the hospital, where there was a branch of the office.

Brunetti had just whispered the words, 'A licence to steal', when Vianello came into his office without bothering to knock.

'They just got a call downstairs,' Vianello said without preamble. 'Someone broke into the pharmacy in Campo Sant'-Angelo.'

'One of your pharmacists?' Brunetti asked with undisguised interest.

Vianello nodded but before Brunetti could ask another question, said, 'We're still looking into bank records.'

'Broke in and did what?' Brunetti asked, wondering if this could be an attempt to destroy evidence or throw dust in the eyes of anyone taking an interest in the pharmacy.

'Whoever called said she opened the door and didn't even bother to go in when she saw what had happened. She called us immediately.'

'But she didn't say what happened?' asked Brunetti with ill-disguised exasperation.

'No. I asked Foa to take us over. He's got the launch waiting.' When Brunetti remained at his desk, Vianello said, 'I think we should go. Before anyone else gets there.'

'Interesting coincidence, isn't it?' Brunetti asked.

'I'm not sure what it is, but I doubt either one of us thinks this is a coincidence,' Vianello answered.

Brunetti glanced at his watch and saw that it was almost ten. 'Why was she just getting there now? Shouldn't they have opened an hour ago?'

'She didn't say, or if she did, Riverre didn't tell me. All he said was that she called and said someone had broken into the place.' In response to the growing impatience in Vianello's voice, Brunetti got to his feet and joined him at the door. 'All right. Let's go and have a look.'

The quickest way was for Foa to turn into Rio San Maurizio and then take them to Campo Sant'Angelo. They crossed the *campo* and approached the pharmacy. Light filtering in from outside illuminated the posters on display in the two shop windows, though no lights appeared to be on inside. Brunetti's eye was drawn to a pair of sleek, tanned female thighs which presented themselves to the beholder, proof of the ease with which cellulite could be banished in a single week. Next to them a white-haired couple stood side by side on a spun-sugar beach, each gazing longingly into the eyes of the other, their hands joined; behind them glistened a tropical sea, on the sand below them a box of arthritis medicine.

'Is this the only entrance?' Brunetti asked, pointing to the intact glass door between the two windows.

'No, the staff uses a door down the *calle* around that side,' Vianello answered, displaying a dubious familiarity with the workings of the pharmacy. Following his own directions, the Inspector led Brunetti to the left and then into a *calle* that led back towards La Fenice.

As they approached the first door on the right, a woman of about Brunetti's age stepped from the doorway, asking, 'Are you the police?'

'*Sì*, Signora,' Brunetti answered, introducing himself and then Vianello. She could have been any of hundreds of Venetian women her age. Her hair was cut short and dyed dark red; her weight was concentrated in her torso, but she had the sense to disguise this with a box-cut jacket over a matching tan T-shirt. Good calves showed under a knee-length brown skirt, and she wore brown pumps with low heels. She carried the remnants of a summer tan and wore little makeup beyond pale lipstick and blue eye shadow.

'I'm Eleonora Invernizzi. I work for Dottor Franchi.' Then, as if to prevent them from taking her for one of the pharmacists, she added, 'I'm the saleswoman.' She did not extend her hand and gazed back and forth at the two men.

'Could you tell us what happened, Signora?' Brunetti asked. She was standing in front of the closed wooden door that presumably led into the pharmacy, but Brunetti made no move towards it.

She shifted the strap of her bag higher on her shoulder and pointed to the lock. Both of them could see the damage: someone had jimmied open the door, with such force that the wood was splintered and stuck out jaggedly above and below the keyhole, suggesting that a crowbar had slipped a few times before it found sufficient purchase to spring the lock and allow the door to be pushed open.

Signora Invernizzi said, 'If I've told him once, I've told the dottore a hundred times that this lock is an invitation to thieves. Every time I tell him, he says, yes, he'll change it, get a *porta blindata*, but then he doesn't, and then I tell him again, and still he doesn't do it.' She pointed to the metal grate that covered a small window in the door. 'I touched it there when I pushed the door open,' she said. 'Otherwise, I haven't touched anything. I didn't even go inside. I just looked and then called you.'

'That was very wise, Signora,' Vianello said.

Brunetti stepped up to the door and placed his palm on the point where the woman said she had put hers. He gave a gentle push, and the door swung easily inward until it stopped with a bang against the wall.

Ahead of them Brunetti saw a narrow corridor and an open door, above which glowed a dim red security light. It was when he lowered his eyes to the floor that he saw why Signora Invernizzi had called the police. For about a metre in front of the far doorway, the floor was strewn with a tapestry of boxes, bottles, and phials, all of which had been stomped on, shattered, and flattened. Brunetti took a few steps until he stood just at the edge of the mess. He extended his right foot and with his toe kicked things aside to clear a place to set his foot, then stepped forward and repeated the process until he reached the second doorway, where the corridor turned right, towards the front of the pharmacy.

Brunetti crossed the corridor and went through the door on the other side into what appeared to be the pharmacists' work space, where mess became catastrophe. Dangerous looking pieces of dark brown glass patterned the floor, among them shattered fragments of what had once been majolica apothecary jars. On one piece, tiny rosebuds wound themselves in a garland among three letters: 'IUM'. Liquids and powders had bled together into a thick soup that smelled faintly of rotten eggs and something astringent that might be rubbing alcohol. Some liquid had burned its way down the front of a cabinet, leaving a wave of corroded plastic behind. A cancerous circle in the linoleum tiles in front of the cabinet exposed patches of cement floor. Two jars still stood on the shelves, but the rest had been swept to the ground, where all but one had broken. Brunetti raised his head instinctively to back away from the fiery smell and found himself looking at the crucified Christ, who had also turned his head away from the stench.

From behind him, Brunetti heard Vianello call his name; he followed the Inspector's voice to the main room of the pharmacy. Perhaps to avoid being observed from outside, whoever had broken in had confined most of his attentions to the area behind the counter and thus farthest from the windows. Here too the counters had been swept clean. All of the drawers had been pulled from the cabinets and tossed to the floor; packages and bottles had been strewn about, then apparently stamped on. Cash register and computer screen were thrown on top of them. Like a tongue lolling from a dog's mouth, the cash drawer lay halfway out of the register and bent to one side: coins and small-denomination bills had vomited from it.

'*Mamma mia*,' exclaimed Vianello. 'I don't think I've ever seen anything like this. Even that guy who went into his ex-wife's new house didn't do this much damage.'

'Her new husband stopped him, remember?' Brunetti said.

'Ah, yes. I'd forgotten. But even so, it was nothing like this.' In emphasis, Vianello pointed at the jumble of bottles and boxes that filled the space behind the counter to the height of their shins.

They heard a noise behind them and spun around to see Signora Invernizzi standing in the doorway, her bag clasped to her chest. '*Maria Vergine*,' she whispered. 'Do you think it was drug addicts again?'

Given the extent of the damage, Brunetti had already excluded that possibility. Addicts knew where the drugs were kept and knew what they wanted. They usually took the drugs, checked the cash register for anything that had been left there overnight, and let themselves out quietly. This had none of the signs of theft: quite the contrary, the money had not been touched. The destruction they gazed on spoke of rage, not greed.

'No, I don't think so, Signora,' Brunetti answered. He glanced at his watch and asked, 'Why is it that no one's come in this morning, Signora? Aside from you, that is?'

'We had the *turno* last week; open day and night. We don't have to open until three-thirty today, but I came in to restock the shelves before we do. It's not much, but Dottor Franchi said it's good if the other doctors get a half-day off after working like that.' She grew suddenly thoughtful at the reference to her employer and added, 'I hope he gets here soon.'

'You called him?' Vianello asked.

'Yes, as soon as I called you. He was in Mestre.'

'And what did you tell him, Signora?'

She seemed puzzled by the question. 'The same thing I told you: that someone had broken in.'

'Did you tell him about all of this?' Brunetti asked, gesturing in a wide circle at the devastation that surrounded them.

'No, sir, I didn't see it,' she reminded him. She lowered her bag and looked around for a place to put it. Finding no clean surface, she hooked it over her arm and said, 'I suppose I didn't want to be the one to tell him, even about what I saw from the door.' Then, as if she'd suddenly remembered something, she set her bag on the littered counter and quickly left the room without explanation.

Brunetti signalled Vianello to remain and followed Signora Invernizzi. She headed back down the corridor and paused outside a door that Brunetti and Vianello had passed without opening. She opened it and reached in to switch on the light. Whatever she saw in there caused her to raise her hands to her face and shake her head. Brunetti thought he heard her mutter something, and instantly he feared that the violence had found a human target.

Stepping up beside her, he took her arm and led her gently away from the doorway and from whatever it was that had so shocked her. Once she had started back towards the main room, he returned to the door and went inside. It was small, each side no more than three metres long, and must once have served as a storeroom or closet. Two walls held bookshelves, but all of the books were now on the floor. The solid wooden desk had once held a computer, but both computer and desk had been tipped on to the floor. The desk, probably because of the solidity of its construction, had suffered nothing more than a pair of parallel scratches on its surface, but the computer had not escaped harm. Pieces of the screen crunched under Brunetti's feet, and wires protruded from its eviscerated case. The keyboard appeared to have been snapped in half, though the plastic case continued to hold the two sides together. The rectangular metal case that contained the hard drive had been hit repeatedly with what he assumed was the crowbar that had been used to force entry. The metal had been deeply dented, and sharp-edged wounds gaped here and there. One corner had been smashed in, as if an attempt had been made to prise the box open. But the best the assailant had achieved was to force loose part of the back panel; inside, Brunetti could make out a flat metal board with tiny coloured dots soldered to its surface. If the other destruction had been vandalism, this was attempted murder.

Brunetti heard footsteps behind him and assumed it was Vianello. He noticed a smear of red on a piece of metal prised up from the back panel and crouched down to take a closer look. Yes, it was blood that appeared to have been wiped away hurriedly, leaving a small trace and a darker stain where the blood had flowed into the seam between the back panel and the frame. Nearby, on the white cover of a book, there was what appeared to be a single red drop, surrounded by tiny red splashlets.

'Who are you? What are you doing here?' a man's voice demanded angrily behind him.

Brunetti pushed himself quickly to his feet and turned to face the man. He was shorter than Brunetti, but thicker, especially in the arms and chest, as though he worked at a heavy physical job or had spent a lot of time swimming. He had hair the colour of apricots, thinning in front and exposing a great deal of forehead. His eyes were light, pale green perhaps, his nose thin, his mouth tight with irritation at Brunetti's continued silence.

'I'm Commissario Guido Brunetti,' Brunetti said.

The man could not hide his surprise. With evident effort, he removed the aggression from his face and replaced it with something softer.

'Are you the owner?' Brunetti asked mildly.

'Yes,' the other man answered, and, his manner warming further, extended his hand. 'Mauro Franchi.'

Brunetti shook the man's hand with conscious briskness. 'Signora Invernizzi called the Questura to report the break-in, and because my colleague and I were already in the area, they called us,' Brunetti said, speaking with the faintest hint of irritation, as if a commissario had better things to do with his time than rush off to the scene of something so ordinary as a break-in. Brunetti had no idea what made him downplay the presence of someone of the rank of commissario at the scene, but he preferred that Dottor Franchi not begin to speculate.

'How long have you been here?' Franchi asked, and again it

seemed to Brunetti the sort of question he should really be asking.

'A few minutes,' Brunetti answered. 'But time enough to see the damage.'

'It's the third time,' Franchi surprised him by saying. 'We're no longer safe to conduct business in this city.'

'Third time what?' Brunetti asked, ignoring Franchi's other comment. Before the other man could answer, they heard footsteps approaching from the front of the pharmacy.

Franchi wheeled around, and when Vianello appeared at the door, Signora Invernizzi a step behind, Brunetti said, 'This is my colleague, Inspector Vianello.' Franchi nodded to Vianello but did not extend his hand. He stepped out into the corridor and approached Signora Invernizzi. At a gesture from Brunetti, Vianello joined him in the smaller room. Brunetti pointed to the smear of blood on the back of the metal case and to the spots on the book.

Vianello went down on one knee. Brunetti watched his head turn slowly from left to right, and suddenly Vianello's hand shot out and he said, 'There's another one.' When Vianello pointed to it, Brunetti saw the spot on the dark tile. 'Well, if we ever get someone for it, we can do a DNA match, I suppose,' Vianello said, sounding sceptical at the thought that the test would be used for a case this minor. Or perhaps that they would ever arrest anyone for the crime.

A moment later, they heard the other two, talking softly, move off towards the front room. Franchi's voice floated back, and Brunetti thought he heard the phrase, 'My mother won't . . .'

'Invernizzi say anything?' Brunetti asked.

'Only what a job it will be to clean up and put it all back together,' Vianello answered. 'And then she mentioned the insurance and said how impossible it is to get them to pay for anything. She started telling me about the daughter of a friend of hers who was knocked off a bicycle ten years ago, and the case still isn't settled.'

'Is that why you came back here?' Brunetti asked with a smile.

Vianello shrugged. 'She kept asking me if she should call the other people who work here and ask them to come in to help clean up.'

'How many of them are there?'

'Two other pharmacists and the cleaning woman. Aside from the owner, that is.'

'Let's go see what he's decided,' Brunetti said and started out of the room. He paused at the door and added, 'Call Bocchese and have him send a scene of crime crew over, will you?'

'The computer?' Vianello asked.

'If that's how the appointments were made, then I think we should take it along with us,' Brunetti answered.

In the larger room, Franchi and the woman stood on the far side of the counter, in the area used by customers. The pharmacist's hand was raised, pointing to the wall behind the counter, from which all of the drawers had been ripped.

'Should I call Donatella? Or Gianmaria, Dottore?' Brunetti heard her ask.

'Yes, I suppose so. We have to decide what to do with the boxes.'

'Should we try to save some of them?'

'Yes, if we can. Anything they haven't torn open or stepped on. And, with the rest, start a list for the insurance.' He said it tiredly, Sisyphus looking at the rock.

'You think it was the same ones?' she asked.

Franchi glanced at Brunetti and Vianello and said, 'I hope the police can find that out, Eleanora.' As if hearing how close to sarcasm his tone was, he added, 'The ways of the Lord are many.'

'You said three times, Dottore,' Brunetti said, ignoring the piety. 'Do you mean this has happened twice before?'

'No,' Franchi answered, waving his hand at what lay all around them. 'But we've been robbed twice. Once it was a break-in, when they took what they wanted. The second time they came in during the day. Drug addicts. One of them had his hand in a plastic bag and said he had a gun. So we gave him the money.'

'Best thing to do,' volunteered Vianello.

'We had no intention of causing them trouble,' Franchi said. 'Let them take the money, so long as no one's hurt. Poor devils; I suppose they can't help themselves.' Did Signora Invernizzi turn and give him a strange look when he said this?

'So you think this was another robbery?' Brunetti asked.

'What else could it be?' Franchi asked impatiently.

'Indeed,' Brunetti agreed. No need, certainly, to raise that question just now.

The pharmacist raised his hands in a gesture rich with resignation and said, '*Va bene.*' He turned to Signora Invernizzi. 'I think the others should come in; you might as well start here.' He held up his thumb and began to count on his fingers as he said, 'I'll call ULSS and report this, and the insurance company, then when we have a list, we can order replacement stock, and then I'll see about getting a new computer by tomorrow morning.' The resignation in his voice could not cover the anger.

The pharmacist walked to the counter and leaned over to

pick up the phone, but the receiver had been ripped away. Franchi pushed himself off from the counter, walked around it, and headed into the corridor. 'I'll phone from my office,' he called back over his shoulder.

'Excuse me, Dottore,' Brunetti said in a loud voice. 'But I'm afraid you can't go into your office.'

'I can't what?' Franchi demanded, wheeling to face Brunetti.

Brunetti joined him in the corridor and explained, 'There's evidence in there, and no one can enter until we check it.'

'But I need to use the phone.'

Brunetti pulled his *telefonino* from the pocket of his jacket and handed it to the doctor. 'Here, Dottore; you can use this.'

'But the phone numbers are in there.'

'I'm sorry,' Brunetti said with a smile that suggested that he was as much a victim of rules as was the pharmacist. 'I'm sure if you dial twelve, they'll give you the numbers. Or you could call my secretary and she'll find them for you.' Before Franchi could protest, Brunetti added, 'And I'm afraid there's no sense in asking your colleagues to come in, Dottore, at least not until the scene of crime team has been here.'

'There was none of that last time,' Franchi said in a voice pitched between sarcasm and anger.

'This seems quite a different matter from a simple burglary, Dottore,' Brunetti said calmly.

Franchi took the *telefonino* with obvious bad grace but made no attempt to use it. 'What about the other things in there?' he asked, jerking his head back towards his office.

'I'm afraid the whole area has to be treated as a crime scene, Dottore.'

Franchi's face reflected even greater anger, but he said only, 'All of my records are in that computer: all of the financial information about my suppliers and all my own billing and the ULSS files. The insurance policy. I can probably get another computer delivered by this afternoon, but I'll need the disc to transfer the records.'

'I'm afraid that's impossible, Dottore,' Brunetti said, biting back the temptation to use a bit of computer jargon he had often heard and thought he understood: 'backup'. 'I don't know if you saw, but whoever did this broke the computer open. I doubt you'd be able to retrieve anything from it.'

'Broke it open?' Franchi asked, as though it were a phrase new to him and he weren't sure what it meant.

'Prised it open at one end is a more accurate description, wouldn't you say, Vianello?' Brunetti asked the Inspector, who had just come into the room.

'That metal box thing?' Vianello asked with ox-like stupidity. 'Yes. He broke it trying to get at whatever's in it.' It sounded as if the Inspector considered the computer as little different from a piggy bank. Changing the subject, he said, 'Bocchese's on the way.'

Before Franchi had time to ask, Brunetti explained, 'The scene of crime team. They'll want to take fingerprints.' With a gracious nod to Signora Invernizzi, who had followed their conversation with some interest, Brunetti said, 'The Signora was careful not to come inside after she opened the door, so if any prints were left, they're still here. The technicians will want to take yours,' he continued, addressing them both, 'so that they can exclude them from what they find. And those of the other people who work here, of course, but that can certainly wait a day.'

Signora Invernizzi nodded, followed by Franchi.

'And I'd prefer that you not disturb anything until my men have gone over it,' Brunetti added.

'How long will that take?' Franchi asked.

Brunetti looked at his watch and saw that it was almost eleven. 'You could come back at three, Dottore. I'm sure they'll be finished by then.'

'And can I . . .' Franchi started to ask but then thought better of it and said, 'I'd like to go out and have a coffee. I'll come back later and they can take my fingerprints, all right?'

'Of course, Dottore,' Brunetti agreed.

He waited to see if the pharmacist would invite Signora Invernizzi to accompany him, but he did not. He handed Brunetti's *telefonino* back to him, then moved around Vianello and went down the corridor and to the exit, disappearing without a word.

'I'd like to go home, if I may,' the woman said. 'I'll come back in an hour or so, but I think I'd like to go home and lie down for a while.'

'Of course, Signora,' Brunetti said. 'Would you like the Inspector to go with you?'

She smiled for the first time and shed ten years as she did so. 'That's very kind. But I live just across the bridge. I'll be back before lunch, all right?'

'Certainly,' Brunetti said and walked her to the door into the *calle*. He stepped outside with her, wished her goodbye and stood there as she walked away. Where the *calle* opened into Campo Sant'Angelo, she turned and gave him a little wave.

Brunetti returned her wave and went back into the pharmacy.

17

'"That metal box thing," Lorenzo?' Brunetti asked. 'Is that some sort of advanced cyber-speak for "hard drive"?' He thought he did quite well in disguising his pride in being able to use the term so casually.

'No,' Vianello answered with a grin, 'It's my attempt to convince Dottor Franchi that he is dealing with a technical illiterate—if not two—and make him believe that neither one of us would think to wonder why he was so interested in holding on to his hard drive.'

'By keeping it from us, that is?' Brunetti asked.

'Exactly,' Vianello answered.

'What do you think's on his computer?'

Vianello shrugged. 'Something he doesn't want us to see: that's for certain. It could be the fake appointments.' Vianello considered the question a little longer and added, 'Or he's looking at websites or chatting in places where he ought not to be.'

'Is there a way you can find out?' Brunetti asked.

Did Vianello smile? 'I couldn't,' he said, and before Brunetti could ask, added, 'nor could Signorina Elettra.' He saw Brunetti's surprise and went on. 'It's physical damage to the hard drive, and neither one of us is able to work with that, recovering information when the disc's been damaged. You need a real technician for that.'

'But you know someone?' Brunetti prompted.

'She does.' A strange expression flitted across Vianello's face: Brunetti had seen something like it on the faces of men who had killed out of jealousy. 'She won't tell me who he is.' He sighed. 'I imagine she'll want to pass it on to him.'

'Then I'll have Bocchese take it back with him,' Brunetti said, his mind busy with speculation about the hard disc and what it might contain. With a certain chagrin, he realized how limited his imagination was. 'If she takes it to this person, do you think he'll be able to find what's on there?' he finally asked Vianello.

'It depends on how bad the damage is,' the Inspector answered. Then he added, speaking very slowly, 'But Signorina Elettra did say he's very good and that she's learned a great deal from him.'

'But nothing else about him?'

'He could be the former governor of Banca d'Italia, for all I know,' Vianello answered, then smiled and added, 'He's got a lot of free time now, hasn't he?'

Brunetti pretended not to have heard.

Bocchese and the scene of crime team showed up after about twenty minutes, and Vianello and Brunetti stood around for an hour or so while the door, the counters, and the computers were photographed and dusted for fingerprints. Brunetti explained about the bloodstains and the hard disc and asked Bocchese's men to take everything back to the Questura.

Signora Invernizzi returned a little after noon and stood on the customer side of the counter while one of the technicians took her fingerprints. Dottor Franchi came in while she was still there and, with far less grace, also had his taken. He asked when they would be finished because he wanted to get his pharmacy ready to open the next day, if possible. Bocchese's assistant told him that they would be gone in an hour, and Franchi said he would go and find a *fabbro* to change the lock on the side door. Brunetti waited to see if Signora Invernizzi would bring up the subject of *una porta blindata*, but she did not.

When both of them were gone, Brunetti went back to the small room, where Bocchese was busy scraping a drop of blood from a point low on the wall. On the floor beside him lay a sealed plastic evidence bag, the book with the other drop of blood already inside it.

'You get a look at the whole place?' Brunetti asked when Bocchese glanced up at him.

'Yes.'

'And?'

'And somebody doesn't like him,' came Bocchese's reply. Then, after a moment, 'Or doesn't like pharmacists, or computers, or boxes of medicine or, for all I know, cash registers.'

'Always trying to interpret things, aren't you, Bocchese, and make them fit into some master plan?' Brunetti asked with a laugh. To the technician, a cigar was always a cigar, and a series of events was a series of events and not cause for speculation.

'What about the blood?' Brunetti asked.

'There's something that looks like a piece of skin and a bit of leather caught under this flange that got pulled up from the back,' Bocchese said, pointing with the tips of a pair of tweezers to where Brunetti had seen the streak of blood on the casing of the hard drive.

'And that means?' Before Bocchese could answer, Brunetti said, 'If you tell me it means there's a piece of skin and a piece of leather there, I'll never let you sharpen Paola's kitchen knives again.'

'And tell her I refused, I imagine?' Bocchese asked.

'Yes.'

'Then I'd say,' the technician began, 'that he had trouble prising at it with the crowbar, or whatever it was, tried to move the tip of it to a more effective place, and tore his glove and cut his hand in the process.'

'Cut it badly?'

Bocchese took some time to answer this. 'I'd say no. It was probably only a small cut.' He anticipated Brunetti's thought and said, 'So, no, I wouldn't bother to call the hospital and ask if anyone's come in to have a hand sewn up today.' After a moment, with audible reluctance, Bocchese added, 'And I'd also say that this is a very impatient as well as a very angry person.'

'Thanks,' Brunetti said. 'After you take a sample of the blood on that,' he added, pointing at the hard disc, 'could you see that it goes to Signorina Elettra?'

As if he found this the most normal thing in the world, Bocchese nodded and returned his attention to the bloodstain.

At the front of the shop, Brunetti found Vianello talking with one of the photographers. 'You ready to go?' he asked.

Brunetti explained to the technician that the owner would be back soon with a locksmith. As he and Vianello walked past the door to the side room, Brunetti called goodbye to Bocchese, who was still on his knees, leaning over to study the electric socket.

Outside, Vianello asked, 'Want to walk?' and it seemed like the best of ideas to Brunetti.

The day, which had started foggy and damp and in a very bad mood, had decided to treat itself to some sun. Without discussion, Brunetti and Vianello turned right and crossed the bridge towards Campo San Fantin. They passed the theatre without really seeing it, both eager to reach Via XXII Marzo and then the Piazza, where the promise of warmth would surely be fulfilled.

As they approached the Piazza, Brunetti watched the people they passed, at the same time half listening to Vianello's lesson on how information was preserved on the hard disc of a computer and how it was possible to retrieve it, even long after the user thought it had been erased.

He saw a group of tourists approach and judged them to be Eastern Europeans, even before he gave the decision any conscious thought. He studied them as they walked past him: sallow complexions; blond hair, either natural or assisted in that direction; cheap shoes, one remove from cardboard; plastic jackets that had been dyed and treated in an unsuccessful attempt to make them resemble leather. Brunetti had always felt a regard for these tourists because they *looked* at things. Probably too poor to buy most of what they saw, they still gazed about them with respect and awe and unbridled delight. With their cheap clothes and their bad haircuts and their packed lunches, who knew what it cost them to come here? Many, he knew, slept for nights on buses in order to spend a single day walking and looking and not shopping. They were so unlike the jaded Americans, who had of course seen bigger and better, or the world-weary Western Europeans, who also believed they had but were too sophisticated to say so.

As they entered the Piazza, the Inspector, who appeared not to have registered the tourists, said, 'The whole world's gone mad with fear of avian flu, and we have more pigeons than people.'

'I beg your pardon,' Brunetti said, his attention still on the tourists.

'I read it in the paper two days ago,' Vianello said. 'There's about sixty thousand of us, and the current population of pigeons—well, the one given in the paper, which is not the same thing—is more than a hundred thousand.'

'That can't be possible,' Brunetti said, suddenly disgusted by the thought. Then, more soberly, 'Who'd count them, anyway, and how'd they do it?'

Vianello shrugged. 'Who knows how any official number is determined?' Suddenly his mood brightened, either at the growing warmth of the Piazza or the absurdity of the subject, and he asked, 'You think there are people working for the Comune who are paid to go around and count pigeons?'

Brunetti considered this for a moment and answered, 'It's not as if pigeons stay in the same place all day long, is it? So some of them might have been counted twice.'

'Or not at all,' Vianello suggested and then added, suddenly venomous, 'God, I hate them.'

'Me, too,' Brunetti agreed. 'I think most people do. Loathsome things.'

'But just touch one of them,' Vianello went on, heated now, 'and you've got the *animalisti* screaming about cruelty to animals and our responsibility to all God's little creatures.' He threw up his hands in disgust or confusion. Brunetti was about to mention his surprise that such talk could come from the Questura's own paragon of all things environmental, when his eye shifted to the façade of the Basilica and those absurdly asymmetrical cupolas, the whole lopsided glory of it.

Brunetti stopped walking and put his hand up to quiet Vianello. In an entirely different voice, almost solemn, he asked, 'We're lucky, aren't we?'

Vianello glanced aside at Brunetti and then followed his

gaze to San Marco and the flags whipping in the breeze, the mosaics above the doors. The Inspector stood there for some time, looking at the church, then glanced to the right, across the water and towards San Giorgio with its ever-vigilant angel. In an entirely uncharacteristic gesture, Vianello raised his free arm and moved it in an arc that encompassed the buildings around them as well as those across the water, then he turned to Brunetti and patted his arm, quickly, twice. For a moment, Brunetti thought the Inspector was going to speak, but he remained silent and moved away towards the Riva degli Schiavoni and the sun-splashed walk down to the Questura.

They decided to stop and have lunch on the way but would not do so until they had put at least two bridges between themselves and San Marco. Vianello knew a small trattoria on Via Garibaldi, where they had penne with a sauce of peppers, grilled *melanzane*, and pecorino affumicato, followed by a baked roll of turkey breast filled with herbs and pancetta.

During the meal, Vianello attempted to explain the basic operating principles of the computer but was forced to abandon the attempt halfway through the pasta. He was reduced to saying, 'She'll have this guy look at it, and then we'll see what's possible.'

Neither wanted dessert, even though the owner swore that the pears in the cake came from his own trees on Burano. Brunetti signalled for coffee, his mind still on the tangible reality of the pharmacy. 'No normal person did that,' he said with no prelude.

'Vandals aren't normal people,' answered Vianello. 'Neither are drug addicts.'

'Come on, Lorenzo, think about what we saw there. It's not a couple of kids on a railway bridge with a can of spray paint.'

The coffee came and Brunetti spent a great deal of time stirring sugar into it, recalling the scene inside the pharmacy.

Vianello finished his own coffee and set down the cup. 'All right,' he said, 'I agree. But why would someone want to do a thing like that? If anything, the doctors he's involved with would do anything to keep us from paying attention to him, or to them.'

'Are we agreed,' Brunetti asked, 'that it's not a coincidence, that he's not just any pharmacist or any store chosen at random?'

Vianello let out a puff of air to show how unlikely he considered this.

'Then why?' Brunetti asked.

'Let's hope Elettra's friend can tell us that,' Vianello said and raised his hand to call for the bill.

18

Autumn advanced. The days grew shorter, and after the clocks went back, they grew shorter still. As happened every year, Paola grew snappish during the first days when darkness arrived sooner, causing her husband and children to keep their heads down until her usual spirits returned, when family life would revert to normal.

Brunetti had transferred his professional attention to his ongoing cases, and the eye he kept on the Pedrolli case grew increasingly inattentive. Though he twice called the social services, he was unable to discover the whereabouts of the child. The reports he wrote grew shorter and then ceased entirely for lack of information, but still he could not banish Dottor Pedrolli from his mind. Weary of the need to seek information indirectly and always having to find arcane ways to induce people to divulge what they knew, Brunetti checked his notebook for the number of Marvilli's office and dialled it.

'Marvilli.'

'Captain, this is Brunetti. I'm calling about Dottor Pedrolli.'

'I'm afraid you might be too late, Commissario.'

'Why is that?'

'The case has been pretty much closed.'

'Could you tell me what that means, Captain?'

'That all of the major charges against him have been dropped.'

'Leaving which ones?'

'Only falsification of a state document.'

'The birth certificate?'

'Yes. It's unlikely to get him anything more than a fine.'

'I see.'

'Is that all, Commissario?'

'No. I have only one question, really: it's why I called you.'

'I'm not sure I can answer any other questions about this case, Commissario.'

'Mine is a simple one, Captain, if you'd hear it.'

'Very well.'

'How is it that you knew about Pedrolli in the first place?'

'I thought I told you that.'

'No, Captain, you didn't.'

'The documents I was given before the operation referred to an anonymous phone call.'

'An anonymous phone call? You mean someone can call and make an accusation, and the Carabinieri . . . they will respond?'

'I think I know what you stopped yourself from saying, Commissario: that the Carabinieri will break into a person's home in response to an anonymous phone call? . . . Are you still there, Commissario?'

'Yes, I am, Captain. Let me repeat my question, if I may.'

'Of course.'

'Could you tell me why you chose to respond to this particular call in the way you did?'

'Even with your graceful rephrasing, Commissario, I'm not sure I should answer that question, especially now that it looks as if very little, if anything, will come of the whole thing.'

'I'd be very grateful if you would, Captain. More to satisfy my personal curiosity than anything else. If the charges have been dropped, then . . .'

'You sound like you mean that, Commissario, about your personal curiosity.'

'I do.'

'Then I can tell you that the person who made the call—at least according to the report I read—provided certain information that added credibility to his claim that the Pedrolli adoption was illegal.'

'"His?"'

'The report I read referred to a man.'

'I'm sorry to have interrupted you, Captain.'

'It's nothing . . . Apparently, he gave the name of the woman, the name of the hospital where the child was born, and the probable date of birth. He also mentioned that money had changed hands.'

'And was this enough?'

'Enough for what, Commissario?'

'To convince you that the caller was telling the truth?'

'My guess, Commissario—and it is only a guess—is that the fact that he knew the woman's name and the other details was enough to convince my colleagues to investigate the accusation or at least to see if this woman's name was on the birth certificate of Dottor Pedrolli's child and if it was, to go and question her about the circumstances.'

'How long did it take them to do that?'

'Do what, Commissario?'

'Question her.'

'I don't remember exactly, but I think the call came in about a week before we . . . before we went to Dottor Pedrolli's. As it turned out, the Verona command was working on similar cases at the same time. It seems they aren't related; that is, Pedrolli's isn't related to the others.'

'So it was just bad luck for Pedrolli?'

'Yes, I suppose you could say that, Commissario.'

'And convenient for you, as well?'

'If you'll allow me to say this, Commissario, you sound as if you think we'd do something like that without being sure.'

'I'm afraid you're right, Captain.'

'We don't do these things rashly, Commissario. And for what it's worth, I have a child, a girl. She's only one.'

'Mine are older.'

'I don't think that changes anything.'

'No, probably not. Is there any news of him?'

'Dottor Pedrolli?'

'The baby.'

'No, there isn't. And there can't be: you must know that. Once a child is in the care of the social services, we're not given any further information.'

'I see . . . Tell me one last thing, Captain, if you will.'

'If I can.'

'Is there any way that Dottor Pedrolli could ever . . . ?'

'See the baby?'

'Yes.'

'It's not likely. I'd say impossible. The boy isn't his, you see.'

'How do you know that, Captain? If I might ask.'

'May I say something without risk of offending you, Commissario?'

'Yes. Certainly.'

'We're not a gang of jackbooted thugs here, you know.'

'I hardly meant to suggest . . .'

177

'I'm sure you didn't, Commissario. I simply wanted to make this clear, first.'

'And second?'

'To tell you that, before the operation was authorized, the mother of the baby testified that the child was her husband's and not that of the man whose name was on the birth certificate.'

'So she could get her child back?'

'You have a very idealised vision of motherhood, Commissario, if I might make that observation. The woman made it clear that she did not want the baby back. In fact, this is one of the reasons my colleagues in Cosenza believed her.'

'Will it affect her chances of being allowed to stay here?'

'Probably not, no.'

'Ah.'

'"Ah"', indeed, Commissario. Believe me, the baby's not his. We knew that before we went in there that night.'

'I see. Well, then . . . thank you very much, Captain. You've been very helpful.'

'I'm glad to learn you think so, Commissario. If it would put your mind at rest, I could send you a copy of our report. Shall I email it to you there?'

'It would be a great kindness.'

'I'll do it now, Commissario.'

'Thank you, Captain.'

'You're welcome. *Arrivederci*.'

'*Arrivederci, Capitano*.'

A copy of the deposition arrived less than an hour later. It had been made by the Albanian woman whose name was on the birth certificate of Pedrolli's son. It had been signed four days before the Carabinieri raid and had been compiled over two days of testimony. She had been located by a simple computer search, in Cosenza, where she had, two days after registering the birth of her child to an Italian father, been granted a *permesso di soggiorno*. When questioned, she originally maintained that her child had been sent back to Albania to live with his grandparents. It was, she insisted, sheer coincidence that her husband, also Albanian and illegally resident in Italy, had bought a car two days after she was released from the hospital: he had been working as a mason, she explained, and had been saving money for months in order to buy the car. Nor was there any connection between her son's disappearance and the three months' deposit her husband had paid on an apartment the same day he bought the car.

Later in the questioning, she began to insist that the Italian man, whose name she could not remember and whom she had a certain difficulty in describing, was the father of the child, but when she was threatened with arrest and deportation unless she told the truth, she changed her story and claimed that an Italian man who said his wife was unable to have a child had contacted her in the weeks just before she gave birth. Her first version suggested that the man had found her on his own; no one had introduced him to her. But when the possibility of extradition was mentioned to her again, she said that he had been introduced to her by one of the doctors in the hospital—she could not remember which—who said that the man who wanted to talk to her was also a doctor. After the child was born, she had agreed to let the doctor's name be on the birth certificate because she believed her son would have a better chance at a decent life if he were raised as an Italian, in an Italian family. She finally admitted that the man had given her some money, but as a gift, not a payment. No, she could not remember how much it had been.

The woman and her husband were now under house arrest, though the husband was allowed to continue to work: the question of her *permesso di soggiorno* was being examined by a magistrate. When he finished reading, Brunetti was left wondering why whoever had questioned her had so easily accepted her explanation of how Pedrolli had contacted her: he might just as easily have descended from a cloud. 'Had been introduced to her by one of the doctors in the hospital,' the woman had stated. But which one? And for what reason?

At a certain point, Brunetti realized that—in a manner frighteningly reminiscent of Bianca Marcolini—the woman had expressed no interest in the child or in what had happened to him. He slipped the papers into his desk drawer and went home.

Before dinner Brunetti managed to return to the travels of the Marquis de Custine. With the French aristocrat as guide and companion, he found himself in St Petersburg, contemplating the Russian soul, which de Custine observed was 'intoxicated with slavery'. Brunetti let the open book fall to his lap as he considered these words and was brought out of his reverie by Paola, who sat down beside him.

'I forgot to tell you,' she said.

Brunetti dragged himself back from the Nevsky Prospekt and said, 'Tell me what?'

'About Bianca Marcolini.'

'Ah, thank you,' he said.

'I asked around, but not a lot. Most people know the name because of the father, of course.'

Brunetti nodded.

'I asked my father about him. I told you he knew him, didn't I?'

Brunetti nodded again. 'And?' he asked.

'And he said Marcolini is a man to be reckoned with. He made his fortune himself, you know.' She paused, then added, 'Some people still find that an intoxicating idea.' Her voice was rich with a disdain that only those born into great wealth can experience.

'My father says he has friends everywhere: in local government, in regional government, even in Rome. In the last few years, he's come to control an enormous number of votes.'

'Suppressing a news story would be easy for him, then?' Brunetti asked.

'Child's play,' she said, a phrase that struck Brunetti with an odd resonance.

'And the marriage?'

'"Chiesa dei Miracoli garlanded with flowers": the usual. She works as a financial adviser for a bank; he's the assistant *primario* in *pediatria* at the Ospedale Civile.'

None of these statements seemed to have merited the excitement Brunetti thought he heard in her voice, something experience told him came from revelations still unspoken. 'And the non-official news?' he asked.

'The baby, of course,' she said, and he registered that she was finally in her stride.

'Of course,' he repeated and smiled.

'The gossip among their friends was that he had had a short affair with a woman—not even an affair: just a few days—when he was in Cosenza for a medical conference. I've asked a number of people who know them, and that's the story I was told every time.'

'Was it your father who told you about this?'

'No,' she answered instantly, surprised that he would think her father capable of gossip. Then, in explanation, she offered, 'I saw my mother this afternoon and asked her about them.' Paola had come by her inquisitiveness about other people's lives honestly: similarly, the Contessa's emeralds would some day be hers.

'So this is the official story?' he asked.

She had to think for a while before she answered, 'It sounds true and people seem to believe it is. After all, it's the sort of thing they want to believe, isn't it? It's the stuff of film, cheap fiction. The erring husband returns to the hearth and the long-suffering wife forgives him. Not only forgives him, but agrees to take the little cuckoo into the nest and raise it as their own. Heart-warming reunion, the rebirth of love: Rhett and Scarlett together again for ever.' She paused a moment and then added, 'It certainly plays better than saying that they went down to the market, bought a baby, and brought it home.'

'You sound more mordantly cynical than usual, my dove,' Brunetti said, picking up her hand and kissing the tips of her fingers.

She pulled her hand away, but with a smile, and said, 'Thank you, Guido.' Then, in a more serious tone, she continued, 'As I said, people seemed to believe it, or at least wanted to. The Gamberinis know them, and Gabi told me that they went to dinner there about six months after they brought the baby home. Well . . . he brought the baby home, but she said the re-union might not have continued so happily.'

'You really love gossip, don't you?' he asked, wishing she had brought him a glass of wine.

'Yes, I suppose I do,' she answered, sounding surprised at the realization. 'You think that's why I love reading novels so much?'

'Probably,' he said, then asked, 'In what way not a happy re-union?'

'Gabi didn't actually say. People usually don't. But it was pretty clear from what she said, well, more from the way she said it. You know how people are.'

How he wished that were true, Brunetti thought. 'Did she speculate about the reason?'

Paola closed her eyes, and he watched her replay the conversation. 'No, not really.'

'Would you like a glass of wine?' he asked.

'Yes. And then we can have dinner.'

He took her hand and kissed it again by way of thanks. 'White or red?' he asked.

She chose white, probably because of the risotto with leeks, which started the meal. The children had recently gone back to school, so they spent much of the meal reporting on what their classmates had done during the summer. One girl in Chiara's class had spent two months in Australia and returned disgruntled that she had traded summer for winter and then returned to autumn. Another had worked at an ice-cream shop on the island of Santorini and came back with a passable knowledge of spoken German. Raffi's best friend had backpacked from New-foundland to Vancouver, though the quotation marks with which Raffi pronounced 'backpacked' was rich with a sugges-tion of trains and aeroplanes.

Brunetti did his best to follow the talk that swirled above the table, but he found himself constantly distracted by the sight of them, assailed by an overwhelming sense of possession: these were his children. Part of him was in them, the part that would go on into their children, and then into the next generation. Try as he might, however, he could recognize little of his physical self in them: only Paola seemed to have been copied. There was her nose, there the texture of her hair and that unruly curl just behind her left ear. As she spoke, Chiara waved a hand to dismiss something that had been said to her, and the gesture was Paola's.

The next course was *orata* with lemon, further reason to justify the choice of white wine. Brunetti began eating, but halfway through his portion, his attention was drawn again to Chiara, who was now in full denunciation of her English teacher.

'The subjunctive? Do you know what she told me when I asked about it?' Chiara demanded, voice rich with remembered astonishment as she glanced round the table to see that the others were prepared to respond in similar vein. When she had their attention, she said, 'That we'd get to it next year.' The noise with which she set down her fork gave ample expression of her disapproval.

Paola shook her head in sympathy. 'Next year,' she repeated, the conversation somehow having crossed over into English. 'Unbelievable.'

Chiara turned to her father, hoping perhaps that he would express similar amazement. But she stopped and studied his unresponsive face. She tilted her head to one side, then to the other. Finally she said in an entirely conversational voice, as if in response to a question he had posed. 'I left it in school, *Papà.*' When he said nothing, she said, 'No, I didn't bring it home with me today.'

As if emerging from a trance, Brunetti said, 'I'm sorry, Chiara. What didn't you bring home today?'

'My second head.'

Utterly at a loss as to what might have occurred at the table while he was staring at his children, Brunetti said, 'I don't understand. What second head?'

'The one you've been looking for all night, *Papà*. I just wanted to tell you I didn't bring it home: that's why you don't see it.' To emphasize this, she raised her hands to either side of her head and waved the fingers in the empty air on either side of it.

Raffi guffawed, and when he looked at Paola, she was smiling.

'Ah, yes,' Brunetti said with some chagrin, returning his attention to his fish. 'I hope you left it in a safe place.'

There were pears for dessert.

19

It was late the following afternoon when Vianello came into Brunetti's office, his expression rich with the delight that comes of having been right when others have thought you wrong.

'It's taken a long time, but it was worth it,' the Inspector said. He came over to Brunetti's desk and placed some papers on it.

Brunetti narrowed his eyes and raised his chin by way of enquiry.

'Signorina Elettra's friend,' Vianello explained.

She had many friends, Brunetti knew, and he could not recall which one was at the moment contributing to her extralegal activities. 'Which friend?'

'The hacker,' Vianello explained, surprising Brunetti by the ease with which he pronounced the 'h'. 'The one we gave the hard disc to.' Before Brunetti could ask, Vianello added, 'Yes, I got it back to Dottor Franchi the next day, but not before her friend had made a copy of everything that was on it.'

'Ah, that friend,' Brunetti said and reached for the papers. 'What's Franchi been up to on his computer?'

'No kiddie porn and no Internet shopping: I can tell you that right now,' Vianello answered, though his tiger shark smile did not lessen.

'But?' Brunetti asked.

'But it seems he's found his way into the ULSS computer system.'

'Isn't that how he makes the appointments?' Brunetti asked. 'How the other pharmacists do, too?'

'Yes,' Vianello agreed and pulled up a chair. 'He does, and they do,' he said, prodding at Brunetti with a tone that forced him to ask another question.

Which he did. 'And what else does he do when he's in there?'

'According to what Signorina Elettra's friend told us, it would seem that he's found a way to bypass their log-in.'

'Which means what?'

'It gives him access to other parts of their system,' Vianello said and waited for Brunetti's reaction, as though he thought Brunetti should leap to his feet and cry 'Eureka!'

He feared his confession would lower him in Vianello's estimation, but Brunetti knew he couldn't bluff his way through this one, so he said, 'I think you'd better explain it to me, Lorenzo.'

The little Spartan boy with the fox eating away at his vitals could have kept no straighter a face than did Vianello. 'It means he can access the central computer and examine the medical files of anyone for whom he has the ULSS number.'

'His clients?'

'Exactly.'

Brunetti put his elbow on his desk and rubbed his hand across his mouth a few times as he considered the implications of this. Access to those files meant access to all information about medication, hospitalization, diseases cured or under treatment. It meant that an unauthorized person would have access to potentially secret parts of another person's life.

'AIDS,' Brunetti said. After a long pause, he added, 'Drug rehabilitation. Methadone.'

'Venereal diseases,' contributed Vianello.

'Abortions,' added Brunetti, then added, 'If they're his clients, he knows whether they're married, about their family lives, where they work, who their friends are.'

'The friendly family pharmacist; known you since you were a kid,' added Vianello.

'How many?' Brunetti asked.

'He's looked into the files of about thirty of his clients,' Vianello said, pausing to allow Brunetti to register the implications of this. 'Her friend says he won't be able to send us the actual files until tomorrow.'

Brunetti let out a low whistle, then drew their attention back to the original reason for their interest in Dottor Franchi. 'And the appointments?'

'He's made more than a hundred in the last two years.' Before Brunetti could express his surprise at the number, Vianello said, 'That's only one a week, remember.'

Brunetti nodded. 'Has this friend of Signorina Elettra... does he have a name, by the way?' he asked.

'No,' Vianello said in a curiously bland voice.

'Have you checked to see which of these appointments actually took place?' Brunetti asked.

'He sent her the final list of the appointments only this morning,' Vianello said. 'And it seems that all of the appointments Franchi made were kept.' When Brunetti said nothing, the Inspector continued, 'She's already run a check on the other pharmacists. One of them has scheduled only seventeen appointments in the last two years, and all of them were kept: we spoke to the people. Andrea doesn't use the system, so he's off the list. In the other case, she checked the record of appointments in the files in the hospitals here and in Mestre, and in almost all cases the people were listed as having shown up for the appointments he scheduled.' Vianello could barely contain his excitement when he said, 'But one of the pharmacists scheduled three appointments for people who didn't need medical help.'

'Tell me, Lorenzo,' Brunetti said to save time.

'They're dead,' Vianello said.

'You mean, from what happened to them during the appointments?' asked an astonished Brunetti, wondering how something like this could have happened and he not be aware of it.

'No. They were dead when the appointments were made.' Vianello allowed himself to savour, and Brunetti to grasp, that information, and then he continued, 'It looks like he got careless, the pharmacist, and just started punching in the patient numbers of customers at the pharmacy: perhaps he thought they had moved away or perhaps . . .' and here Vianello gave the small pause he always made before he dropped what he considered to be a bomb. 'Perhaps he's starting to lose his memory. At that age.'

'Gabetti?' asked Brunetti.

'None other,' responded a grinning Vianello.

'All right, Lorenzo. You win,' Brunetti said with a smile. 'Tell me about the appointments he scheduled for these dead people.'

'In each case, the doctor recorded on his computer that he had seen the patient, made a diagnosis—it was always something innocuous—and then billed the health service for the appointment.'

'Very careless,' Brunetti agreed. 'Or very bold. What about the doctors?'

'It's always the same three, and in each case they recorded

the appointments and requested payment,' Vianello said. Almost reluctantly, Vianello added, 'Franchi never scheduled an appointment with any of those three doctors.'

'I wonder what else he was doing, though,' Brunetti said, then asked, 'Why can't her friend send the files until tomorrow?'

'Computer things,' said Vianello.

'I'm not a Neanderthal, you know.' Though Brunetti smiled as he said this, he came across as no less defensive.

'Signorina Elettra told me it has to do with the way Franchi protected the files: each one requires a different code to get into it, and then you have to go back and find the patient number, using a different access code . . . do you want me to go on?' Vianello asked.

Brunetti's smile became rueful. 'Tomorrow?'

'Yes.'

'Until then?'

'Until then, we'll keep calling the patients Gabetti made appointments for and asking them if they were satisfied with the treatment they received. And then we can think about asking the doctors to come in and have a word with us.'

Brunetti said, 'No, I'd like to wait until we know what Franchi is up to. Are you sure he wasn't suspicious that you held on to his computer for a day?'

It looked as though Vianello had to stop himself from clapping his hands in delight when he heard the question. 'I had Alvise take it back,' he said.

Brunetti laughed out loud.

He left the Questura at five, his conscience at peace at the thought that his wife, who had said she would bring him more information about Pedrolli, was unlikely to do so by coming to his office. Whatever she had learned, Brunetti was forced to admit that it had probably become irrelevant by now. Whatever charges might be brought against Pedrolli, they were likely to be of the kind that would evaporate at the wave of a cheque-book or at some other manifestation of Bianca Marcolini's father's power.

He let his feet and his whim take him where they pleased, and after a time he found himself standing at the foot of the bridge that led to the entrance to Palazzo Querini Stampalia. The man at the desk knew Brunetti and waved aside his attempt to pay for a ticket.

He went upstairs to the gallery, where he had not been for some time. How he loved to look at these portraits, not so much because of their beauty as paintings but for the resemblance of so many of them to people he saw every day. Indeed, the portrait of Gerolomo Querini, painted almost five hundred years ago, bore an almost photographic likeness to Vianello—well, to what Vianello had looked like as a younger man. He savoured these faces and looked forward to encountering them again in the order he had become accustomed to over the years.

His favourite was the Bellini *Presentation in the Temple*, and, as always, he allowed himself to come to it last. And saw that child, the swaddled Jesus, being passed back to his mother by the high priest Simeon. The baby's body was bound tight by the encircling strips of cloth, his arms trapped to his sides with only the tips of his fingers wriggling free. At the sight of him, Brunetti's thoughts returned to Pedrolli's child, similarly bound, if by the decisions of the state. The mother of the child in the painting held him protectively in both hands; the look she

191

passed to the high priest across the infant's bound body was cool and sceptical. Brunetti noticed for the first time how her scepticism was echoed in the faces of everyone else in the painting, especially in the eyes of a young man on the far right, who gazed out at the viewer as if to ask how he could expect anything good to come of what was going on here.

Abruptly Brunetti turned from the painting and walked back to the portraits in the other rooms, hoping that the more tranquil faces on the portraits by Bombelli and Tiepolo would erase the uneasy feeling that had come over him at the sight of that trapped child.

Brunetti was unusually inattentive during dinner, nodding when Paola or the children spoke with one another and contributing little to the conversation. Afterwards, he returned to the living room and to St Petersburg, where he encountered his Marquis in a reflective mood, observing of Russia that it was a place where 'the taste for the superfluous holds sway over a people who are still unacquainted with the necessary'. Brunetti closed his eyes to consider the contemporary truth of this.

He heard Paola's footsteps and, without opening his eyes, said, 'Nothing changes, nothing at all.'

She recognized the book and said, 'I knew nothing good could come of your reading that book.'

'I know it's not politically correct, especially when the leaders of our two great countries are such good buddies, but it sounds like a dreadful place then, and it sounds like a dreadful place now.' He heard the clink of glasses and, opening one eye, saw her place two on the table in front of him.

'Read Tolstoy,' she advised him. 'He'll make you like it more.'

'The country or the book?' Brunetti asked, eyes still closed.

'Time for gossip,' she announced, ignoring his question. She tapped his feet and he pulled them back to create room enough for her to sit.

He opened his eyes then and took the glass she handed him. He sipped, took a deep breath and inhaled the essence of grappa, and sipped again. 'Is that the Gaia?' he asked.

'We've had the bottle since Christmas. With any luck we'll get another one this year, so I see no reason we shouldn't drink it.'

'Do you think there's grappa in heaven?' Brunetti asked.

'Since there's no heaven, no, there's no grappa in heaven,' she answered, then added, 'which is even more reason to drink it while we can.'

'I'm helpless in the face of your logic,' Brunetti said, emptied his glass, and handed it to her.

'I'll be back in a moment.'

'Good,' Brunetti said and closed his eyes again.

Brunetti felt, rather than saw, Paola get up from the sofa. He listened as she went into the kitchen, heard her moving around and then come back into the living room. Glass clinked against glass, liquid poured, and then she said, 'Here.'

Suddenly curious about how long he could keep his eyes closed, Brunetti stuck his hand in the air, fingers waving. She gave him the glass, he heard another clink, another glug, and then he felt the sofa shake as she sat back down.

'*Salute*,' she said, and he took a sip from the glass he couldn't see. Again he had a foretaste of heaven.

'Tell me,' he asked.

'You're welcome,' she answered and then segued seamlessly into, 'At the beginning, people thought Pedrolli was nervous or embarrassed that they would make jokes about him, but as soon as it became obvious how crazy he was about his son, there was no chance that anyone would make fun of him. The only talk was nice talk, or so I was told.'

'And the Rhett and Scarlett reunion you said didn't work?'

'I didn't say it: I was told it,' she corrected him. 'According to a number of people, he was always the loving partner, and she was the one who was loved, right from the beginning. But after the son arrived, the equilibrium changed.'

'How?' he asked, sensing from her voice that the answer to this would not be the obvious one that the wife neglected the husband for the new child.

'He transferred his affection to the son . . . or so I was told,' she said, reminding Brunetti of how careful Paola always was to provide citations for her gossip.

'And where did the wife transfer hers?' he asked.

'Not to the child, apparently,' she said. 'But that would be understandable, I suppose, if the baby wasn't hers to begin with and if her husband began to pay more attention to the baby than to her.'

'Even if she didn't much want these attentions any longer?' Brunetti asked.

Paola leaned against him and rested her elbow on his knees. 'That doesn't make any difference, Guido. You know that.'

'What doesn't?'

'Whether she wanted his affections or not. She still wanted to be the object of them.'

'That doesn't make any sense,' he said.

She was silent for so long that Brunetti finally opened his eyes and looked at her. She had her face buried in her hands and was shaking her head from side to side.

'All right, what have I said?' he asked.

She gave him a level look. 'Even if a woman isn't happy to

have them, she still doesn't want them to go to anyone else,' she said.

'But it's their son, for heaven's sake.'

'His son,' Paola corrected him, then added for emphasis, 'Not theirs, but his.'

'Perhaps not,' Brunetti said, then told her the contents of the Carabinieri report.

'Who the biological father was really doesn't make any difference,' Paola insisted. 'To Pedrolli, the boy is his son. And from what I heard today, my guess is that she never really thought of the child as hers.'

How much had Pedrolli actually told his wife? She claimed that he had told her the truth, but what *was* the truth? Brunetti imagined that the Albanian woman, threatened with extradition, would have told the authorities whatever it was she thought they wanted to hear and whatever would make them view her with greatest sympathy. If they asked her if Dottor Pedrolli had promised to raise the boy as his son, this was at least something she could take credit for, if only because it demonstrated a desire to ensure that her son would have a better life. Far better to admit to this, even if money had changed hands, than to admit she had sold her son to someone without much caring where the child would end up.

And what of Pedrolli? Was he to endure his life like the parents of children who are the victims of actual kidnap-pings? To wonder—for ever—if the child was alive or dead? To spend the rest of his life searching for that remembered face in the face of every child, teenaged boy, man of about the right age?

'"Oh, to lose all father now,"' Brunetti said.

20

Brunetti's sleep was disturbed, not by excess of grappa, but by thoughts of the Pedrolli child. How much would he remember of those first months of his life? What was the future psychological cost of being taken from a loving home and placed in a public institution?

Between sleeping and waking, Brunetti told himself repeatedly to let it all go, to forget Pedrolli, to forget the sight of the man as he lay in the hospital bed, and most of all to forget about his son. Brunetti was uninterested in either the legal or the biological realities: it sufficed for him that Pedrolli had claimed the child as his own and that the child's natural mother had been willing to let him go. And that the doctor loved the child.

What he could not fathom were the feelings of Bianca Marcolini, but he did not feel able, during that long night, to wake Paola, sleeping quietly beside him, and ask her what a woman would feel. Why should Paola understand it any better than he? Were he to ask, she would probably assail him for the most blatant sort of sexist thinking: surely a man could understand a woman's feelings? But that was precisely what troubled Brunetti, the absence in Bianca Marcolini of what Paola would, again, assail him for thinking of as a woman's feelings. If the reports given to Paola were accurate, then Bianca Marcolini had shown little evidence of maternal feelings to the people Paola had talked to or to Brunetti himself.

Some time before six, an idea came to Brunetti of how to learn more about Bianca Marcolini and her feelings towards the child. Soon after he thought of it, he drifted off to sleep, and when he woke again, the idea was still with him. He lay there, looking at the ceiling. Three bells rang: soon it would be seven and he would get up and make coffee, bring some back to Paola. She had a class that morning and had asked him to wake her before he went to work.

Well, this was before he went to work, wasn't it? 'Paola,' he said. He waited, repeated her name, and waited a longer time.

The bells began to ring the hour: Brunetti took this as a sign that he could wake her now. He turned, put his hand on her shoulder and shook it gently. 'Paola,' he said again.

There was the faintest tremor of movement. 'Paola,' he repeated. 'Could your father arrange for me to meet Giuliano Marcolini?' The last bell chimed, and the world returned to silence.

'Paola, could your father arrange for me to see Giuliano Marcolini?'

The bundle beside him turned away. He put his hand on her shoulder again, and the bundle moved even further.

'Paola, could . . .'

'If you say that again, I'll drown the children.'

'They're too big.'

There was some thrashing about, and then he saw the side of her face. One eye opened.

'I'll bring you coffee,' he said amiably and got out of bed. 'And then we'll talk.'

Though the promise was not easily won from her, Paola agreed to phone her father and ask him if he would arrange a meeting.

Brunetti knew that he could, as a police officer, have arranged one himself, but he knew it would be more easily done, and he would be more gracefully received, were the request to come through the agency of Conte Orazio Falier.

Paola told him she would phone the Count that afternoon: her father was in South America, and she had to find out where exactly he was to be able to figure out the time difference before she called him.

Thus it was that Brunetti, thinking of his father-in-law, was momentarily confused when Vianello came into his office in mid-morning, saying, 'Pedrolli's on the list.'

Brunetti looked across at the Inspector and asked, 'What list?'

'The list on the computer. Dottor Franchi's. He's been a customer there for the last four years.'

'Of the pharmacy?'

'Yes.'

'Pedrolli?'

'Yes.'

'And Franchi has seen his medical records?' It was only then that Brunetti noticed the file in Vianello's hand.

'It's all in here,' Vianello said. He came and stood next to Brunetti and put the file on the desk. He opened it and shuffled through the stack of papers, pulling out four or five. Brunetti saw short paragraphs of very small print, numbers, dates. Glancing down the first page, he saw Latin terms, more dates, brief comments that made little sense to him.

Vianello spread the papers out on the desk so that they could look at all of them at the same time. 'This goes back only seven years,' Vianello said. 'That's as far back as they could be traced.'

'Why?'

Vianello raised a hand. 'Who knows? The original files were lost? They haven't got that far back in computerizing the records? You name it.'

'Have you read it?' Brunetti asked.

'The first two paragraphs,' the Inspector said, his eyes on the third.

Together, they read down the first sheet of paper, then the next, and then the remaining pages. Pedrolli's visits to fertility specialists appeared to have begun three years before, the year after his marriage.

At the bottom of two of the pages were what looked to Brunetti to be lab reports: he saw lists of names and lists of numbers which made little sense to him. He did recognize the words 'cholesterol' and 'glucose', though he had no idea what the numbers beside them meant in terms of Pedrolli's health.

The last page was a report, apparently emailed to ULSS from a clinic in Verona and dated two years ago.

'Probable malformation of the sperm ducts due to trauma experienced in adolescence,' Brunetti read. 'Sperm production normal, present in testicles, but obstruction of tubes results in total sterility.'

'Poor devil, eh?' said Vianello.

Sexual behaviour is the ichor, the very life-blood, of gossip. Remove it, and there is relatively little left to chew over in the lives of other people, certainly very little of any interest, aside from their money or their work or their health. Some people might take an interest in those things, but none of them possesses the all-consuming fascination of sexual behaviour and its consequences. The story of Pedrolli's affair and the subsequent birth of his child—to make no mention of his wife's noble acceptance of that child—was the sort of thing that would make the rounds.

But here was proof that Pedrolli, regardless of gossip, could not have been the father of the child and so must have acquired the baby in some other way. One had but to indicate the word 'sterility' to the police, and it would not be long before Pedrolli would be listed among those to be investigated for illegal possession of a child he clearly could not have fathered. Since his name was on the birth certificate along with the mother's, she could be easily located, and then it was only a matter of time before the forces of the state could be expected to arrive to save the child. A person who valued virtuous behaviour would almost be constrained to make such a thing known to the authorities, wouldn't he? Well, unless perhaps a certain sum were to change hands, perhaps at regular intervals?

Brunetti reassembled the sheaf of papers, careful to keep them in order. 'What else is in there?' he asked, pointing to the file.

'Pucetti and I have already come across HIV and drug rehabilitation, even a surgeon with a history of hepatitis B.'

'A gold mine, really,' Brunetti said.

'I'm afraid so,' Vianello answered.

'Have you gone through them all?'

'No, only about half. But I came up here as soon as I saw that Pedrolli was a client of his.'

'Good,' Brunetti said. 'How many of you are working on this?'

'Just me and Pucetti,' Vianello said.

'How do you know what you're finding?' Brunetti asked, tapping the medical reports with the back of his fingers.

'He's at one of the computers. And when he doesn't know what something is, he checks the medical dictionary.'

'Where'd he get that?' Brunetti enquired.

'The whole thing's on a disc: her friend sent it when he sent us these lists. He thought it would make things easier for us.'

'Thoughtful fellow,' observed Brunetti.

'Yes,' Vianello answered without true conviction.

'Go back and see what else you can find, all right? I want to read through this again.'

Vianello moved away from the desk but stopped, looking less than fully persuaded.

'Go on,' Brunetti said, gesturing towards the door. 'I'll come down soon.'

He glanced through the papers but with no great interest: he had learned what he needed to know the first time he read them. He looked out the window, suddenly unable to remember, not only what time of day it was, but the season. He got up and went over to the window, opened it. The air was cool, the grass across the way tired and dusty and in need of the rain that seemed to be in the air. His watch showed that it was almost one. He picked up the papers and went downstairs, only to be told that Vianello and Pucetti had gone out for lunch. Paola would be out, so Brunetti was not planning to eat at home. He tried not to feel sorry for himself that his colleagues had not asked him to join them and returned to his office. He dialled the number at the hospital of Ettore Rizzardi, the *medico legale* of the city, planning to leave a message, and was surprised when the doctor answered the phone.

'It's me, Ettore.'

'Hmm?'

'And good afternoon to you, too, Dottor Rizzardi,' Brunetti said in a voice he made sound as mindlessly cheerful as he could.

'What is it, Guido?' the doctor asked. 'I'm in the middle of something.'

'Malformation of the sperm ducts due to a trauma in adolescence?' Brunetti asked.

'No kids.'

'One hundred per cent?'

'Probably. Next question?'

'Fixable?'

'Perhaps. Any more questions?'

'Personal, not medical,' Brunetti answered. 'About Pedrolli, the paediatrician.'

'I know who he is,' Rizzardi said with some asperity. 'Lost his son.'

'What did you hear about how he got his son?'

'Story I was told said he brought him back from some woman in Cosenza.'

'What, exactly, did you hear?'

'I told you I was busy with something,' Rizzardi said with exaggerated patience.

'In a minute. Tell me what you heard.'

'About Pedrolli?'

'Yes.'

'That he went to a medical conference in Cosenza, and while he was there he met a woman—one of those things that happen—and then he found out some time later that she was pregnant. And he did the right thing by her and accepted paternity.'

'How did you find out about this, Ettore?'

There was a long pause before Rizzardi said, 'I suppose the story just started to spread round at the hospital.'

'Who started it?'

'Guido,' Rizzardi said with exaggerated politeness, 'It was more than a year ago. I don't remember.'

'Then how did Pedrolli find out?' Brunetti asked. 'Do you know that?'

'Find out what?'

'That she was pregnant? The woman who was questioned couldn't even remember his name, so how did she find him? He certainly didn't leave her his business card, did he? So how did she find him or how did he find out she was pregnant?' Brunetti insisted, his curiosity running away with him.

'I can't answer any of those questions, Guido,' Rizzardi said, impatience slipping back into his voice.

'Could you ask around?'

'I'd rather not,' Rizzardi surprised him by saying. 'He's a colleague.' Then, as if to make up for that, the doctor suggested, 'Why don't you come and ask him yourself?'

'Is he there?'

'I saw him in the bar this morning, and he was wearing his lab coat, so it would seem so,' Rizzardi said. Brunetti heard another voice in the background, sounding insistent or angry. Rizzardi said, 'I've got to go,' and hung up.

Brunetti was on the point of deciding that he would call Vianello on his *telefonino* and join his colleagues for lunch, but just at that moment, his own *telefonino* rang.

'*Pronto*,' he said and saw that it was Paola's office number. 'Did you manage to track down your father?'

'No, he found me. He said he couldn't sleep because of the time difference, so he called to see how we are. He's in La Paz.'

Ordinarily, the name of the city would have caused Brunetti to joke and ask if her father were there to arrange a deal in cocaine, but the mounting evidence that many, if not most, of the calls made on *telefonini* were intercepted and recorded dissuaded him from doing so. Instead, Brunetti contented himself with a neutral, 'Ah.'

'And he'll see you at three.'

'Marcolini?'

'Certainly not my father,' she said and hung up.

That left Brunetti just under two hours. If he was able to speak to Pedrolli now, he might be better prepared to meet the doctor's father-in-law. Perhaps from Pedrolli he could get some sense of whether a man as powerful as Marcolini would use his connections to find a way to return the child to Pedrolli and his wife. Since the child's natural mother seemed to want no part of him, perhaps the authorities would... Brunetti stopped himself from pursuing this thought. He could not stop himself, however, from remembering how Pedrolli had cradled his missing son in his empty arms, and it made him a victim of his own sentimentality.

He wrote a note to Vianello, saying he was going to the hospital to speak to Pedrolli and then to Marcolini; he left it downstairs on the Inspector's desk. It had begun to rain, so Brunetti ducked back inside to take an umbrella from the stand where the staff always deposited those umbrellas left behind by visitors.

Brunetti was glad of the rain, however inconvenient it proved to him or anyone else. The autumn had been a dry one, as had the summer, and Chiara had redoubled her efforts as water monitor of the family. Infected by her constant reminders about the waste of water, Brunetti now found himself asking barmen to turn off taps left running to no purpose, a request which always earned him astonished glances both from staff and from other customers. What surprised him was the frequency with which he found himself having to do it.

When he reached the hospital, all thought of lunch abandoned, he followed the signs to *pediatria*. He heard it before he saw it, in the wail of a screaming baby that flooded down the staircase and grew louder as he approached.

The waiting room was empty, but the sound penetrated even the heavy double doors separating him from the ward. Brunetti pushed one of them open and went into the corridor. A nurse emerging from one of the rooms came immediately towards him. 'Visiting hours have finished,' she said above the screams.

Brunetti took his warrant card from his pocket, showed it to her, and said, 'I'd like to speak to Dottor Pedrolli.'

'He's with a patient,' she said sharply, then added, 'Haven't you people done enough to him?'

'When will he be free?' asked an imperturbable Brunetti.

'I don't know.'

'Is he here?' Brunetti asked.

'Yes, in 216.'

'I'll wait, then, shall I?' Brunetti asked.

At a loss what to do, she turned and walked away, leaving Brunetti standing by the door. It was then he noticed that the cries of the child had ceased and felt a slackening of the tension in his heart.

After some time, a bearded man in a white jacket emerged from a room halfway down the corridor and started in Brunetti's direction. Had he seen him on the street, Brunetti would not have recognized Pedrolli. The doctor was taller than he had seemed lying on the hospital bed, and the bruise on his face had all but disappeared.

'Dottor Pedrolli?' Brunetti asked as the man grew closer.

Startled, the doctor looked up. 'Yes?'

'I'm Commissario Guido Brunetti,' he said, extending his hand. 'I came to visit you when you were in hospital.' Then, smiling, Brunetti added, 'As a patient, I mean.'

Pedrolli took the extended hand. 'Yes, I remember your face, but I'm afraid I don't remember much else. That was when I still couldn't talk, I think. I'm sorry.' His smile was awkward, almost embarrassed. His voice, which Brunetti was hearing for the first time, was deep and resonant, a true baritone.

'Could I speak to you for a moment, Dottore?' Brunetti asked.

Pedrolli's gaze was level, untroubled, almost uninterested. 'Of course,' he said. Pedrolli led Brunetti into the corridor and then down to one of the last doors on the left. Inside, Brunetti saw a desk with a computer, a few chairs ranged in front of it. The windows behind the desk looked out on the same horizontal tree Brunetti had noticed on his last visit. One wall was covered with bookshelves filled with medical texts and journals.

'Here's as good as any place,' Pedrolli said, pulling a chair out for Brunetti. He took the other chair and sat facing him. 'What is it you'd like to know?' Pedrolli asked.

'Your name has come to our attention, Dottore,' Brunetti began.

Almost unconsciously, Pedrolli reached up and touched the side of his head. 'Is that meant to be an understatement?' he asked with an expression he seemed to be struggling to make appear pleasant.

Brunetti smiled in return but continued, 'This isn't connected in any way to why I saw you last time, Dottore.'

The look Pedrolli gave Brunetti was sharp, but then he quickly looked away.

'That investigation was in the hands—and remains in the hands—of the Carabinieri. I'm here to ask you about another investigation that is being carried out by my department.'

'The police, then?'

'Yes, Dottore.'

'What sort of investigation is that, Commissario?' he asked with a more than faintly ironic emphasis.

'Your name has appeared in connection with an entirely un-related matter. I've come to ask you about that.'

'I see,' Pedrolli said. 'Perhaps you could be more specific?'

'It has to do with fraud here at the hospital,' Brunetti said, de-ciding to raise this first, before introducing the idea that he might be the victim of blackmail. Pedrolli relaxed just minimally.

'Fraud of what sort?'

'False appointments.' He saw the contraction of Pedrolli's eyes and went on, 'There are doctors here who are apparently scheduling appointments for patients they know will not keep those appointments; in some cases pharmacists schedule the appointments, and then the health service is charged for them, though they never take place. In at least three cases, the patients for whom the appointments were scheduled are dead.'

Pedrolli nodded affirmatively, then pressed his lips together. 'I'd be a liar if I said I'd never heard about this, Commissario. But it doesn't happen in this department. My *primario* and I see to that.'

Though Brunetti's impulse was to believe the doctor, he still asked, 'How?'

'All patients—well, their parents, since our patients are all children—who have appointments scheduled have to sign in with the nurse on duty, and at the end of her shift, she checks that list against the computer list of the patients who were actually seen by every doctor in the department.' He saw Brunetti's response and said, 'I know, it's very simple. It adds about five minutes of work to the nurse's day, but it eliminates any possibility of falsification.'

'It sounds as though you set up your system specifically to avoid the possibility, Dottore,' Brunetti said. 'If I might say that.'

'I think you should say that, Commissario: that's exactly why we did it.' Pedrolli waited a moment until Brunetti's gaze met his, and then said, 'Word travels in a hospital.'

'I see,' Brunetti said.

'Is that all you wanted to ask me about?' Pedrolli said, beginning to shift his weight forward on his chair.

'No, Dottore, it isn't. If you'd have a moment's patience...'

Pedrolli relaxed back into his chair and said, 'Of course,' but he looked at his watch as he said it. Suddenly Pedrolli's stomach made a thunderous groan and he gave that same almost embarrassed smile. 'I haven't had lunch yet.'

'I'll try not to keep you too long,' Brunetti said, hoping that his own stomach would not begin to echo the doctor's.

'Dottore,' Brunetti began, 'are you a customer at the pharmacy in Campo Sant'Angelo.'

'Yes. It's the one nearest to where I live.'

'You've used it for years?'

'Since we moved there, about four years ago. No, a bit more than that.'

'Do you know the pharmacist well?' Brunetti asked.

A long time passed before Pedrolli said, pronouncing his words carefully, 'Ah, the exquisitely moral Dottor Franchi.' Then he added, 'I suppose I know him as well as any doctor knows a pharmacist.'

'Could you tell me what you mean by that, Dottore?'

Pedrolli shrugged. 'Dottor Franchi and I have diverging views of human weakness, I fear,' he said with a wry smile. 'He tends to take a sterner view than I do.' He gave a small smile. When Brunetti said nothing, Pedrolli continued, 'As to how well I know him professionally, I ask him if patients of mine are collecting their prescriptions, and occasionally I go in to write and sign prescriptions when I've told someone over the phone to take a certain medicine.'

'And for yourself, Dottore? Do you buy things there?'

'I suppose I do; toothpaste or things we need in the house. Occasionally I'll get things my wife asks me to buy for her.'

'Do you get your prescriptions made up there?'

Pedrolli considered this question for a long time and finally said, 'No, I don't. I get any medicine I need here at the hospital.'

Brunetti nodded.

Pedrolli smiled, but it was not the same smile as before. 'Would you tell me why you're asking these questions, Commissario?'

Ignoring the question, Brunetti asked, 'In all these years, you've never had to get a prescription made up there?'

Pedrolli gazed off into the middle distance. 'Maybe, once, not too long after we moved in. I had flu, and Bianca went out to get medicine for me. She came back with something, but I don't remember if I needed a prescription for it.'

Pedrolli gazed away, his eyes narrowed in an attempt to recall, and he seemed about to speak when Brunetti interrupted to ask, 'If it had required a prescription, would that information have to be put into your medical records, Dottore?'

Pedrolli gave him a long look, and then suddenly his face went blank, as though someone had turned him off. Life returned in the form of a quick glance that Brunetti could not read. 'My medical records?' he finally asked, but it was not a question, not the way he said it. 'Why do you ask about them, Commissario?'

Brunetti saw no reason not to tell him, so long as he did not mention blackmail. 'We're looking into the inappropriate use of medical information, Dottore.'

He waited to see how Pedrolli would respond to this hint, but all the doctor did was blink, shrug, and say, 'I'm not sure that means anything specific to me.' It seemed to Brunetti that, behind the calm expression the doctor appeared to have nailed to his face, he was busy considering what Brunetti had just said, perhaps considering the possibilities towards which it might lead.

Brunetti realized that he had so far failed to raise with Pedrolli the chance of his son's return. He began again but in an entirely different tone of voice. 'What I would really like to do is talk to you about your son.'

He thought he heard Pedrolli gasp. Certainly the noise he made was stronger than a sigh, though the doctor's face remained impassive.

'What about my son would you like to know?' Pedrolli asked in a voice he struggled to control.

'Reports I've received suggest that the boy's natural mother is unlikely to make a claim that he be returned to her.' If Pedrolli understood the real meaning of this, he gave no sign of it, so Brunetti continued, 'And so I wondered if you had thought of pursuing the case in the courts.'

'What case?'

'Of having him returned to you?'

'How did you think that might be achieved, Commissario?'

210

'Your father-in-law is certainly a man... well, a man with many connections. Perhaps he could...' Brunetti watched the other man's face, waiting to see some play of emotion, but there was none.

The doctor glanced at his watch and said, 'I don't mean to be impolite, Commissario, but these are matters which concern my family and me, and I would prefer not to discuss them with you.'

Brunetti got to his feet. 'I wish you well, Dottore. If I can ever be of help to you, I'd like to offer it,' Brunetti said, extending his hand.

Pedrolli took it, briefly looked as if he was going to say something, but remained silent.

Brunetti said he knew the way out of the hospital and left, planning to stop and have something to eat before his next meeting, with the doctor's father-in-law.

21

Brunetti stopped in a trattoria at the foot of the second bridge between the hospital and Campo Santa Marina but, finding that there was no table free, contented himself with a glass of *vino novello* and a plate of cicchetti, standing at the bar to eat them. Conversation swirled around him, but he overheard none of it, still recalling Pedrolli's surprise when asked about his medical records, or had it been at the suggestion that inappropriate use might have been made of them?

The *fondi di carciofi* were delicious, and Brunetti asked for two more, then another *polpetta* and another glass of wine. When he was finished, he was still not satisfied, though he was no longer hungry. These pick-up meals that he was often forced to eat were one of the worst things about his job, along with the too-frequent early morning calls, such as the one that had begun this story for him. He paid and left, cut behind the Miracoli and down towards Campo Santa Marina.

Paola had not had to tell him where the office of Marcolini's party was: its location was etched into the minds and hearts of every Venetian, either by fame or by shame. Lega Doge was one of the separatist political parties that had sprung up in the North in recent years, their platform the usual primitive cocktail of fear, rancour, and resentment at the reality of social change in Italy. They disliked foreigners, the Left, and women with equal ferocity, though their contempt in no way lessened their need for all three: the first to work in their factories; the second to blame for the ills of the country; and the third to prove their masculinity by serving in their beds.

Giuliano Marcolini was the founder of Lega Doge—Brunetti blanched at the thought of referring to Marcolini as the 'ideologue' because of its suggestion that the party might be involved with ideas. He had managed in the course of twenty years to turn his small plumbing supply business into a chain of megastores: for all Brunetti knew, the workers who had refitted his own bathroom four years earlier had obtained their fixtures from a Marcolini outlet.

Some wealthy men bought soccer teams; others acquired new wives or had their current ones rebuilt; some endowed hospitals or art galleries: it was Brunetti's destiny to live in a country where they began political parties. In obvious imitation of other separatist parties, Lega Doge had chosen a flag displaying a rampant animal; with the lion, however, having already given its allegiance to another party, the griffin, though it had appeared seldom in Venetian history and was an infrequent subject in its iconography, had been dragged into service. The party's colours were purple and yellow, and its salute a clenched fist thrust above the head, embarrassingly reminiscent, at least to anyone with a sense of history—which clause thus excluded most members of the party—of the Black Power salute given by American athletes at the 1968 Mexico Olympics. One waggish journalist of the Left, upon first seeing the salute, asked if this were meant to represent the legendary tight-fistedness of the Veneti, and the first appearance of the purple and yellow flags and matching T-shirts had, alas, coincided with the use of the same colours in the spring collection of a notoriously gay designer.

But the intensity of Marcolini's rhetoric and the faith of his listeners had easily overcome these initial obstacles, and within six years of its establishment, Lega Doge had already won the mayorships of four towns in the Veneto and numerous seats on the city councils of Verona, Brescia, and Treviso. Politicians in Rome had begun to pay attention to Signor Marcolini and his... the Right talked of his ideas, while the Left referred to his opinions. He was courted by those politicians who thought Marcolini might be useful to them, causing Brunetti to reflect upon the observation made of Hitler by the leader of one of the political parties he would subsequently sweep into oblivion: 'Goodness, the man can talk: we could use him.'

As he entered Campo Santa Marina, Brunetti considered who he should appear to be when he arrived. Gruff, of course, a real man who took no nonsense from women or foreigners; well, unless the foreigners were men and Europeans and could speak a civilized language like Italian, though real men spoke in dialect, didn't they? He hadn't known that morning that he would be speaking to Marcolini, or he would have dressed for the occasion, though for the life of him, Brunetti could not imagine the appropriate costume for an appearance at the offices of Lega Doge. Something faintly military, with just a hint of dominance: Marvilli's boots, perhaps?

He crossed in front of the hotel and turned into Ramo Bragadin. The first door on the right opened on to a courtyard and a flight of stairs leading to the offices of Lega Doge. A marble-cutting workshop was located on the ground floor, and Brunetti wondered what the noise would be like upstairs. The bell was quickly answered by a clean-shaven young man wearing a tweed jacket and black jeans.

'Guido Brunetti,' he said, omitting his title and putting out his hand. 'I have an appointment with Signor Marcolini.' Brunetti was careful to pronounce the Italian precisely, as though it did not come to him naturally.

The young man, who had a face so thin that his eyes looked even closer together than they were, smiled in return and shook Brunetti's hand. In dialect, he responded, 'He'll be free in a moment, Signore. If you follow me, I'll take you back to his office.'

Brunetti greeted the switch to dialect with an audible sigh, relieved of the burden of speaking in a foreign language.

Brunetti had no idea how a plumbing millionaire would choose to decorate the offices of his political party, but what he saw here seemed just about right. One wall of the corridor down which the young man led him had windows that looked out on to the houses opposite and back towards Campo Santa Marina. The other wall was covered with pairs of crossed Lega flags on long wooden poles, about the size of those carried at the head of the Palio parade and thus somewhat outsized for the not very high corridor. There were a few shields, obvious modern copies of medieval originals, which looked like they were made from heavily shellacked papier mâché. The young man preceded him into a large room, the ceiling of which contained a newly and quite excessively restored fresco of some celestial event attendance at which had clearly necessitated the baring, not only of swords, but of great areas of pink female flesh. White stucco decorations encircled the painting with a nervous halo while pastel swirls spread menacingly away from it towards the corners of the room.

Six chairs made of a wood so highly glossed it succeeded in looking like plastic stood against one wall, and above them was a gold framed print of Vittorio Emanuele III inspecting the troops, perhaps before some disastrous First World War battle. As he studied the scene, Brunetti realized that one of two things had happened: either the artist had added twenty centimetres to the King's height, or most of the men who fought on the Italian side in the First World War were dwarfs.

'It's before Caporetto,' the young man said.

'Ah,' Brunetti let escape him, 'a significant battle.'

'There are sure to be more,' the young man said in a voice so full of longing that Brunetti had to stop himself from staring at him.

'No doubt,' Brunetti said, then gave a nod of manly satisfaction in the direction of the pictured scene.

A red plush sofa that looked as if it had begun life in a French brothel stood against the far wall, and above it were more prints, these of actual battles. The weapons differed, but all of them managed to bring to his knees a young man in uniform who held the Italian flag aloft with one hand while clutching at his heart with the other.

On the table in front of the sofa lay a series of purple and yellow pamphlets and booklets, their covers all bearing the distinctive griffin, flying protectively over the Italian flag. Brunetti looked up from them and smiled at the young man.

Before either could speak, a voice called out something from behind a door at one end of the room, prompting the young man to hurry towards it, saying over his shoulder, 'He'll see you now.'

Brunetti followed him. The young man stepped inside and snapped his heels together in the balletic equivalent, Brunetti thought, of the clenched-fist salute. 'Signor Brunetti to see you, Commendatore,' he said, and actually bowed to usher Brunetti in.

As soon as Brunetti passed in front of him, the young man stepped back into the other room, pulling the door shut behind him. Brunetti heard his footsteps click away into the distance. He glanced across the room at the figure just getting to his feet . . . And recognized the man who had been in the hospital with Patta.

Brunetti hid his surprise by raising his hand to cover his mouth as he cleared his throat. He turned his face away and coughed once, twice, then continued towards the desk, allowing himself an embarrassed smile.

In another culture, Giuliano Marcolini might have been described as fat: Italians, however, graced with a language from which euphemism springs with endless sympathy, would describe him as 'robusto.' He was shorter than Brunetti, but his barrel-like chest and the stomach visible below it made him look shorter still. He wore a suit similar to the one he had been wearing when Brunetti had first seen him, but even the vertical grey stripes of this one could not disguise his girth. The extra flesh on his face ironed out all wrinkles and made him look not significantly older than Brunetti.

His eyes were deeply recessed, the clear eyes of a Northerner, though he was tanned dark as an Arab. His ears were particularly large and seemed even more so because of the shortness of his hair. His nose was long and thick, his hands those of a labourer.

'Ah, Commissario,' he said, getting to his feet. He came across the room, moving gracefully for so thick a man. Brunetti took his hand with a smile that he did not allow to falter as Marcolini tried to crush all of the bones in his hand. Brunetti returned the pressure, increased it, and Marcolini let go, smiling appreciatively at whatever had just taken place.

He waved Brunetti to a chair identical to those in the other room, grabbed another one and pulled it round to face Brunetti. 'What can I do for you, Commissario?' Marcolini asked. Behind him was a wooden desk, the surface covered with files, papers, a telephone, and a number of photographs in silver frames, their backs to Brunetti.

'Find a doctor to look at my hand,' Brunetti said with a chuckle he made sound very hearty while he waved his hand in the air between them.

Marcolini laughed out loud. 'I like to get the sense of a man when I meet him,' he said. 'That's one way to do it.'

Brunetti kept to himself the suggestion that smiling politely and introducing himself might perhaps serve as well and would certainly be less painful. 'And?' Brunetti asked. 'What do you think?' He spoke dialect and put a rough edge on his voice.

'I think maybe we can talk to one another.'

Brunetti leaned towards him, started to speak, and then consciously stopped, as if he had thought better of it.

'What?' Marcolini asked.

Brunetti said, 'My job seldom lets me speak like a real man. Openly, that is. We're in the habit of being careful about what we say. Have to be. Part of the job.'

'Careful what you say about what?' Marcolini asked.

'Oh, you know. I wouldn't want to express an opinion that would offend anyone or that would sound aggressive or offensive in any way.' Brunetti spoke in a sort of patter, as though these were things he had been forced by rote, and against his will, to learn to say.

'To be politically correct?' Marvilli asked, pronouncing the foreign words with a thick accent.

Brunetti made no effort to disguise the scorn in his laughter.

'Yes, to be politically correct,' he answered, pronouncing the words with an accent just as strong as Marvilli's.

'Who do you have to be careful about?' Marvilli asked as though he were genuinely interested.

'Oh, you know. Colleagues, the press, the people we arrest.'

'You have to treat them all the same way, even the people you arrest?' Marvilli asked with manufactured surprise.

Brunetti answered with a smile he tried to make as sly as possible. 'Of course. Everyone's equal, Signor Marcolini.'

'Even *extracomunitaria*?' Marcolini asked with ham-fisted sarcasm.

Brunetti confined himself to a puffing noise rich with disgust. He was a man who could not yet trust himself with words, but who wanted this fellow spirit to know how he felt about foreigners.

'My father called them niggers,' Marcolini volunteered. 'He fought in Ethiopia.'

'Mine was there, too,' Brunetti, whose father had fought in Russia, lied.

'It started so well. My father told me they lived like princes. But then it all fell apart.' Marcolini could not have sounded more cheated if all those things had been taken away from him, as well.

'And now they're all here,' Brunetti said with fierce disgust, oh, so slowly lowering the cards from in front of his chest. He threw up his hands in a gesture redolent of helpless disgust.

'You're not a member, are you?' Marcolini asked, apparently not thinking it necessary to be more specific.

'Of the Lega?' Brunetti asked. 'No.' He allowed a short pause and then added, though it was by now clearly no more necessary than Marcolini's identifying of the Lega, 'Not a formal member, at any rate.'

'What does that mean?' Marcolini surprised him by asking.

'That I think it's wisest to keep my political ideas to myself,' Brunetti said, a man refreshed at finally being able to speak the truth. But then, to avoid any possible confusion, he added, 'At least it's best to do so while I'm at work or working.'

'I see, I see,' Marcolini said. 'But what brings you here, Commissario? Conte Falier called and asked if I'd meet you. You're his son-in-law, aren't you?'

'Yes,' Brunetti agreed in a neutral voice. 'As a matter of fact, it's about *your* son-in-law that I'd like to speak to you.'

'What about him?' Marcolini asked instantly, with some curiosity but little enthusiasm.

'My department got drawn into his trouble with the Carabinieri,' Brunetti said, his voice suggesting displeasure at the memory.

'How?'

'The night of the raid, I was called to the hospital to see him.'

'I thought that was the Carabinieri,' Marcolini said.

'Yes, it was, but our office never processed the notice from the Carabinieri, so when it happened, we were called.' Affecting the voice of an irritated bureaucrat, Brunetti added, 'It wasn't our case, but I was told a citizen had been attacked.'

'So you went?'

'Of course. When they call you, you have to go,' Brunetti said, pleased with how much he sounded like the little drummer boy.

'Right. But you still haven't told me why you're here.'

'I'd like, first, to be completely frank with you, Signore,' Brunetti said.

Marcolini's nod was surprisingly gracious.

'My superior doesn't like it that we've been mixed up in Carabinieri business, so he's asked me to look into it.' Brunetti paused, as if to check that Marcolini was following him, and at the older man's nod, he went on. 'We've been given different stories about the child. One version says it's Pedrolli's child by some *extracomunitaria* woman he met in the South,' he said, managing to put as much contempt as he dared into the words, '*extracomunitaria*' and 'South'. He saw this register with Marcolini and went on, 'Then there's the other story that says it was this woman's child by her husband.' He paused to let Marcolini speak.

'Why do you want to know about this, Commissario?'

'As I told you, Signore, if it's not Pedrolli's child, then we think we should leave it to the Carabinieri.' He smiled, then went on. 'But if the child is his, then some intervention from my superiors, as well as from you, might make enough difference to help.'

'Intervention?' Marcolini asked. 'Help? I don't know what you're talking about.'

Brunetti put on an expression of limpid good will. 'With the social services, Signore. The child will probably end up in an orphanage.' This was fact, leaving Brunetti to continue with the fiction. 'It might be possible, in the end—and for the child's good—for him to be returned to his parents.'

'His parents,' Marcolini exploded, his voice stripped of all affability, '. . . are a pair of Albanians who sneaked into this country illegally.' He paused for effect and then repeated, 'Albanians, for the love of God.'

Rather than respond to this, Brunetti changed his expression to one of the most intense interest, and Marcolini went on, 'The mother is probably some sort of whore; whatever she is, she was willing enough to sell the baby for ten thousand Euros. So if he's put in an orphanage and kept away from her, it's all the better for him.'

'I didn't know that, Signore,' Brunetti said, sounding disapproving.

'I'm sure there's a lot about this you don't know and that the Carabinieri don't know,' Marcolini said with mounting anger. 'That his story about his affair in Cosenza is a lie. He went down there for some sort of medical conference, and while he was there, he made a deal to buy the baby.' Brunetti managed to express surprise at hearing this, as if he were hearing about it for the first time.

Marcolini got to his feet and walked behind his desk. 'I could understand if it really happened the way he said in the beginning. A man has needs, and he was away for a week, so I'd understand if he'd knocked her up. And then at least it would be his son. But Gustavo's never been the type who knows how to have a good time, and all this was was some little Albanian bastard his mother brought to market, and my son-in-law was stupid enough to buy it and bring it home.'

Marcolini picked up one of the photos on his desk and brought it back with him. Standing over Brunetti, he pressed the frame into his hand. 'Look, look at him, the little Albanian.'

Brunetti looked at the photo and saw Pedrolli, his wife and, between them, a tow-headed infant with a round face and dark eyes.

Marcolini paced away, turned at the wall, and came back to Brunetti. 'You should have seen him, the little cuckoo, with his square Albanian head, flat at the back the way they all are. You think I want my daughter to be his mother? You think I'm going to let something like that inherit everything I've worked for all my life?' He took the photo back and tossed it face down on to his desk. Brunetti heard the glass shatter, but Marcolini must not have heard it or must not have cared, for he snatched up another one and thrust it at Brunetti.

'Look, there's Bianca when she was two. That's what a baby is supposed to look like.' Brunetti gazed at the photo of a tow-headed infant with a round face and dark eyes. He said nothing but was careful to nod in appreciation of whatever it was he was meant to detect in the photo. 'Well?' demanded Marcolini. 'Isn't she? Isn't she what a baby's supposed to look like?'

Brunetti handed it back, saying, 'She's very beautiful, Signore. Then and now.'

'And married to a fool,' Marcolini said and let himself down heavily into his chair.

'But aren't you worried for her, Signore?' Brunetti asked in a voice he struggled to fill with concern.

'Worried about what?'

'That she'll miss the baby?'

'Miss it?' Marcolini asked, and then he put his head back and laughed. 'Who do you think made me make the phone call?'

22

Brunetti could neither hide nor disguise his astonishment. His mouth hung open for a second before he thought to close it. 'I see,' he said, but in an unsteady voice.

'Surprised you, didn't I?' Marcolini said with a deep laugh. 'Well, she surprised me, too, I have to confess. I thought she'd taken to the child: that's what kept me quiet for so long, though the older he got, the more I saw him turning into a little Albanian. He didn't look like one of us,' he said, his voice earnest. 'And I don't mean me and Bianca or my wife: he just didn't look like an Italian.'

Marcolini looked to see if he had Brunetti's attention, and though he certainly had that, Brunetti did his best to make it look as if he had his approval, as well. 'But I wasn't sure because, well, she seemed to take to him, and I didn't want to do anything or say anything that would hurt her feelings or make things difficult between us.'

'Of course,' Brunetti said with a friendly smile, one father to another. Then he prodded, 'But?'

'But then one day she was at home—my home, our home, that is. The day there was that story in the paper about that Romanian woman who sold her baby. Down in the South,' Marcolini added with particular contempt. 'That's where everything happens. They don't know the meaning of honour.'

Brunetti nodded, as though he had never heard a greater truth spoken.

'I said something. I was angry, and as soon as I said it, I was afraid I might have said too much. At any rate, that's when she told me that they had done the same thing, well, that she thought that's what Gustavo had done. Anyway, the baby wasn't his.' Marcolini broke off, as if to see that Brunetti was still following his story. Brunetti made no attempt to disguise his mounting interest.

'Until that time, I swear I still thought the baby was Gustavo's, and that he looked the way he did because of the mother: that her influence was stronger than his. Like with Blacks: you just need a little bit, and the genes take over.' From the way Marcolini spoke, he might as well have been Mendel, explaining the rules that governed his peas.

'But then Bianca told me what had really happened. Some colleague of his—someone he was at medical school with—was working in Cosenza, and one of his patients was going to have a baby and wanted to, well, to give it up.'

'For adoption?' asked an artfully ingenuous Brunetti.

'You can call it that if you want,' Marvilli said with a complicit smile. 'So Gustavo went down to talk to his friend and to this woman, and when he came back he explained things to Bianca, and she agreed because she said Gustavo said it was the only chance they'd ever have to have a baby. She told me she really didn't want to, but he persuaded her. They were too old to be allowed to adopt a baby—maybe an older child, but not a baby—and the tests always said they couldn't have children.' Marcolini stopped and gave a short, barking laugh. 'That's about the only thing we ever got out of Gustavo's being a doctor: he could at least interpret all the figures on the tests. So Bianca agreed.'

'I see,' Brunetti muttered. 'So he went and got the baby?'

'Yes. It's easy enough down there, to do things like that. He went into the Anagrafe and said it was his baby, and the woman signed it with him, confirming that it was.' Marcolini cast his eyes at the ceiling in a manner Brunetti judged melodramatic, then continued. 'She probably doesn't even know how to read and write, but she signed the document, and then the baby was his. And he gave her ten thousand Euros.' Marcolini's anger was no longer melodramatic, but real. 'It was only later that he told Bianca how much he paid. The fool.'

It was evident from his manner that he had something further to add, so Brunetti sat quietly, the look of intense interest still on his face, and Marcolini continued, 'For the love of God, he could have got it for less. That other guy—the one with the Romanian—got it for a *permesso di soggiorno* and an apartment for the mother to stay in. But no, Dottor Gustavo has to be the *gran signore* and give her ten thousand Euros.' Lost for words, Marcolini threw his hands in the air, then went on. 'She probably spent it on drugs or sent it back to her family in Albania. Ten thousand Euros,' he repeated, clearly unable sufficiently to express his disgust.

'And when he brought it back, I saw immediately what was wrong with it, but, as I said, I thought it was the mother's influence. You'd think all babies look alike, but this one . . . I knew right away that it wasn't one of us. You just have to look at those little eyes and that head.' Marcolini shook his own head in disbelief, and Brunetti murmured in assent and encouragement, hoping to keep the man talking.

'But Bianca's my daughter,' Marcolini continued, and it seemed to Brunetti now that he was talking to himself as much as to his listener. 'And I thought she wanted the child, too.

Then that day she told me what she really felt, and that the baby was just a chore for her, something she had to take care of and that she really didn't want. It was Gustavo who was crazy for him, couldn't wait to get home so he could play with him. Paid no attention to her any more, just to the baby, and she didn't like that.'

'I see,' Brunetti said.

'So I said something like, "Just like in the papers today, huh?" because of what we'd been talking about. I meant that Gustavo got the baby the same way, but Bianca thought I meant the way the police found out.'

'A telephone call?' Brunetti asked, making himself sound very proud at having figured it out.

'Yes, a telephone call to the Carabinieri.'

'And that's when she asked you to make the call, I imagine,' Brunetti said, knowing he would not believe it until he heard Marcolini spell it out.

'Yes, call them and tell them Gustavo had bought the baby. After all, the woman's name was on the birth certificate along with his, so it would be easy for them to find her.'

'And that's just what happened, isn't it?' Brunetti asked. He forced himself to imbue his voice with approval, even a small measure of enthusiasm.

'I had no idea what would happen after they found out,' Marcolini said. 'And I suppose Bianca didn't, either. She said she was terrified the night they came. She thought they were terrorists or robbers or something.' Marcolini's voice had grown unsteady as he considered his daughter's suffering. 'I didn't expect them to go breaking into the house the way they did.'

'Of course not,' Brunetti agreed.

'God knows how much they frightened her.'

'It must have been terrible for them,' Brunetti allowed himself to say.

'Yes. I didn't want that to happen, *per carità*.'

'I can certainly understand that.'

'And I suppose they shouldn't have been so rough with Gustavo,' Marcolini added in a lacklustre voice.

'No, of course not.'

The clouds parted and Marcolini's voice warmed. 'But it solved the problem, didn't it?' he asked. Then, as if suddenly aware who he had been speaking to, he asked, 'I can trust you, can't I?'

Brunetti pulled his face into a broad smile and said, 'You needn't ask that, Signore. After all, our fathers fought together, didn't they?' Then, stunned by the realization, he added, 'Besides, nothing you did was actually illegal, was it?'

'No, it wasn't, was it?' Marcolini asked with a sly smile, obviously having long since arrived at this truth. He reached over and gave Brunetti's shoulder a friendly, manly squeeze.

Brunetti was suddenly conscious of how easy it would be, now, to keep Marcolini talking. All he would have to do was ask him more questions, and Marcolini was sure to answer them, perhaps even honestly. It was a common enough phenomenon, though Brunetti had most frequently observed it among the people he was questioning in regard to crimes they were accused of having committed. The point came when the subject believed he had won the sympathy of his questioner and, in return, placed his trust in him. After this, people would even confess to crimes about which no questions had been asked, almost as if there was no length to which they would not go in order to maintain the good will of their listener. But Marcolini, as the man himself had agreed with great pleasure, had committed no crime. Indeed, he had acted as would any conscientious citizen and had reported one to the police.

It was this thought that forced Brunetti to his feet. He clung to the remnants of the role he was playing as he said, 'I'm very grateful for your time, Signor Marcolini.' He forced himself to extend his hand and said, 'I'll report to the Questore what you've told me.'

The older man stood and took Brunetti's extended hand. He smiled in a friendly manner, then turned and moved towards the door. At the sight of Marcolini's thick, expensively clothed back, Brunetti found himself overcome by the desire to strike him. He saw himself knocking the older man to the floor, but that would serve no purpose unless he were also able to kick the man, and he knew he could not do that. So he followed Marcolini across the room.

The older man opened the door and stood aside to let Brunetti pass. Marcolini raised a hand, and Brunetti knew he was going to clap him on the shoulder or pat him on the arm. The thought filled him with something close to horror; he knew he could not stand that. He quickened his pace and slipped past Marcolini, took two steps and then turned, as though surprised that the other man had not followed close behind him.

'Thank you for your time, Signore,' Brunetti said, squeezing out a last smile.

'Not at all,' Marcolini said, rocking back on his heels and folding his arms across his chest. 'Always happy to be of help to the police.'

Brunetti tasted something metallic, muttered words even he did not understand, and left the building.

23

Outside, Brunetti felt himself assailed by a chorus of Furies whispering, 'Eighteen months, eighteen months, eighteen months.' They had had the child for eighteen months, and then Bianca Marcolini had asked her father to arrange to have it taken away, as though the little boy were an unwanted piece of furniture or a kitchen appliance she had bought on warranty and had decided to return.

By the time either one of his children was eighteen months old, Paola could have told Brunetti they resulted from her union with the postman, the garbage man, the parish priest, for all he cared, and he would have loved them none the less. Brunetti pulled himself up short: here he went again, judging the entire world by his own experience, as if there were no other standard with which to measure human behaviour.

He continued walking towards the Questura, but however much he tried to rid himself of the sound of these voices, he failed to do so. He was so distracted that he almost bumped into Patta, who was coming out of the main door.

'Ah, Brunetti,' the Vice-Questore said, 'coming back from a meeting, are you?'

Brunetti slapped an expression of distracted busyness on his face. 'Yes, Dottore, I am, but don't let me keep you from yours.' How else to make polite note of the fact that the Vice-Questore was leaving for home two hours early?

Brunetti felt it best that Patta should not learn what he was up to, especially not that he had just been asking questions of the leader of a political party of growing significance in the Veneto. Patta believed that only waiters had the right to ask questions of politicians; everyone else should only stand and wait.

'What sort of meeting?' Patta asked.

Brunetti recalled the description the Marquis de Custine had given of the customs officers at the port of St Petersburg and said, 'Someone was complaining about the port, that the customs officers were taking bribes or making it difficult for people who didn't pay them.'

'Nothing new there,' Patta said with little patience, pulled on his gloves, and turned away.

When Brunetti reached the first floor, he went to the officers' room and was relieved to see Vianello and Pucetti. He gave no thought to whether they had discovered anything about the pharmacist, nor whether they could help him resolve this case: Brunetti was simply happy to be in their company and to know that they were men who would share his visceral disgust at what Marcolini had just told him.

He came into the office quietly. Vianello looked up and smiled, then Pucetti did the same. Their desks were covered with papers and files; an ink smear ran across Pucetti's chin. Strangely, Brunetti found himself too moved at the sight of them to speak: two entirely normal men, sitting at their desks and doing their jobs.

Vianello's smile, however, was that of a predator that has just glimpsed the dappled brown coat of a fawn at the edge of the forest glade. 'What is it?' Brunetti asked.

'Have you seen Signorina Elettra?' the Inspector enquired.

Brunetti noticed that Pucetti was looking at him with much the same grin.

'No. Why?'

'Signor Brunini's companion had a phone call last night.'

It took Brunetti a moment to process this information: the *telefonino* he had bought and the number he had given at the clinic, the number of Signor Brunini, the phone Signorina Elettra had said she would see to answering.

'And?' asked Brunetti.

'And the caller said he thought he might be able to be of help to Signor Brunini and, of course, to the Signorina.'

'That's all?' Brunetti asked.

'Signorina Elettra could not help becoming emotional when he gave her the news.' Brunetti did not respond, so the Inspector went on. 'She kept saying, "a baby, a baby," until the man said that, yes, he was talking about a baby.'

'And now what? Did he leave a number?'

Vianello's smile grew broader. 'Better. He agreed to meet her and Signor Brunini. She told me that, even when he told her where and when they should meet, she was still unable to stop her tears.'

Brunetti could not help smiling. 'And?'

'And I wondered what you wanted to do,' Vianello said.

Marvilli had behaved honestly, even generously, towards them: the least they could do was return the favour with a piece of information that might help advance his career. Besides, it could never hurt to have another friend among the Carabinieri. He could call Marvilli himself, but it would be more subtle if the call came from Vianello: that would appear less like what it was: repayment of a personal favour. 'It belongs to the Carabinieri,' Brunetti finally said. 'Would you call Marvilli?'

'And the meeting?'

'Tell him about it. If they want us to go, we will. But it's theirs: they decide.'

'All right,' Vianello said but made no move for the phone. 'It's not until the day after tomorrow,' he said.

Brunetti cleared his throat and addressed himself to the reason he had come. 'You finished with the names that were on Franchi's computer?'

'Just now,' Vianello said. 'We've gone through the files and found about a dozen with information that someone might be interested in.'

How wonderfully diplomatic the Inspector was being today, Brunetti thought. 'You mean blackmail them about?' he asked.

Pucetti laughed, turned to Vianello and said, 'I told you it was better just to say it.'

Vianello went on. 'I think we should divide the files among the three of us and go and talk to them.'

'Not on the phone?' Pucetti asked, unable to disguise his surprise.

Brunetti spoke before Vianello had time to answer, conscious of what sort of information might be in those files. 'The first contact, yes, to see if there is reason to talk to them, and then in person.' He pointed at the folders. 'Is any of it criminal?'

Vianello put his hand out horizontally and waggled it a few times. 'There are two who are taking an awful lot of tranquillizers, but that's the doctors' fault, not theirs, I'd say.'

It sounded pretty tame to Brunetti. 'Nothing better?' he asked, struck by how strange the word sounded.

'I've got one that might be,' Pucetti said diffidently.

Both men turned to look at the young officer, who rooted

around in the files on his desk and finally pulled one out. 'It's an American woman,' he began.

Shoplifting, was Brunetti's immediate unspoken thought, but then he realized that a pharmacist was unlikely to have information about that.

'Well,' temporized Pucetti, 'it's really maybe her husband.'

Vianello sighed audibly, and Pucetti said, 'She's been into the Pronto Soccorso five times in the last two years.'

Neither of them said anything.

'The first time was a broken nose,' said Pucetti, opening the file and running his finger down the first page. He flipped it over and started down the second. 'Then, three months later, she was back with a very bad cut on her wrist. She said she cut it on a wine glass that fell into the sink.'

'Uh huh,' Vianello muttered.

'Six months passed, and then she was back with two broken ribs.'

'Fell down the stairs, I suppose?' Vianello offered.

'Exactly,' answered Pucetti. He flipped over another page and said, 'Then her knee: torn ligaments: tripped on a bridge.'

Neither Brunetti nor Vianello said anything. The sound of the next page turning was loud in the silence from the two men.

'And then, last month, she dislocated her shoulder.'

'Falling down the stairs again?' asked Vianello.

Pucetti closed the file. 'It doesn't say.'

'Are they residents?' Brunetti asked.

'They have an apartment, but they come as tourists,' Pucetti answered. 'She pays her hospital bills in cash.'

'Then how'd she get on his computer?' Brunetti asked.

'She went into the pharmacy to get painkillers the first time,' Pucetti said.

'Quite a lot of them, it would seem,' Vianello muttered.

Ignoring Vianello's remark, Pucetti completed his explanation, 'And so she's in his computer.'

Brunetti considered the wisdom of pursuing this but decided against. 'Let's begin with Venetians or, at least, Italians, and see if we can get anyone to speak to us. If they realize we know whatever it is he's been blackmailing them about, then they might tell us. And we might find out who broke into his pharmacy, as well.'

'There's the blood samples,' Vianello said, reminding them but not sounding at all optimistic that any results would be ready yet. 'It might be easier if we could match that sample with the blood type of someone in the files. They've been with Bocchese since the break-in.'

'Or in some lab,' Brunetti said. He grabbed the phone and dialled Bocchese's number. The technician answered.

'Those blood samples?' Brunetti said.

'Thank you, Dottore, for asking. I'm fine. Glad to hear you are, too.'

'Sorry, Bocchese, but we're in something of a hurry here.'

'You're always in a hurry, Commissario. We scientific types know how to take life more easily. For example, we have to wait for specimens to come back from laboratories, and that teaches us the virtue of patience.'

'When will they be back?'

'The results should have been here yesterday,' Bocchese said.

'Can you call them?'

'And ask them what?'

'To tell you whatever they found in the blood.'

'If I call them and they have it, they can just as easily send me the information by email.'

'Would you call them,' Brunetti said in a voice he struggled to keep as placid and polite as he could, 'and ask them if they'd send you the results?'

'Of course. I'd be delighted. Shall I call you back if I get anything?'

'You are kindness itself,' Brunetti said.

Bocchese snorted and hung up.

Neither of the others bothered to ask, both aware of the sovereign truth that Bocchese worked at a rhythm set by and known only to himself.

Brunetti replaced the phone with studied patience. 'The ways of the Lord are infinite,' was the only thing he could think of to say.

'How shall we do this?' Vianello asked, displaying no apparent interest in the ways of the Lord.

'Do you know any of the people on the list?' Brunetti asked.

Vianello nodded and picked up one of the files. Pucetti searched until he found the file he was looking for.

'Let me have a look,' Brunetti said. He took the list of names and read through it, recognizing two, a young woman colleague of Paola's he had met once and a surgeon at the hospital who had operated on the mother of a friend of his.

Given the time, they agreed that the best thing they could do now was for each of them to call the people they knew and arrange appointments for the following day. Brunetti went up to his office and read through the files. Dottor Malapiero had first been prescribed L-dopa three years before. Even Brunetti recognized this as the drug most commonly used against the first symptoms of Parkinson's.

As for Paola's colleague, Brunetti had met Daniela Carlon once, a chance meeting, when he and Paola had joined her for a coffee and a conversation that had turned out to be far more pleasant than he had anticipated. The immediate prospect of listening to a professor of English literature and a professor of Persian was not one that had at first thrilled Brunetti, but the discovery that Daniela had spent years in the Middle East with her husband, an archaeologist still working in Syria, had changed that. Soon, they were talking about Arrian and Quintus Curtius, while Paola looked on silently, upstaged for once in the discussion of books but not at all troubled by that fact.

According to her records, Daniela Carlon had been hospitalized for an abortion two months before, the foetus in its third month. And according to what Brunetti remembered of their conversation, which had taken place shortly before, her husband had been in Syria for the previous eight months.

Brunetti chose to do the easy call first and learned from the doctor's wife that Dottor Malapiero was in Milano and would not be back for two days. He left no message and said that he would call again.

Daniela answered the phone and, after her initial confusion that Brunetti had called, and not Paola, asked, 'What is it, Guido?'

'I'd like to talk to you.'

The pause that followed stretched out until it was too long and embarrassingly significant.

'It's about work,' Brunetti added awkwardly.

'Your work or mine?'

'Mine, unfortunately.'

'Why unfortunately?' she asked.

This was exactly the situation Brunetti had wanted to avoid, having the conversation on the telephone, where he could not observe her responses or weigh her expressions as they spoke.

'Because it has to do with an investigation.'

'A police investigation?' she asked, making no attempt to disguise her astonishment. 'What have I got to do with a police investigation?'

'I'm not at all sure; that's why I'd like to discuss this in person,' Brunetti said.

'And I'd like to discuss it now,' she said, her voice suddenly hard.

'Perhaps tomorrow morning?' he suggested.

'I'm not free tomorrow morning,' she said, offering no details. When Brunetti said nothing, she went on, 'Look, Guido, I have no idea why the police might want to talk to me, but I'll admit that I'm curious.'

Brunetti knew when a person would not concede. 'All right,' he said. 'It's about your medical records.'

'What about my medical records?' she asked coolly.

'They say that you terminated a pregnancy three months ago.'

'Yes.'

'Daniela,' he began, feeling himself like a suspect, 'what I want to know is if anyone . . .'

'Knows about this?' she completed the question for him, her voice blistering with rage. 'Other than that creepy little pharmacist, that is?'

Brunetti felt the hairs on the back of his neck rise. He fought to keep control of his voice and said, 'He called?'

'He called Luca's mother. That's who he called,' she shouted down the phone, all restraint gone. 'He called her and asked if she knew what her daughter-in-law had done, if she knew that her daughter-in-law had been in the hospital and had destroyed a baby, that she had been pregnant.'

Brunetti's fingers tightened on the phone. She started to cry, and Brunetti listened to her sobbing for more than a minute.

Finally he said, 'Daniela, Daniela, can you hear me? Is there anything . . .' The only response was the continued sound of her sobbing. Brunetti thought of calling Paola and asking her to go to Daniela's home, but he did not want to involve Paola in this, did not want her to know he had made this call and done what he had done.

After some time, Daniela stopped crying and Brunetti listened to her sniff, then to the strangely comforting sound of her blowing her nose, then her voice returned. 'It was . . .'

'I don't want to know,' Brunetti said, too loudly. 'I don't want to know anything about it, Daniela. It's none of my business and none of the police's business.'

'Then why are you calling me?' she demanded, still angry but at least no longer in tears.

'I want to know what Dottor Franchi wanted.'

'God knows what he wanted,' she said angrily. 'That everyone should be a quiet little castrato, just like him.'

'Did he call you?'

'I just told you: he called my mother-in-law. No, he didn't call me. He called her. Can I make that any clearer?'

'Did he ask for money?'

'Money?' she asked and then started to laugh, a strange sound hard to distinguish from her crying. After a time she stopped and said, 'No, he didn't want anything, no money, no sex, no anything. He just wanted the sinner to be punished.'

'I'm sorry, Daniela,' he said, meaning that he was sorry both for her pain and for having asked her about it.

'I'm sorry too,' she answered. 'Is that enough?' she asked.
'Yes, it is.'
'You don't want to know anything about it?'
'I told you: it's none of my business.'
'Then goodbye, Guido. I'm sorry we had to talk about this.'
'I am, too, Daniela,' he said and put down the phone.

24

Her voice broke him. Brunetti set the receiver down softly, as if afraid it would break, too. He got to his feet and, with the stealth of a burglar, went down the stairs and outside. The rain had cleaned the streets a few days previously, but already the grit and dirt had returned; he felt them underfoot, or perhaps that was his imagination and the streets were clean and the only dirt came from the things his work made him privy to. People passed him, looking entirely normal and innocent and untouched; some of them looked quite happy.

It was as he was walking into Campo Santa Marina that he realized his body had contracted into something that felt like a long, tight knot. He stopped at the *edicola* and stood quietly for a while, looking at the covers of the magazines on display through the glass, all the while rolling his shoulders in an attempt to loosen them. Tits and ass. Paola had again observed, months ago, that he should spend a day counting the times he saw tits and ass: in the newspapers, in magazines, in ads on the vaporetti, on display in every kind of shop window. It might help him understand, she suggested, the attitude of some women towards men. And here he found himself contemplating evidence, though, strangely enough, he was comforted by the sight of all that lovely flesh. How lovely tits were; how his hand longed to touch that well-curved ass. How much better than what he had just heard, the narrow life-denying nastiness of it. So let there be tits and let there be ass and let them lead people to make small children and to love them.

The thought of having children brought Daniela Carlon back into his mind, though he would rather not have thought about what she had told him. Over the years, he had come to believe that he could have only a second-class opinion about abortion and that his gender deprived him of a vote on the subject. This in no way affected his thoughts or his visceral feelings, but the right to a decision belonged to women on this one, and it behove him to accept this and keep his mouth shut. On the other hand, this was only theory and had little relevance to the raw pain he had heard in her voice.

He felt something against his leg, and he looked down to see a mid-sized brown dog sniffing at his shoe, rubbing its flanks contentedly against his calf. It looked up at him, seemed to smile, and returned to his shoe. At the other end of its lead was a young boy, only a little bit taller than the dog.

'Milli, stop that,' he heard a woman's voice call, and then she came up to the boy and took the lead from his hand. 'I'm sorry, Signore, but she's still a puppy.'

'And loves shoes?' Brunetti asked, his good spirits lifted by the appealing absurdity of the situation.

She laughed, and he saw that her teeth were perfect in her well-tanned face. 'It seems so,' she said. She extended her hand to her son and said, 'Come on, Stefano. Let's take Milli home and give her a treat.'

The boy extended his free hand and, with some reluctance, she gave him back the lead.

The dog must have sensed the tremors of the change of command, for she scampered off, tossing her back legs high in the air in the manner of small dogs, though she ran off slowly enough to allow the boy to be towed after her without danger of his falling.

His heart lifted and remained that way for a moment until his thoughts scampered on and found themselves faced with Dottor Franchi. What was it that Pedrolli had called him, 'exquisitely moral'? To form such a judgement, Pedrolli must have heard talk or, just as likely, listened to the pharmacist as he spoke about his clients or the wider world, or whatever subject would enable a listener to form that opinion of him. Thinking back, Brunetti remembered the startled look Signora Invernizzi had given Franchi when he had remarked on the drug addicts' inability to help themselves.

Was he a chameleon, then, Dottor Franchi, keeping his judgements to himself when he thought they might offend someone whose good opinion he sought, only to reveal them to those he considered his inferiors? In Brunetti's experience, it was not uncommon for people to behave in this fashion. Was this one of the reasons why people married, then, to free themselves to say what they thought and thus spare themselves the terrible exhaustion of leading a double life? Then what of Bianca Marcolini: what life could she lead if any day, any moment, her husband were to discover what her father had done at her urging? It had been so easy to lead Marcolini into boasting about his phone call; surely, she must have known that, sooner or later, her husband would learn what had actually happened. No, not what had happened, but why it had happened. The bolt struck Brunetti then: Pedrolli would never learn what had happened to the child, only why it had.

He became aware that the tension had returned to his shoulders and that he was still standing in front of the *edicola*, gazing open-mouthed at the naked bodies on the covers of the magazines.

In a chill moment of lucidity, he saw what Paola meant: they were there, on display, these young women, naked and undefended and inviting any attention a man might please to give them.

Trapped, his eyes moved to the left and fell on a column of bright-coloured covers, each of which displayed a bare-breasted woman in a posture of submission: some bound with straps, some with ropes, and some with chains. Some looked frightened; some looked happy; they all looked excited.

He pulled his eyes away and looked at the façade of Palazzo Dolfin. 'She's right,' he said under his breath.

'You going to stand there all day talking to yourself?' he heard someone ask in a loud, angry voice. He drew his attention away from the building and turned. The news vendor was standing less than a metre from him, his face red. Again he asked, 'You going to stand there all day? What's next, you put your hands in your pockets?'

Brunetti raised a hand to defend himself, to explain, but then he let it drop and walked away, out of the *campo* and towards his home.

He had heard that people who had pets often found them at the door of their homes when they returned from work, that animals had some sixth sense that alerted them to the approach of what they no doubt thought of as their pet humans. When he reached the top of the steps and began to hunt for his keys, the door opened to reveal Paola, just inside. He could not disguise his joy at seeing her.

'Bad day?' she asked.

'How did you know?'

'I heard you coming up the stairs and it sounded like the tread of a weary man, so I thought it might help if I opened the door and told you how it lifts my heart that you are here.'

'You know, you're right about the tits and ass in magazines,' he blurted out.

She tilted her head to one side and studied his face. 'Come in, Guido. I think you might need a glass of wine.'

He smiled. 'I capitulate to you about something we've argued about for decades, and all you can do is offer me a glass of wine?' he asked.

'Why, what did you want instead?'

'How about some tits and ass?' he asked, making a grab for her.

After dinner, he trailed her down to her study. He had drunk little wine with dinner and had no desire now save to sit and talk and listen to what she might have to say about something he still did not know how to refer to: the Pedrolli disaster was perhaps as good as he could manage.

'The pharmacist in Campo Sant'Angelo?' she asked when he had finished telling the story—in what he hoped was a chronological, but what he feared was a garbled, manner.

Brunetti sat beside her, his arms folded across his chest. 'You know him?'

'No. It's out of the way for me. Besides, it's one of those *campi* where you don't think of stopping, isn't it? You just walk across it on your way to Accademia or Rialto: I've never even bought one of those cotton shirts from the place by the bridge.'

Brunetti's inner map focused on the *campo*, viewed first from the entrance from the bridge and then from Calle della Mandola. A restaurant where he had never eaten, an art gallery, the inevitable real estate agency, the *edicola* with the chocolate Labrador.

He was summoned from these cartographical considerations

by Paola, who asked, 'You think he'd do that? Call and tell people about his clients?'

'I used to think there were limits to what people were capable of doing,' Brunetti said. 'But I don't think that any more. Given the right stimuli, we're all probably capable of anything.' He listened to that statement echo, realized the extent to which it was a response to the events of the day, and said quickly, 'No, that's not right, is it?'

'I hope not,' Paola said. 'But doesn't he take some sort of oath, like a doctor, not to reveal certain things?'

'I think so. But I'm sure he's too clever to do this sort of thing openly. All he'd have to do is make a phone call to ask after someone's health: "Is Daniela back from the hospital yet?" "Could you tell Egidio it's time to renew his prescription?" And if anything embarrassing or shameful were revealed by these calls, well, it was just the faithful family pharmacist, trying to be helpful, showing his concern for his patients' well-being, wasn't it?'

Paola considered this, then turned and put her hand on his arm. 'And it would let him go on thinking of himself in the same way, wouldn't it? If anyone questioned him, he could maintain—not only to them but to himself—that it was merely an excess of zeal on his part.'

'Probably.'

'Nasty little bastard.'

'Most moralists are,' said Brunetti wearily.

'Is there anything you can do about it, or about him?' she asked.

'I don't think so,' Brunetti said. 'One of the strange things about all of this is that, no matter how sordid and disgusting any of it is, the only thing Franchi's done that's illegal is look at those files, and he'd be sure to argue—and believe—that he was simply acting in the best interests of his clients. And Marcolini was doing his duty as a citizen, wasn't he? So was his daughter, I suppose.' Brunetti gave more thought to all of the things that had happened and said, 'And with Pedrolli, the violence of the Carabinieri wouldn't even be judged criminal. They had a judge's order to make their arrests that night. They did ring the doorbell, but the Pedrollis didn't hear it. And Pedrolli admits that he attacked the Carabiniere first.'

'All this pain, all this suffering,' Paola said. They sat quietly side by side for some time. Finally, Brunetti pushed himself to his feet, went back into the living room and retrieved his copy of the *Lettere della Russia*, and came back to her study. In the short time he was absent, like water seeking the lowest point, Paola had spread out on the sofa with a book, but once again she pulled her feet back to make room for him.

'Your Russians?' she asked when she saw the book.

He sat down beside her and began to read where he had left off the night before. Paola studied his profile for a moment, then stretched out her feet and slipped them on to his lap, under his book, and returned to her own.

The weather worsened the next day, first with a sudden drop in temperature, followed by a torrential rainstorm, both of which cleaned the streets, first of tourists, then of any dirt that remained. Some hours later the sirens announced the first *acqua alta* of the autumn, worsened by a fierce *bora* that sprang up and blew in from the north-east.

Umbrellaed, hatted, booted, and raincoated, a disgruntled Brunetti arrived at the Questura and made what he thought was *una brutta figura* at the entrance, pausing to shake himself free of water in the manner of a dog. He looked around and saw that the floor was wet for at least a metre in every direction.

Heavy-footed and unwilling to talk to anyone, he made his way up the stairs to his office.

He stuffed the umbrella upright behind the door. Let the water run down on to the wooden floor: no one would see it back there. He hung his raincoat in the *armadio*, tossed his sodden hat on the top shelf, and then sat on a chair to remove his boots. By the time he finally sat behind his desk, he was sweaty and ill-tempered.

The phone rang. '*Sì,*' he said with singular lack of grace.

'Should I hang up and call back after you've had time to go out for a coffee?' asked Bocchese.

'It wouldn't make any difference, and I'd probably be carried away by the *acqua alta* if I tried to go down to the bar.'

'Is it that bad?' the technician asked. 'I got here early, and it wasn't bad when I came in.'

'Supposed to peak in an hour, but yes, it's bad.'

'You think any tourists will be drowned?'

'Don't tempt me, Bocchese. You know our phones are tapped, and what we say might get back to the Tourist Board.' He felt suddenly cheered, perhaps because of Bocchese's unwonted chattiness or perhaps by the thought of drowned tourists. 'What have you got for me?'

'HIV,' the technician said and then, into the resulting silence, 'That is, I've got a blood sample that is HIV positive. Or, to be even more precise, I've got the results from the lab—finally—saying that the sample I sent them is positive. B negative blood type, which is relatively rare, and HIV, which is not as rare as it should be.'

'The blood from the pharmacy?'

'Yes.'

'Have you told anyone?'

248

'No. The email just came in. Why?'

'No reason. I'll talk to Vianello.'

'It's not his blood, is it?' Bocchese asked in a neutral voice.

The question so stunned Brunetti that he could not stop himself from barking, 'What?'

A long silence ensued at the other end, after which a curiously sober Bocchese said, 'I didn't mean it that way. With a sample, we don't know whose it is.'

'Then say it that way,' Brunetti said, still shouting. 'And don't make jokes like that. They're not funny,' he added, his voice still rough, taken aback by the surge of anger he felt towards the technician.

'Sorry,' Bocchese said. 'It's an occupational hazard, I think. We see only pieces of people or samples of people, so we make jokes about them, and maybe we forget about the actual people themselves.'

'It's all right,' Brunetti said, then in a calmer voice, added, 'I'll go and tell him.'

'You won't...' the technician began, but Brunetti cut him off by saying, 'I'll tell him the sample's back.' In a softer voice, he added, 'Don't worry. That's all I'll tell him. We'll see if it matches the blood of anyone we have in the files.'

Bocchese thanked him and said goodbye, in a polite manner, and hung up.

Brunetti went down to find Vianello.

It took them almost no time to find the match among the medical files from Franchi's computer and only a few phone calls to find a possible motive. Piero Cogetto was a lawyer, recently separated from the woman, also a lawyer, with whom he had lived for seven years. He had no history of drug use and had never been arrested.

Once Vianello had that hint, it took him only two more phone calls before he found someone who told him the rest of the story: upon learning that he was HIV positive, Cogetto's fiancé had moved out. She claimed that it was the infidelity and not the disease that made her leave, but this had been treated with a certain amount of scepticism among the people who knew her. The second person Vianello spoke to said she had always maintained that she had learned about his disease when someone told her about it by mistake.

Having recounted all this to Brunetti and Pucetti, Vianello asked, 'What do we do now?'

'If he's positive, he can't go to jail,' Brunetti said, 'but at least, if we can get him to admit the break-in, we can close the file on the vandalism and get it off the books.' He realized how very much like Patta he sounded and was grateful that the other men did not mention this.

'You think he'll admit it?' Vianello asked.

Brunetti shrugged. 'Why not? The blood samples match, and a DNA test would probably confirm the match. But he's a lawyer, so he knows there's nothing we can do to him if he's positive.' He was suddenly weary and wanted all this to be over.

'I'd understand if he did do it,' said Pucetti.

'Who wouldn't?' agreed Vianello, giving tacit agreement to the idea that Dottor Franchi had been the person to make the "mistake".

'I'll talk to him if you like,' Vianello volunteered to Brunetti. 'As soon as the water goes down.' Turning to Pucetti, he said, 'Why don't you come along and see what it's like to talk to someone who knows he can't be arrested?'

'Lot of that around,' Pucetti said, absolutely straight-faced.

25

He liked it back here in the lab, working, preparing medicines that would help people and restore them to health. He liked the order, the jars and bottles lined up as he wanted them to be, obedient to his will and following the system he knew was best. He liked the feeling of unbuttoning his lab coat and reaching into the watch pocket of his waistcoat for the key to the cabinet. He wore a suit to work every day, put his jacket on a hanger in his office but left the waistcoat on under his lab coat. No sweaters at work: waistcoat and tie. How else would people know that he was a professional, *un dottore*, if he did not present himself in a serious way?

The others did not. He no longer felt he had the power to make them conform to his standards of propriety regarding dress, though he still would not allow the women to wear skirts shorter than their lab coats, just as he would not permit any of them to wear trainers to work. In the summer, sandals were acceptable, but only for the women. A professional had to dress like one, otherwise where were we?

He ran his fingers down the gold chain until he found the key to the poisons cabinet. He crouched down and unlocked the metal door, comforted by the sound of the key turning in the lock: was there another pharmacy in Venice where they took their responsibility to their clients as seriously as he did? He remembered that he had, some years ago, visited a colleague in his pharmacy and had been invited back to the preparation room. The room was empty as they entered, and he had seen that the door to the poison cabinet was standing open, the key in the lock. It was only by the exercise of great restraint that he had prevented himself from commenting on this, from pointing out the tremendous risks of such negligence. Why, anyone could get in there: a child slipping away from its mother, a person bent on theft, a drug addict. Anyone, and God forbid what might happen then. Wasn't there a movie, or was it in a book, where a woman goes into a pharmacy and eats arsenic that has been left unattended? Some poison; he couldn't remember which. But she was a bad woman, he remembered, so perhaps it was right.

He pulled out the bottle of sulphuric acid, stood, and placed it carefully on the counter, then slid it slowly back until it touched the wall, safely away from harm. He did the same with other bottles, sliding each carefully back and lining them up so that their labels were to the front and clearly legible. There were small containers: arsenic, nitroglycerine, belladonna, and chloroform. He lined them up, two to the left and two to the right of the acid, turning each carefully so that the skull and crossbones on the labels were visible. The lab door was shut, the way he always left it: the others knew to knock and ask to come in. He liked that.

The prescription lay on the counter. Signora Basso had been suffering from the same gastric problem for years, and he had filled out this prescription at least eight times, so there was really no need to consult the written prescription, but a true professional did not toy with such things, especially when it was something as serious as this. Yes, the dosage was the same: the hydrochloric acid was always mixed one to two with pepsin, then added to twenty grammes of sugar and the resulting mixture added to two hundred and forty grammes of water. What might differ from prescription to prescription was the number of drops Dottor Prina prescribed for use after each meal, and that depended on the results of the Signora's tests. He was responsible for the reliability and the consistency of the solution. How else could the missing gastric juices be replicated in Signora Basso's stomach?

She, poor thing, had suffered for years, and Dottor Prina said the condition was common in her family. She was worthy of all of his help and sympathy, poor woman, and not only because she was a fellow parishioner at Santo Stefano and a member of his mother's rosary society. She did her duty and bore her cross in life in silence, not like that other one, Vittorio Priante, little more than a glutton. Fat-faced and flat-footed, all he could talk about, every time he came in, was food and food and food, and then about wine and grappa, and then again about food. Only by lying about his symptoms could he have deceived a doctor into prescribing the acid solution to help him with his digestion, and that made him a liar, as well as a glutton.

But the profession made demands like this on a person who was loyal to it. He could easily have altered the solution, made it stronger or weaker, but that would be to betray his sacred trust. No matter how much Signor Priante might deserve punishment for his excesses and dishonesties, that was in the hands of God, not in his. From him all of his patients would receive the care he had sworn to provide them; he would never allow his personal certainties to affect that, not in any way. To do so would be to be unprofessional, and that was unthinkable. Signor Priante, however, might well have emulated his own moderation at table. His mother had taught him that: indeed, she had taught him moderation in all things. Tonight was Tuesday, so they would have gnocchi that she had made with her own hands and then a grilled slice of chicken breast, and then a pear. No excess, and one glass of wine: white.

No matter how immoral, no matter how lascivious the behaviour of his clients, he would never think of allowing his own ethical standards, or his standards in anything, to affect his professional behaviour. Even someone like Signora Adami's daughter, only fifteen but already twice prescribed medicines against venereal diseases: he would never think of treating her in anything but a manner that remained true to his oath. To do so would be both unprofessional and sinful, and both of those things were anathema to him. But the girl's mother had a right to know the path her daughter was treading and the place where it was likely to lead her. A mother had the duty to protect the purity of her child: he had never doubted that truth. Thus it was his duty to see that Signora Adami knew of the dangers faced by her child: it was his moral duty, never at variance with his professional duty.

Think of someone like Gabetti, bringing disgrace on the entire profession by his greed. How could he do something like that, betray his trust, use the faith placed in him by the entire medical system to set up those false appointments? And how shocking that doctors, medical doctors, had been party to such corruption. The *Gazzettino* had carried a front page story that morning, even a photo of Gabetti's pharmacy. What would people think of pharmacists if one of them were capable of something as vile as this? Yet the law was to be made mock of once again. The man was too old to be sent to jail, and so it would all be settled quietly. Some paltry fine, perhaps he would be barred from the profession, but he would never be punished, and crimes such as this, indeed, most crimes, merited punishment.

He opened one of the upper cabinets and lifted down the ceramic mixing bowl, the middle-sized one, the one he used for prescriptions of 250 cc. From one of the lower cabinets he took an empty brown medicine bottle and placed it on the counter. He reached into the upper cabinet for plastic gloves, pulled them on, and then reached into the poison cabinet for the bottle of hydrochloric acid. He set it on the counter in front of him, twisted the glass stopper and placed it in a low glass dish kept there especially for this purpose.

Chemistry is not random, he reflected: it followed the laws established for it by God, as God has established laws for all creation. To follow those laws is to partake in a small way in the power God exercises over the world. To add substances in the proper sequence—first this one and then that one—is to follow God's plan, and to give those substances to his patients was to do his duty, fulfilling his part in that vast plan.

The syringe was in the top drawer, wrapped for its single use in a clear plastic package. He tore it open, checked the plunger, pushing and emptying the air from it to see that it moved freely. He inserted the needle into the bottle of acid, slipped his left hand down to steady it, and drew the plunger slowly up, bending down to read the numbers on the side. Carefully, he pulled the tip of the needle out, wiping it gently against the side of the bottle, then held it over the ceramic dish. Fifteen drops, and no more.

He had reached eleven when he was distracted by a noise behind him. Was it the door? Who would open it without knocking first? He could not remove his eyes from the tip of the syringe, for if he lost count, he would have to clean out the dish and start again, and he didn't want to empty that acid, no matter how minimal the amount, into the city water supply. People might laugh at such caution, but even fifteen drops of hydrochloric acid might do some unknown harm.

The door closed, more quietly than it had opened, as the last drop fell into the dish. He turned and saw one of his patients, though he was really more of a colleague than a patient, wasn't he?

'Ah, Dottor Pedrolli,' he said, unable to disguise his reaction. 'I'm surprised to see you here.' He phrased it that way, carefully, so as not to offend a medical doctor, a man whose education and responsibilities placed him in a rank above his own. He addressed Pedrolli as '*Lei*', a vocal sign of the respect he paid to all medical doctors, no matter how many years he might have worked with them. Outside of the pharmacy, perhaps, he would have liked to use '*tu*' with doctors and thus demonstrate the closeness of their professional association, but they all continued to address him formally, and so formality had become natural to him over the years. He took it as a sign of their respect for him and his position and had come to take pride in that. He stripped off the plastic gloves and put them in the wastepaper basket before extending his hand to the doctor.

'I wanted to talk to you, Dottor Franchi,' the other man said in a soft voice after they shook hands. He seemed agitated, Dottor Pedrolli, which was unusual, since he had always seemed such a calm man.

'Who let you in?' Franchi asked, but he was careful to ask the question mildly, in a tone indicative only of curiosity, not of irritation. Only some sort of medical emergency could induce one of his staff to override his instructions about the door.

'Your colleague, Dottor Banfi. I told him I had to see you about a patient.'

'Which one?' the pharmacist asked, genuinely alarmed that one of his patients might be sick or in peril. He began to run through the names of the children he knew were in Dottor Pedrolli's care: perhaps it was one with a longstanding condition, and by guessing who it was, he could save precious seconds in preparing the medicine, could be of greater service to a sick person.

'My son,' Pedrolli said. It made no sense. He had heard, with great astonishment, about the Carabinieri and what had happened at Dottor Pedrolli's home. Surely, the child could no longer be considered a patient.

'But I thought...' Franchi began, and then came the thought that the child might have been returned. 'Has he...?' he began but didn't know how to finish the question.

'No,' said Pedrolli in his typically soft voice. It sounded strange here, in this small room which usually made sounds larger. 'No, he hasn't,' the doctor said and regret flowed across his face. 'And he won't.'

'Then I'm afraid I don't understand,' Franchi said. Suddenly conscious of the syringe in his hand, he placed it on the counter, careful to see that the tip did not touch the surface. He saw that Pedrolli watched as he placed it there, and he saw the doctor's professional glance range over the bottles on the counter. Pedrolli was a fellow professional and would surely appreciate his carefulness, the disciplined orderliness of his workshop, a sure reflection of the disciplined orderliness of his work; indeed, of his entire life.

'I'm preparing a pepsin mixture for a patient,' he explained in answer to no question from Pedrolli, hoping the doctor noticed the way he declined to use the patient's name. With a gesture towards the bottles ranked up against the wall, he said, 'I didn't want to risk taking a bottle out from the back of the cabinet while the others were still there, in front of it, so I took them all out. For safety.' A doctor would appreciate this kind of caution, he was sure.

Pedrolli nodded, seemingly uninterested. 'I'm also a patient here, aren't I?' he surprised the pharmacist by asking.

'Yes. Of course,' he agreed. He took it as a compliment that a doctor, a fellow professional but nevertheless senior to him, had chosen him as his pharmacist, though it was really the doctor's wife who was his client. And the child, of course, though no longer.

'That's why I came,' Dottor Pedrolli said, again confusing the pharmacist.

'I still don't understand,' Franchi said. Could the loss have upset the balance of this man's mind? Ah, poor man, but perhaps understandable after so much trouble.

'You have my records, then?' Pedrolli surprised him by asking.

'Of course, Dottore,' he answered. 'I have records for all of my clients.' He liked to think of them as his patients, but he knew he had to refer to them as clients, to show that he knew his proper place in the order of things.

'Could you tell me how it is you come to have them, Dottore?' Pedrolli asked.

'Have them?' Franchi repeated stupidly.

'My medical records.'

But he had said only 'records', surely, not 'medical records.' The other man had not understood. 'I don't mean to correct you, Dottore,' he began, though he did, 'but I have your records for this pharmacy', he said, choosing his words very carefully. 'It would not be proper for me to have your medical records.' That was true enough, thus to say so was not to lie.

Pedrolli smiled, but it was not a reassuring thing to see. 'I'm afraid that's not what I heard.'

'From whom?' asked an indignant Franchi. Was he, a professional, a man who had lawyers, judges, engineers, and doctors among his patients, was he to be subject to such an accusation?

'From someone who knows.'

Franchi's face grew hot. 'You can't come in here and make that sort of accusation.' Then, remembering the status of the person to whom he spoke, he forced his voice to a more accommodating tone. 'That's completely inappropriate. And unjust.'

Pedrolli took a short step back; strangely, the distance seemed to increase the difference in height between them: the doctor now loomed above the pharmacist. 'If you'd like to talk about inappropriate and unjust accusations, Dottor Franchi,' the other man began in a reasonable voice, one that spoke of patience, 'perhaps we could talk about Romina Salvi.'

Franchi took some time to prepare his face and his voice. 'Romina Salvi? She's a client of mine, but I don't know what you're talking about.'

'Who has been taking lithium for six years, I believe,' Pedrolli said with a small smile, the kind that encouraged confidence in a patient.

'I'd have to check her records to be sure of that,' Franchi said.

'That she's taking lithium or that it's been six years?'

'Either. Both.'

'I see.'

'I don't understand what all this is about, Dottore,' Franchi said fussily. 'And if you don't mind, I'd like to get back to what I was doing. I don't like to keep my clients waiting.'

'She was going to marry Gino Pivetti, one of the lab technicians at the hospital. But somehow his mother learned about the lithium and about her depression, and she told her son. He didn't know: Romina had never told him. She was afraid he would leave her.'

'I don't see how any of this concerns me,' Franchi interrupted. He reached for another pair of plastic gloves, hoping that his desire to return to work would both impress the other man and suggest that there was no purpose in continuing this conversation, and that it was time for him to leave. But Dottor Franchi could hardly ask a medical doctor to leave, could he?

'And that's what did happen: he left. So there will be no children who might disrupt God's plan of perfection by developing manic depression like their mother.'

Politeness kept Franchi from answering that this was a very good thing: God's creatures should emulate His many perfections, not pass on an illness that distorted the divine plan. He uncapped the empty glass bottle and set the cap carefully upside down so as to eliminate any chance of contamination from the counter, unlikely as that was.

'I've been thinking about this for some time, Dottor Franchi,' Pedrolli said, his voice more animated now. 'Ever since I learned that my medical file was here and began to think about the information that was in it.'

Hoping to demonstrate how close he was to losing his patience, Franchi moved the mixing bowl a few centimetres closer to him, as if he were about to begin preparing the solution, and said, 'I'm afraid none of this makes any sense to me, Dottore.' He reached up and opened one of the cabinets, took down the bottle of pepsin, the suspension solution that formed the next part of the preparation. He unscrewed the cap and placed it in a separate glass dish.

'And Romina Salvi? Does it make any sense to you that someone made a phone call that destroyed her life?' Pedrolli asked.

'Her life has not been destroyed,' Franchi said, now making no attempt to disguise his exasperation at what Pedrolli was saying. He reached for the syringe and moved it carefully out of the way. He said, 'Her engagement has perhaps been broken off: that has hardly destroyed her life.'

'Why not?' Pedrolli asked with sudden anger, 'Because it's only emotions? Because no one's in hospital, and no one's dead?'

Franchi had suddenly had enough of this, enough of this talk of emotions and destroyed lives. A life lived in the shadow of the Lord could not be destroyed.

He turned to Pedrolli. 'I told you some time ago, Dottore, that I don't understand what you're talking about. What I do understand is that Signorina Salvi suffers from a disease that could be transmitted to any children she might have, so it is perhaps better that this engagement has been broken off.'

'With your help, Dottore?' Pedrolli asked.

'Why do you say that?' Franchi asked with what sounded almost like indignation.

'According to Gino's mother, someone asked her if she weren't concerned for grandchildren. They live in Campo Manin, don't they? So this must be their pharmacy. And where else was she likely to hear such an expression of concern?'

'I do not gossip about my clients,' Franchi said in the absolute tones of a man who would neither lie nor gossip.

Pedrolli looked at him for a long time, studying his face, looked for so long that Franchi, to escape his gaze, turned back to his work. He took out another syringe and ripped open the package, the noise an echo of his anger. He tested the syringe, then inserted the tip into the smaller bottle. Slowly, he began to draw up the liquid.

'You wouldn't, would you?' Pedrolli asked, astonished to have so lately realized this. 'You wouldn't lie and you wouldn't gossip about a client. You really wouldn't, would you?'

This was barely worthy of comment, but Franchi looked aside long enough to say, not without disgust at the other man's opacity, 'Of course not.'

'But you *would* make a phone call if you thought a client of yours was doing something you judged immoral, wouldn't you?' Pedrolli spoke slowly, working it out word by word as he spoke. 'You really would, just as you'd warn Gino's mother. You wouldn't actually *say* anything, would you? But after they heard of your concern and the reasons for it, they'd know just what was going on, wouldn't they?' He stopped, and contemplated the man in front of him, as if seeing him for the first time in all these years.

Franchi shifted his grip on the syringe and wrapped his fingers round it, as though it were the handle of a knife. He pointed it in the general direction of the other man, all patience exhausted. What was all this about, and why was Dottor Pedrolli so concerned about this woman? Surely she wasn't one of his patients. 'Of course I would,' he finally said, forced to speech by anger. 'Don't you think I have a moral obligation to do that? Don't we all, when we see evil and sin and deceit and we can do something that will prevent it?'

If he had slashed at Pedrolli with the syringe, the other man

262

could have been no more stunned. He raised one hand, the palm towards Franchi, and in a tight voice, asked, 'Only prevent it? And if it's too late to prevent it, do you think it's right to punish it?'

'Of course,' Franchi said, as if explaining a matter of exquisite simplicity. 'Sinners should be punished. Sin must be punished.'

'So long as no one's in the hospital and no one's dead?'

'Exactly,' Franchi said with his usual fussiness. 'If it's only emotions, it doesn't matter.'

He turned back to his work. He was calm, competent, a man busy with his professional duties.

Who knows what Pedrolli saw then? A little boy in duck-patterned pyjamas touching his own nose? And who knows what he heard? A small voice saying *Papà*? What matters is what he did. He stepped forward and with an angry swing of his arm pushed the pharmacist aside. Franchi, concentrating on the syringe and avoiding injuring himself with it, tangled his left foot with his right and fell to one knee, breathing a sigh of relief at having managed to keep the syringe away from his body.

He looked up at Pedrolli, but what he saw was the large glass bottle in the doctor's hands moving towards him, and then he saw the liquid splash from it, his own outstretched hand, and then darkness and pain.

26

'Dottore, I'm afraid our conversation this time has to be different from the others.'

'I understand that.'

'The first time I spoke to you, I was in the hospital to speak to you as the victim of a crime, and the second time it was to question you about someone I suspected of committing one. But this time I must tell you that you are being questioned in relation to a crime you are accused of committing and that our conversation is being recorded and videotaped. My colleague, Inspector Vianello, is here with me as an observer, and at the end of our conversation, a written record will be presented to you for signature . . . Do you understand this, Dottore? . . . I'm afraid you have to speak, Dottore. For the tape.'

'Oh, I'm sorry. I'm afraid I wasn't paying attention.'

'Would you like me to repeat what I've just said?'

'No, that's not necessary. I understand what you said.'

'Before we begin, Dottore, would you like anything to drink? A glass of water? A coffee?'

'No, thank you.'

'If you'd like to smoke, there's an ashtray there.'

'Thank you, Commissario, but I don't smoke. But of course if either of you would like . . .'

'Thank you, Dottore. May we begin?'

'Of course.'

'On the morning of the sixteenth, did you visit the pharmacy of Dottor Mauro Franchi in Campo Sant'Angelo?'

'Yes, I did.'

'Could you tell me why you went there?'

'I wanted to speak to Dottor Franchi.'

'Was this for medical reasons, about a patient of yours, perhaps?'

'No. It was a personal matter.'

'Would you . . . Excuse me, Dottore?'

'I suppose in a way, yes, it was about a patient, but one of his, not mine. And while I was there, we also discussed a woman who was a customer of his, but not my patient.'

'Would you tell me who this woman was, Dottore?'

'I'd rather not. She really doesn't have anything to do with any of this.'

'I'd prefer to be the judge of that, if I might, Dottore.'

'Yes, I'm sure you would, Commissario. But I'm afraid that, in this case, I believe I'm a better judge. So I'd prefer not to tell you her name.'

'Would you tell me, then, why you wanted to speak to Dottor Franchi about her?'

'Hmm, I suppose there's no harm in that. I know her *fidanzato*, well, the man who was once her *fidanzato*. He's a friend of mine.'

'What else can you tell me about her?'

'I was thinking how to put it. They were engaged, these two young people. But the mother of my friend somehow learned that the girl, the woman, had an illness that might be transmitted to their children. They wanted to have children, you see.'

'Excuse me, Dottore, but I'm not sure I understand why you would want to talk to Dottor Franchi about this.'

'Oh, didn't I tell you? Sorry, sorry. You see, they live, the young man and his mother, quite near to Campo Sant'Angelo.'

'And?'

'Don't you see, Commissario? Don't you see what happened?'

'I'm afraid I can only ask questions, Dottore, not supply answers. I need the information from you, you see.'

'Of course. Then this isn't really a conversation, is it?'

'No, not really, Dottore.'

'It's easy to forget.'

'Yes, I suppose it is.'

'Where were we, Commissario?'

'You were telling me about where your friend and his mother live.'

'Yes, of course. Just behind Campo Sant'Angelo. So Dottor Franchi would be their pharmacist. It was Dottor Franchi who told my friend's mother about the disease.'

'Do you have any certain knowledge of that, Dottore?'

'No, I suppose I don't, not certain knowledge. But during my conversation with Dottor Franchi, he said he thought he had a moral right to prevent evil, and help punish it. And that led me to believe that he did tell her, that he let my friend's mother know, and he knew how she would respond.'

'Did he tell you that he did it, Dottore?'

'No, not directly. He did not. But any thinking person would understand what he was saying. Or, rather, the significance of what he said.'

'Is it correct to say that what Dottor Franchi said led you to believe that he revealed this information to the mother of the man this woman was going to marry?'

'Yes.'

'What was your reaction to this, Dottore?'

'It angered me. The young woman has been ... has been very unwell as a result of the breakup with her *fidanzato*.'

'And the young man?'

'Ah, that's a different story.'

'What does that mean?'

'He's already engaged to another woman, and his new *fidanzata* is pregnant.'

'Does the other woman, his former *fidanzata*, know this?'

'I don't mean to be impolite, Commissario, but do you think it would be possible, in this city, for her not to know?'

'Of course. I understand what you mean. And what was her reaction to this news, do you know, Dottore?'

'She has grown more ... more unwell.'

'Anything else?'

'I think that's enough. I'd prefer not to say anything more.'

'Of course, Dottore. You said that you were there to discuss a patient of Dottor Franchi's. Would you tell me who this patient is?'

'Was.'

'I beg your pardon.'

'Was, not is. He is no longer a patient of Dottor Franchi.'

'Has he moved?'

'In a sense, yes.'

'I'm afraid I don't follow you, Dottore.'

'My son, Commissario. My son Alfredo. He was a patient at Dottor Franchi's pharmacy. But he is no longer a patient there because he no longer lives with me.'

'I see. Thank you, Dottore. Would you tell me why you went to speak to Dottor Franchi about your son?'

'I'm afraid the answer is complicated, Commissario.'

'Then take your time, if you need to.'

'Yes. Yes. Thank you. I'll try to do that. I could begin by saying I've worked at the Ospedale Civile for nine years. Paediatrics. But why am I telling you that? Of course you know that already. Twice in the past, that is, before this incident with the mother of my friend, I'd heard people say things about Dottor Franchi. That he gave certain information to people that they should not have . . . well, that they had no right to have. It was medical information, things Dottor Franchi was said to have learned in the course of his work: about people's illnesses or weaknesses or diseases. At any rate, in some way that was never made clear or explained—and I must admit for the sake of honesty, was never confirmed—this information was said to come to the knowledge of certain other people.'

'Are you talking about blackmail, Dottore?'

'Heavens, no. Nothing like that. He could no more commit blackmail, Dottor Franchi, than he could overcharge a client. He's an honest man, you see. And that's what's wrong with him. He's decided what good is, and what sin is, and when someone does something he believes to be sinful, he thinks that they should be punished for it. No, Commissario, I'm not speaking about specific things I know for a fact that he's done: I told you all I know is rumours and suggestions, the way people always say things. It's more that I know the sort of man he is, the way he thinks, and what he believes his obligations are—to maintain public morality. As I told you, I'd heard this about him twice, but it was always that sort of vague rumour—something someone heard from someone else—that cannot be proven. Or disproven. And so, when I learned that the mother of my friend, who must be a client at the pharmacy, had become aware of medical information, it seemed obvious that the source must have been Dottor Franchi.'

'Did you realize this at the time?'

'What time?'

'The time your friend's mother received the information.'

'No, not then. Only later.'

'And when was that?'

'Later. When I started to think about things.'

'But you had no proof? Did your friend's mother say something to you?'

'No, nothing like that. I had no proof. Besides, if I might add, without offence, Commissario: proof is more your line of work than mine. I was sure, and I suppose that's the same thing.'

'Ah.'

'You don't agree, Commissario?'

'It's not my place here to agree or disagree, Dottore: only to ask you to explain.'

'I see.'

'You were telling me why you went to speak to Dottor Franchi about your son, Dottore.'

'Yes, I was, wasn't I? It's hard to remember what I've been talking about, I suppose. There are so many things to say and to think about.'

'I'm here to listen.'

'My son, then. There's no sense now in trying to pretend he was my son—my natural son, that is. His mother was an Albanian woman I met in Cosenza.'

'Met, Dottore?'

'Was introduced to, if you will. Someone I know—I'd rather not say who he was—knew that she was pregnant and didn't want to keep the baby, so he introduced me to her and I agreed to her conditions.'

'Financial conditions, Dottore?'

'Of course. That was the only thing she cared about. I don't like having to admit this, Commissario, but all she wanted was the money. I don't think she cared about the baby.'

'That's unfortunate.'

'Well, she got the money. Ten thousand Euros, and may it do her some good.'

'That's a generous attitude, Dottore.'

'What wrong did she do, really? Got born in the wrong country. Came to a richer one. Found herself pregnant and didn't want the baby and found someone who did? In a way, perhaps she deserves credit for having taken the money and not come back later to ask me for more.'

'I'm still not sure yet that I see why you went to talk to Dottor Franchi about this.'

'Please, Commissario. There's no need for you to pretend to be stupid. Ever since I came into this room, everything's been about why I went to see Dottor Franchi. In fact, the biggest event in my life, and no doubt in my future, is going to be why I went to see Dottor Franchi.'

'You say, Dottore, that it's all about why you went to see him. Would you tell me, then, why you did?'

'Because of something you told me.'

'I'm afraid I don't understand.'

'You told me that he had my medical records.'

'No, Dottore, I asked you if the information about any prescription you had made up in the pharmacy would be in your medical records.'

'But you mentioned the inappropriate use of information.'

'Yes, I did. But that was because, at the time, as I said before, we had reason to believe that Dottor Franchi might be involved in blackmail.'

'That's not worth considering.'

'I didn't realize you knew him so well.'

'Well enough to say that.'

'And so you went to the pharmacy to talk to him about your son?'

'Yes, I did. Have you seen my medical file, Commissario?'

'Yes, I have.'

'May I ask where you saw it?'

'It was on Dottor Franchi's computer.'

'I thought so. Then why did you tell me he didn't have it?'

'I didn't tell you that, Dottore. I told you that when we spoke the first time—that is, the first time you were able to talk to me—I asked if certain information would be in it. I did not tell you that he had it.'

'But he did have it?'

'Yes, he did. But if you exclude the possibility of blackmail, then he made no use of it.'

'Made no use of the file? Surely, you can't be that stupid, Commissario. Of course he made use of it. It was written there, clear enough for any idiot to read: "total sterility." This is a small town, Commissario; furthermore, Dottor Franchi and I are, in a sense, in the same business.'

'I don't follow you here, Dottore.'

'I mean that he would know the gossip from the hospital. Surely you can follow that, Commissario. He would have heard about my supposed affair when I was at the medical conference, and he'd have been told about the illicit fruit—he'd probably think of it in those terms—of that affair. Other people probably sniggered when I brought Alfredo home, but he wouldn't do that: oh, no, Dottor Franchi would content himself with feeling compassion for the poor weak sinner. But think of his shock when he saw my medical records and realized that I'd been guilty, not of adultery, but of deceiving the state. And surely a man as righteous in the ways of the Lord as Dottor Franchi would think that this was as great a sin.'

'I think you're mistaken, Dottore.'

'What do you mean, I'm mistaken? Alfredo was not my son: I broke the law by lying on an official government form and saying he was mine; I lied when I said I broke my marriage vows: God alone knows which of these would most offend his twisted sense of morality.'

'I think you're mistaken, Dottore.'

'I'm not mistaken. He's that sort of man. He loves to impose his ideas on other people, loves to see them punished for their sins. Look what he did to Romina: she's a zombie, going in and out of Palazzo Boldù every day, drugged out of her mind. And all because she wanted to marry and have children, and Dottor Franchi decided that manic depressives should not marry and have children. And I suppose he decided that liars should not have children, either. Vicious, life-hating bastard.'

'Dottore, please. Nothing's to be gained from this.'

'No, nothing is, I suppose. But still, he's a bastard and he got . . .'

'Have you seen him, Dottore?'

'No, of course not. I've been in here, haven't I, since it happened?'

'Of course. Well, I've seen him.'

'Where?'

'In the hospital.'

'And?'

'And he's there. They don't know what they can do: they have to wait until it heals. There's talk of skin grafts. But . . .'

'But what?'

'But that's not the major problem.'

'What is?'

'His eyes.'

'Both?'

'One's gone. The other, well, maybe they'll be able to save it or maybe there's the possibility of a transplant. And then there's his hand.'

'Yes, he tried to cover his face.'

'I suppose that's instinctive. It could have been much worse.'

'You mean if I hadn't put his face in the sink and turned on the water?'

'Yes.'

'It was the only thing I could think of: it was as instinctive as his trying to protect his face, I suppose. Maybe it's because I'm a doctor. You just do things: you see an injured person and you don't think about it: you just react. You remember what they drilled into you in medical school, and you do it. And I remembered it then, when I saw him, that the only thing to do is run water over it as soon as you can, and keep the water running.'

'The doctors think it made a difference. The grafts might be easier.'

'I see.'

'Dottore, I think I have to explain something to you. You aren't going to believe me. But what I have to tell you is true, no matter how much you don't want to believe it.'

'About Franchi?'

'Yes. In a way.'

'What way?'

'He didn't call the Carabinieri.'

'How can you say that? How can you know that?'

'They got an anonymous call. That's true. But it didn't come from Dottor Franchi.'

'I don't believe you. The mother didn't want the baby; anyway, she knew where to find me if she wanted more money. She never called me, so there's no reason for her to have called the Carabinieri. Besides, if she had called them, it would only get her into trouble. She knew that. She'd never call them.'

'It wasn't the woman.'

'See? I told you.'

'Yes, you did.'

'Well, who was it, then? Who told you?'

'I'm sorry to tell you this, Dottore, but it was your father-in-law. Yes, I know it's a shock, but I know it's true because he told me himself that he did it. I spoke to him some days ago, and he told me. I believe it's true.'

'Giuliano? *Oddio*, why would he do that? Why would he take our baby away?'

'Perhaps he didn't think of it as your baby.'

'What do you mean?'

'Perhaps he found it difficult to think of the baby as yours and your wife's.'

'Commissario; you're not telling me the truth, are you? Or you're not telling me everything you know. If you spoke to him and he told you, then he'd tell you why he did it. He boasts about everything he does, so he'd boast about this, too. Besides, Bianca would never forgive . . .'

'I think you've had enough, Dottore.'

'Enough what?'

'Pain.'

'I'm not the only one. Why don't you tell me the last thing, Commissario, so we can end this conversation?'

'Your father-in-law told me that it wasn't his idea.'

'Oh, no. No. You can't expect me to believe that. She loved him. He was her son in everything, everything but his birth. She loved him. She was his mother. He was her baby. She watched him grow ... Well, what do you say, Commissario? Or do you still want me to believe your lie?'

'I didn't say anything, Dottore: neither lie nor accusation. I didn't suggest it was your wife: you did.'

'Then Franchi didn't ...'

'No, Dottore. He may have told your friend's mother, and we know of other cases where he told people about what was in the medical records of people they knew.'

'But did you ask Franchi?'

'I did, but he didn't answer.'

'Like me, eh?'

'Perhaps a bit. But in his case, I think it's because he can't.'

'Why?'

'The bandages. And they said his mouth was badly burned, as well.'

'My God, my God. What will happen?'

'To whom?'

'To him.'

'They have to wait.'

'And to me?'

'That will depend on your lawyer.'

'Do I have to have one?'

'It would be best.'

'But do I have to have one?'

'No. You have the right to defend yourself, if you please. But it's not a wise choice.'

'I haven't made any wise choices, have I?'

'No, you haven't.'

'I think the best thing is to return where I was, then.'

'I don't understand.'

'I couldn't speak when you saw me in the hospital that first time, but then my voice came back. I wasn't pretending, you know, Commissario. It came back, within a few days. But this time I think I don't want to talk because I have nothing more to say.'

'I don't understand ... Dottore, I really don't understand. Dottor Pedrolli, are you listening? Dottore, can you hear me? Dottore? All right. Vianello, would you open the door, and we'll take the dottore back to his cell.'